AND

A NOVEL BY LANCE CARBUNCLE

This book is a work of fiction. The characters, dialogue, and incidents are drawn from the author's imagination (except where otherwise noted) and should never, under any circumstances whatsoever, be construed as real in this or any alternate universe. Any resemblance to persons living, dead, or undead, is entirely coincidental.

 For information, address Vicious Galoot Books, Co., 412 East Madison Street, Suite 1111, Tampa, Florida 33602.

www.lancecarbuncle.com

The fat and fiery center of the solar system paused and squatted itself directly above the souped-up El Camino as Grundish pulled off of the paved road and onto the overgrown gravel path winding into the woods. Askew, Grundish's copilot, navigator, sidekick, best friend, and punching bag, glanced behind them down the empty paved road, and then up at the growing, whirring form in the distant sky. Neither of the men saw the bullet-riddled *No Trespassing* sign that the owner of the property posted. That's because the sign wasn't there anymore. It was stolen the night before by a minivan full of drunken teenagers whose final haul included a stop sign, two blinking orange lights from barricades, a Stoner Road street sign, and a mailbox shaped like a manatee. The driver of the van, a troubled boy with one ear, thought the sign would look cool on his bedroom wall. Not that the sign would have stopped Grundish and Askew. Their intrusion on the private property was just one more transgression committed in the name of self-preservation. Ripping down the road at full throttle, the El Camino left a plume of dust and unfinished business in their wake.

Grundish thought about his promise to his friend. He thought about how he loved that man, although he would never say it in such terms for fear of sounding like a fag or something. It wasn't like that, though. It was just that

Askew was always there for him, and likewise Grundish for Askew. Life always seemed less interesting when the two were separated. Grundish thought about times they had shared, and laughs, and fights, and drunken nights. Grundish thought about how Askew would have done anything for him. Grundish thought about how he was going to shoot his best friend in the back of the head.

Eastern State Penitentiary was the first true prison to be built in the world. On October 2, 1829, the day that it opened, Cotton Askew was the first person to go through the intake procedure. He was the first person to be placed in a cell; a solitary confinement room made of cement and lighted by a single overhead skylight, the *Eye of God*. Cotton never bought into the idea of being watched by The Almighty through that small glass pane above him. If he did, he would have feared eternal damnation for the acts he committed to get himself thrown in the dank isolation chamber. Upon completing the institutional intake procedures, Cotton was given the designation of Inmate #1. It was the only time in his life that he was first at anything. Before his incarceration, Cotton did manage to marry a desperate and slightly daft woman who was happy to take his name and bear him a son, Bartholomew. And with the birth of his son, Cotton kicked over the first domino in a chain reaction of bad luck and bad decisions on the part of his descendants.

Bart Askew was raised fatherless and by a perpetually drunk sot of a mother. The few lessons that he did learn came from the village men who visited his mother late at night. And they weren't the sort of lessons that would help him develop into a well-adjusted young man. Like his father, Bart picked up the bulk of his life experience when he was introduced to life in Eastern State. Like his father,

Bart did manage to wed and father a child before being incarcerated for a thirty-year stretch.

And so it went from father to son – an unbroken chain of Askew men each begetting a son and then going off to prison as if it were some proud tradition. It was not at all uncommon for three generations of Askews to be incarcerated in the prison at the same time. The devastating cycle continued and probably would have gone on indefinitely had the penitentiary not closed down in 1971.

Darrell Askew was the last of the Askew men to know Eastern State. One year before the joint was closed for good, Darrell was granted parole and given another chance at life. When the front gate clanked shut behind him, Darrell made two promises to himself: one, he would never allow himself to be penned up like an animal ever again; two, his son was going to break the Askew curse.

"My old man sat me down when I was seven years old and told me about prison,[1]" sixteen-year-old Leroy Jenkem Askew told Grundish. "And there ain't no fuckin' way I'm ever getting *inprisoned*. He put the fear of the hoosegow in me."

"And what'd he say that's turned you into such a bitch?" asked Grundish who sat in Askew's stained bean bag, paying more attention to scraping grayish mung from beneath a toe nail.

"He told me some shit that made my asshole pucker. I mean, do you know what it's like to be locked up?"

---

[1]San Quentin State Prison, in San Rafael, California is so large that it has its own zip code, 94974.

"Now that's a stupid question," snapped Grundish. "You know that I do."

"Yeah, but you was just sent away to juvee a couple a times and to that rehab instead of jail. I'm talking the big house, man. What do you know of that?"

"Nothing but what I seen on the movies," Grundish waved the nail file in front of him, dismissing Askew's concerns as if waving away the scent of a mildly tangy fart. "It can't be any worse than that shit. And I dealt with all that in juvee. Shit, once I had to fight off a group of four kids who wanted to pop my cherry. I beat 'em all down. Weren't nobody was gonna try to ass-fuck me after that. I'd do the same in the clink. You just gotta know how to handle yourself."

"That's easy for you to say. You're a big mother fucker. You can kick ass. It wouldn't be that easy for me. Look at me," Askew said, rubbing his pot belly and putting his hands over his chest, wiggling the fat. "I'm sixteen and I already got man-titties. They'd love that in prison. My dad told me that young guys in there get turned out right away if they can't stick up for themselves. He knew a guy that got reamed so much that his swollen bunghole looked like a donut, and that was just the guy's first week in there. I'd be some big black guy's bitch getting pimped out for cigarettes and hooch. I can't have that shit. I ain't like you, I couldn't defend myself. And even if you're not a punk, you still have to watch out for some asshole trying to shiv you or shake you down. And then there's the guards. My dad said they're as bad as, if not worse than, the inmates. I cannot do that kind of time. I'd rather die."

"Yeah. You may be right," agreed Askew as he wiped the nail file on the bean bag. "Prison…ah hell, even jail, would probably be more than you could take. So then why you always doing things that could get you in trouble?"

"Because even though I'm *mischevious*, I don't get caught," said Askew, smirking. And it was true. Of all of the many stunts he had pulled, nothing could ever be definitively pinned on him. "Seriously, though. I can never go to prison. And you're my best friend, right?"

"Yeah, right."

"Then you gotta make me a promise," said Askew.

"Anything, Bro. What?"

"Never let me get sent up."

"Now how in the hell am I supposed to be in control of that?" Grundish shrugged and dug in his ear with the nail file. "I can do my best to keep you out of trouble. Help you not get caught. Shit, I'd even help you dispose of a body if it came down to it. But how am I supposed to keep you from going to prison?"

"You could kill me if it looks like, and I mean for sure looks like, I'm going to get caught for something I done that's bad enough to get myself sent away."

"Well, God damn, Askew. Why don't you just make sure you don't do shit that will get you sent away?"

"I'll try. Sure as shit I'll do my best. But I done tol' you about my family history. My daddy, my grandpappy, his daddy before him, *excetra, excetra*. It's a curse. It don't matter if I want to do something. I'm practically bound to screw up eventually."

"Well don't. Just plain and fucking simple, don't," answered Grundish. "And then you don't have to worry about it."

"I'll do my best. But, you gotta promise me," Askew begged. "I'm serious."

"I promise, all right," said Grundish, laughing a little. "If you really fuck up, and it looks like you're gonna get caught, I'll pop a cap in the back of your big ugly dome."

"I'm serious."

"I'm serious, too."

"You're not shitting me?"

"No. I wouldn't shit you, Askew. You're too big of a turd and you'd probably give me bloody hemorrhoids."[2]

"So you swear that you would do it if I am going to get sent away?"

"Yeah, I swear," answered Grundish, rolling his eyes and waving the nail file in front of him in the sign of the cross.

"And," said Askew, with a somber tone equal to that of family members discussing a loved one's terminal disease, "don't let me back out on it."

"What do you mean?"

"I mean don't let me change my mind. I'm telling you now that if I realize that you are going to kill me, I'll probably beg you not to do it. I'll tell you I would rather go to prison. I'll cry like a bitch. Don't listen to me. *Exspecially*

---

[2]Elastic bands can be wrapped around internal hemorrhoids as a cure. This is called *Baron Ligation* or *Rubber Band Ligation*. The band will cut off the blood supply to the hemorrhoid. Within several days the withered hemorrhoid should be sloughed off during the course of a bowel movement.

then, because I will turn cowardly. Do what I'm asking you now. End it for me before they take my freedom."

"All right. All right," replied Grundish. "Would you stop talking about it as if it really is going to happen?"

"You promise?"

"I promise."

"You swear?"

"I fucking swear! Now would you stop talking about it?"

The bluish ink on his arms tells the tale of Grundish's numerous terms of incarceration. The first tattoo, an upside-down cross on his left forearm, was inked by a twelve-year old stick-and-poke artist named Squid in a level three juvenile detention center. Not that Grundish was particularly religious; he just thought the cross looked tough. Looking tough was a good thing for a fourteen-year-old who was confined in close quarters with a mixed bag of deviants, psychopaths-in-training, and lost causes. And while the other punks were indelibly marking misspelled words on themselves with paper clips and a mixture of cigarette ashes and toothpaste, Squid was piercing the flesh on Grundish's left forearm with a sewing needle wrapped in string and dipped in Indian ink. The distinction, though slight, was apparent in the superior quality of Squid's work.

"I once fucked a horse," Squid bragged matter-of-factly as he dipped the needle in a bottle of ink and resumed his work on the cross.[3]

"A horse? Bullshit. I'd think you'd have to be pretty tall to bone a horse," Grundish challenged, "and you're not

---

[3]Bestiality was not illegal in the State of Washington until 2006. In 2006 a law was passed banning sex with animals. The law was the result of a Seattle area man dying from peritonitis as a result of perforation of the colon after being on the receiving end of anal sex with a horse.

exactly Lurch from the Addams Family." The logistics of boning Mr. Ed seemed quite involved to Grundish. He supposed that it was more likely that Squid was just trying to sound crazy so that rumors would start and people would be tweaked out, see him as some sort of twisted freak, and leave him alone.

"You don't have to be tall, you dumb cock-stain. You just need a full feed bag, a stool to climb up on, some good balance, and a gentle horse."

"For real?

"Fuck yeah, for real. And don't act like you wouldn't do the same given the chance," said Squid as if it were a completely reasonable option to couple with a barnyard animal.

"Was it at least a girl horse?"

"Of course it was a girl." Squid squinched up his face in disgust. "What? You think I'm a homo or something?"

He doesn't think about Squid when he looks at the faded cross on his forearm. He doesn't think about juvenile detention, the devil, fighting, or fending off forced sodomy. Nor does Grundish give a thought to the fact that he was innocent of what he was locked up for while the true perpetrator, Askew, was free. That kind of shit didn't matter to Grundish, and he would have done it all again for his best friend. Instead of all of that mess, when he looks at the cross on his forearm, Grundish thinks about horses unfettered by saddles, bridles, bits or tack, frolicking in verdant fields.

Grundish was fifteen when he violated probation by failing a piss test. Instead of juvenile detention again, Mrs.

Grundish was able to convince the juvenile court judge to put her son into a long-term drug rehabilitation center for teens. At six-foot-three and 220 pounds, Grundish was intimidating to the staff members. The kids in the rehab who were from out of town all lived in what the program called foster homes. The homes were actually the houses of other kids in the program. As a newcomer, Grundish was not allowed privacy and was under tight security at all times. Due to his size, he was assigned to the care of group member Scott Flannigan. Scott was nineteen years old and the largest of the kids in the group.

At the end of his first day at Straight, Inc., Flannigan stuffed his fingers down the back of Grundish's jeans and his thumb through the back belt loop. With a tight grip on the back of the pants, and one hand clasping onto one of Grundish's arms, Flannigan walked Grundish out to the parking lot of the rehab. He stuck Grundish in the back seat, closed the door, and got into the driver's seat.

Fixing his rearview mirror on Grundish's face, Flannigan told him, "Don't even try to escape from the car. The child locks are on, and the only way out is through me." Grundish could see Flannigan's mouth in the mirror. He had a smile like a mouthful of broken gravel. The smell from the rotting teeth, like the breath of a sick dog, permeated the car. Despite his tough talk, Flannigan was terrified at the thought of having to try to keep the big kid in his back seat from escaping. There was something in the demeanor that told Flannigan he didn't stand a chance if Grundish wanted out.

"Don't worry," mumbled Grundish, "I ain't got nowhere to go. It's here or juvee. I figure I'm better off putting in my time here. I get to live in a house, eat nice home cooked meals, and sleep in a clean bed. Whatta we have to do? Go into that building everyday and listen to them preach to us about the evils of drugs? Drugs are bad, MMM-kay? I get it. I'll do my six months here, keep my mouth shut, stay out of trouble, and go home."

"Oh-ho-ho no," laughed Flannigan. "It doesn't work like that. This is a six month minimum program. That's minimum. And there's only been one guy who has completed the program in six months. Most of the kids here take at least a year to graduate. There are guys that have been here for over four years."

That night Grundish and Flannigan were locked into Flannigan's bedroom. The plywood that was nailed over the outside of the windows kept out all of the natural light. The windows and closet door were bolted shut. When the bedroom door was closed, Mrs. Flannigan locked it with a deadbolt so that Grundish could not get out. Mrs. Flannigan was nice enough. She told Grundish to call her *Mom*. That just didn't seem right, though. He had a mom with whom he was perfectly happy and not looking to replace.

His first day in group, Grundish was disappointed to learn that he was actually expected to participate in the discussions. When he had nothing to say, they made him stand up while different members of the group yelled at him. One pimple-faced, chipped-toothed thirteen-year-old stood directly in front of Grundish, poking him in the chest and screaming: "You need to get honest. You're a hurting little boy who is crying on the inside. You, Sir, have a drug problem. If you don't deal with it, you are going to end up either dead or in prison."

"No. I ain't got no drug problem," Grundish said. It was true. He smoked a little bit of weed now and again and sometimes used the harder stuff if he was partying and somebody wanted to share their stash. But, Grundish was not chemically dependent. "I'm just here so I don't have to stay in juvee."

The chairs erupted in a sea of flailing arms. They called it motivating. In order to get called on, the kids shook their arms spastically above their heads until the group leader would shout out somebody's name. "Ken," the bearded leader strutting in front of the group shouted, "What do you think of this little bop coming into our group and disrespecting us like this?" Grundish didn't even know what a bop was but he gathered it was a slam.

A skinny kid with a bad hair cut and a bubbling eruption of acne on his cheeks ran across the room and stood inches away from Grundish, looking up into his face and crying. "You are a fucked up guy and you know it. You're just as bad as me. When I was out there using, I would suck a cock just so I could get my fix. I didn't even like the taste of cock. I just needed my drugs. I can tell that you've sucked a cock just to get high. How does that make you feel to know you swallowed cum just so you could get high?" Ken just stood there in front of Grundish, shaking, crying, and staring up into his face.

"I ain't never sucked a dick," Grundish answered the hysterical cock sucker, real slow and low. Looking down at Ken's teary snot-glazed face, all Grundish could think was

I'm gonna snap this faggot's neck if he tries to touch me. As if sensing his thoughts, Ken backed off and sat down.

Again the chairs shook on the floor and arms waved frantically in the air. Person after person stood up and screamed at Grundish. One after another they confessed their sickest acts and accused Grundish of having done the same: I shot my mother up and ate her out while she was unconscious; I killed a rabbit; I fucked my sister; I stuck a hair brush up my ass; I used to eat garlic so I would fart while my boyfriend fucked me up the ass; I worshiped Satan; I cursed God; I worked in a grocery store and used to piss in the pickle barrel; I used to beat off constantly until I came blood in the sink; I tried to kill myself; I cut myself; me and my friends used to jack my dog off and we were so fucked up in our heads that we thought it was funny; I hated my parents; I hated the world; I hated myself. Somehow they all thought that Grundish had done the same things. It wasn't so.

These are some of the most fucked up people I have ever seen, thought Grundish. Sure, Squid claimed that he fucked a horse, but, Grundish never believed him. Each and every one of the deviants in the rehab was credible, though. *This isn't a drug rehab*, he thought, *this is a fucking psyche ward*. It was on that first day that Grundish realized he would never make it through the program.

Two weeks into the stay at Straight, Inc., a new patient was brought before the group. Everybody but Grundish knew him. Everyone was pissed off. They all screamed at him as he stood still, smiling a beautiful happy smile, like he was in a better place. A place where people weren't inches in front of his face with their sour breath, calling him names. The kid's name was Buddy and he ran away from the program. Buddy was a big kid, too. The staff decided that Grundish wasn't going to be a problem and sent Buddy home that night to the Flannigan house.

On the way home, Buddy and Grundish sat in the back of Flannigan's car. "Hey, man, what's your story?" Buddy asked Grundish and smiled that big goofy smile of his.

"Hey, stop talking back there!" Flannigan ordered. "You know the rules, Buddy. You guys are not supposed to be talking to each other."

"Fuck you, Flannigan. What're you gonna do about it?" Buddy challenged.

"I'm gonna turn around, take you back to the building, and have you put in a time out room for a week," said Flannigan.

"Good," laughed Buddy, "that way I won't have to see your stupid snaggle-tooth face." Buddy turned to Grundish, "Seriously, what's your story? You don't look like a queer, or a fucked up junkie like most of the losers in group."

Grundish just shrugged. It was a talent he had, shrugging and not answering. He didn't much see the point in getting involved with Buddy's rebellion. He immediately liked Buddy but didn't want any trouble. *Just do your time and get out*, he thought.

"You know you're not getting out of here unless you tell them what they want to hear," Buddy said.

"Shut up, Buddy!" Flannigan yelled. "You're in enough trouble already. Don't make it worse."

"I've been in here for two years now, and I don't see myself being done with it until I'm eighteen and can sign myself out. You won't get out of here unless you play the game. Oh," Buddy mocked, "I was so fucked up and hated myself so much that I sucked a badger's cock. Please help me because I can't help myself. I'm powerless over drugs and need a higher power to help me. Wahhhh. I hate myself. Wahhhh, wahhhh, wahhh, fucking WAHHHH!"

"You know what we should do?" Buddy continued, nudging Grundish with his elbow. "We should toss fat boy Flannigan out of this old station wagon and get the fuck out of here. Just go out on the road for a while. You're not gonna get out of this program otherwise. They don't let you out. They keep you here until your parents' insurance payments dry up or you become an adult and sign yourself out."

A nervous laugh escaped Flannigan. "Stop fucking around Buddy. If you want to sink down to rock bottom… well, fine…but don't drag this guy down with you."

"Do yourself a favor," Buddy said to Grundish, ignoring Flannigan. "Get the fuck out of here. It'll do nothing but mess your head, and real bad, too. Let's overtake this fat piece of shit in the front seat and split."

Again it was clear to Grundish. He wasn't going to make it through the program. He didn't have the ability to convince them that he had a drug problem. He didn't and he wasn't going to play their game. He could do some short time in juvee and be out, an all-around better deal than spending two years in a warehouse having people yell at him, call him names and accuse him of every sexual perversion imaginable. Grundish didn't even know what docking[4] was, but he was accused of doing it.

[4]Docking = The act of placing the head of ones penis inside the foreskin of another's penis.

"All right," Grundish said. "I am getting out of here but I'm not running away. I just want to go to juvee to do my time. But, I'll help you, Buddy. I like you. Fuck it." Grundish leaned up over the driver's seat and grabbed Flannigan by the neck. With one hard tug he tore Flannigan away from the steering wheel and dragged him into the back seat. Buddy jumped up over the front seat and yanked the steering wheel, cutting the car out of the way of the oncoming traffic. In the backseat Flannigan struggled against the half-nelson Grundish had locked on him. With the car pulled over on the side of the road, Buddy jumped out, opened the back door and helped drag the flailing Flannigan out of the family cruiser.

"Dump him on the ground and let's split in his car," Buddy yelled at Grundish.

"No," grunted Grundish, holding a headlock tight on Flannigan. "Take the keys to the car, lock the doors, and get out of here on foot. I'm not going to be a part of a grand theft auto. I'll hold him long enough for you to get out of here."

Buddy snatched the keys out of the car, locked the doors, and ran off into the woods while Flannigan continued to struggle against the pure muscle clamped around his neck. When Buddy was out of sight, Grundish released Flannigan, shrugged his shoulders and said, "Sorry, man. Now go get the pigs so that they can help you with your car and take me back to juvee." Grundish lay down on the hood of the station wagon and waited for Flannigan to return with the cops.

When he got back to juvee, Grundish got another tattoo, a heart with *Mom* written across it. Nothing original, but it was sincere. Squid was still there and had updated his equipment. Instead of the needle and ink, he now had a contraption made out of a cassette player motor, a guitar string, and various other random parts. The new equipment allowed Squid to put more detail into his work.

Midway through the piece, Squid stopped the makeshift tattoo gun and asked, "you know that shit I told you about fucking a horse?"

"Yeah."

"It ain't true," Squid said, grinning sheepishly. "I was just kind of fucking with your head."

Grundish shrugged his shoulders and sat still so Squid could finish the heart.

His first time in prison, Grundish didn't know what to expect. Despite all of his talk, he was scared. Despite his size, he didn't want to have to have to fight. Grundish could trade blows on the street if he had to and usually came out better than the other guy. Still, there is something about being the new fish that can scare the shit out of the toughest guys. Grundish had an instinct for surviving, though. Somehow he knew to stay away from the screws that caused people trouble. He knew when to stand his ground and when to walk away from other inmates. He didn't run his mouth or talk shit. Mostly he was quiet.

Grundish wasn't thieving, violent, mean, or evil. He didn't rape babies or beat up elderly people. That's not how he ended up in prison. He didn't rob people. He didn't hurt people who didn't deserve hurting. He just liked stuff.

More specifically, he liked other people's stuff. He liked to borrow their stuff. He liked to use their stuff.

Grundish liked stuff. And there were several ways to get stuff. Grundish could have gotten a job, worked hard, saved money, and bought some stuff. That was for suckers. As with most of his life decisions, Grundish took the easy way. With a keen instinct for determining a luxury-laden house where the residents were on vacation or gone for the weekend, Grundish would squat in an opportune dwelling for a day or two. He would sometimes invite Askew along. They would order pay-per-view porn. They would gorge themselves on the best food in the freezer and the most expensive liquor in the house. Grundish might take one or two nice items that he liked. If there was an expensive suit, he would take it and wear it a couple of times and then give it to a homeless person. When he was done with a house, he would find the photo albums or something else of obvious sentimental value and set it out on the kitchen counter with a note saying something like *this is all that matters.*

Grundish was good at his career. But he still got caught sometimes. Whenever he did, the victims would testify at his sentencing that he made them reconsider what really mattered in their lives. They always asked the judge to be lenient. As a result, Grundish never served a sentence of more than a year. Each time he was sent up, Grundish got more ink: a soaring eagle across his back...*FUCK* on the knuckles of his left hand, *KILL* on the knuckles of his right...a rose and a dagger on the palm of his hand[5]...*born*

---

[5]Listen to Cracker's *Euro-Trash Girl*, the hidden track on the CD *Kerosene Hat*. It is incredible.

to lose on his neck…a fire-breathing dragon on his right forearm.

During his final stint in the joint, Grundish made himself a promise. He was never going back to prison. It's not that he made an oath to do no wrong. He simply decided that maybe Askew always had the right idea: just don't get caught. So on the day that he was granted parole for the last time, Grundish made a vow never to get caught with his figurative pants down again.

The apple core flies through the air as if in slow motion. Grundish's reflexes, catlike and precise, react well before his brain gathers what is happening. With the fruit refuse hurtling its way on a collision course with his head, Grundish leaps back and swats the gnarled *malus sylvestris* with his arrow-shaped *HOMES NOW AVAILABLE* sign. Once the offending apple is sauced with a powerful slap of the sign, Grundish's mind catches up with his body and takes account of the incident. *They just threw an apple at me. I'm going to fuck up those rich little brats one of these days*, he thinks, wiping the apple sauce on the grass. This time he got a good look at the driver, with his stringy blond hair and skeevy little mustache. The image is securely filed away in a subfolder of his brain labeled *Payback*.

It is a recurring event. The hulking, tattooed, fur-faced ex-con standing on the street corner, earning minimum wage as a human billboard, holding down an honest job. And that minivan full of kids drives by and bombards him with rotting food products and verbal taunts. Sometimes they shout "loooo-zer" at him. Sometimes it is just loud laughing. It doesn't matter on what street corner the advertising agency places him. It doesn't matter if his arrow-sign is encouraging people to check out great housing bargains or two-for-one pizza deals. The minivan always tracks him down. Grundish often fantasizes about that van breaking down right in front of him; he can visualize himself snapping their skinny necks, one at a time, and leaving behind a pile of smirking, pimple-faced corpses.

For Grundish, every day is enough of a struggle without a hoard of punk teenagers mocking his lot in life. It's not like when he was a kid Grundish aspired to stand on a street corner with an arrow-shaped sign, trying to entice the traffic to turn and check out condominiums which he himself could never afford. No, Grundish didn't really aspire to anything as a youngster. Consequently, he found himself almost ready to turn thirty and working a job that the day-laborers turned up their noses at. But at least he wasn't in prison.

"Don't you just hate punk kids?" asks the unmistakable raspy voice behind Grundish. "I do. Hell, I'll probably be supervising some of those delinquents one of these days. So how are you liking your job, anyway?"

Grundish slowly turns around, wiping the remnants of smashed apple on his pants. It is Miss Velda, his parole officer. Velda, a squat, sturdy lump of femininity, like a wrecking ball that broke off of its chain, is another of the festering boils on the ass of Grundish's life. Not that she tries to give him problems. It's just that she is always appearing behind him out of nowhere and commenting on his state of affairs. Always needing him to do a piss test. "Come on, I need you to go whiz for me," she says, latching onto his solid, tattooed forearm and escorting him to the restroom of the Git'n Go mart.

"Miss Velda, I ain't on drug offender probation, so why do I have to keep taking these tests?" Grundish asks, feigning innocence as best he can. He will never fail a drug test with Ms. Velda. The cannabinoids in his blood and urine will never be detected by the field test. The THC and various illicit chemical compounds are a constant presence in his system, but, Grundish has an ace up his sleeve. Actually he always has a prosthetic penis (nicknamed Steve for no particular reason) tucked in his pants that is filled with clean urine and ready for the testing.[6] Grundish never leaves the security of his trailer without Steve being filled with a fresh, clean, sample. The entire pack makes for an impressive frontal basket presentation.

Ironically, it was the fake schlong that caused Velda to start testing Grundish in the first place. The oversized bulge in the front of his pants caught her eye the first time she met with her charge. From that day forth, Velda regularly showed up requesting a sample. As per the Department of Corrections' supposed regulations, Velda has to witness the actual sample presentation.

"Miss Velda, I'm really uncomfortable having to pee in front of you," Grundish pleads as he unfurls the club-shaped and realistic looking phallus from his pants.

At the sight of what Velda believes to be a fresh slab of throbbing man-meat, Velda's eyes glaze over and a shiver shoots down her spine, pausing in her loin briefly to spark the candle that brews the fondue in her panties. She stands awestruck, as always, at the veiny faux meat-club with its bulbous, purple-tinted head. Grundish's practiced hands

---

[6]There actually is such a product to help people pass drug tests. It is called the *Whizzinator*. The device is available in five flesh colors and includes a prosthetic penis attached to an undergarment resembling a jock strap. It connected to a pouch containing rehydrated urine.

manipulate the prosthetic penis perfectly, draining the clean urine into the specimen cup and even shaking off the last couple of drops for a realistic effect.

From her shirt pocket Velda extracts an expired ketone testing strip (the only evidence of her all protein diet years earlier). "Now hand me the cup, and leave that thing out," she says, pointing the fraudulent strip at the fraudulent dong, "while I test the sample." Her eyes, wide open, topped with a fuzzy unibrow, and locked on the dangling participle, never stray as she stirs the clean urine sample. "Well," Miss Velda briefly glances at the test stick before resuming full dong-focus, "it looks like you're clean, Mister. Good job. You can go ahead and put that thing away. Perhaps we should go somewhere so that we can discuss the terms of your probation and maybe…"

"Miss Velda," Grundish interrupts, "I really have to get back to work. If I'm gone too long, my boss will can me. He knows that if I don't have a job, then I can be violated on my parole. And he gives me a hard enough time about that. I don't want any trouble. I just wanna get back to work."

"Well get back to it then, Mister," she says, swatting him gently on the rump as he starts for the door. Grundish pauses, and in that nanosecond he ponders the shit he puts up with—the kids in the van, the shitty job, strapping on a synthetic penis and a bag of someone else's urine everyday, sexual harassment from Velda, and then the thought of returning to prison—and he decides to keep walking. He can't go back to prison. That is a promise he made to himself. *And a man ain't nothing if he can't at least keep his promises*, Grundish thinks. Swallowing down a gulletful of humility, Grundish clenches his teeth and walks out the door, back to his minimum wage human-directional career. As Grundish returns to his thankless and meaningless work, Miss Velda stays behind in the restroom. She slips her middle finger in and out of the sweaty fat folds she calls a vagina and fantasizes about the molded hunk of silicone strapped to Grundish's crotch.

Grundish and Askew arrive at their trailer at the same time, both carrying the tired slouch of the beaten down. Grundish with a twelve pack of Milwaukee's Best. Askew with a cold supreme pizza left over from a prank order. Two nobodies settling in for a dinner of warm beer and cold pizza.

"You should'a seen her face," Grundish tells his friend, relating the incident with Miss Velda. "Practically drooling and quivering. It was like a dog eying a thick, greasy pork chop. I swear I should just fuck her and get it over with. Maybe I can get my supervision early-terminated. I could just plug up my nose, close my eyes and pretend she's your sister."

"You should give it a try," Askew agrees, ignoring the sister comment. He pops the top on his beer can. "She's a *volumptuous* piece of ass. You could do worse. She's got big plump titties." He wedges a hand under the worn elastic band of his underwear and ponders the situation. "Yeah, but she'd probably be disappointed with that little bitty thing you got between your legs. She's used to seeing that monster thick-dick you keep pulling out in front of her. And then you show her what you really got," he shrugs, "hell, she's *libel* to just go ahead and violate your parole right then and there. Then again, you ain't been laid in a while and you wouldn't have that much time to finish off your sentence."

"Why are you always doing that?" Grundish asks and pops the top on his beer, releasing an ooze of warm foam down the side of the can.

"Doing what?"

"Agreeing with me in one breath, and then disagreeing with me in the next, and then changing course again? It drives me fucking bat-shit sometimes. Can't you just give me a straight answer for once?"

"It's called the *di-electric* process," explains Askew. "Point and counterpoint. *Ying* and yang compete until eventually the true answer becomes apparent. The answer is usually somewhere in between the original points of view. So there you have it."

"Well the *dialectric* process sucks balls. There you have it." Opening the pizza box on the floor in front of him, Grundish extracts a piece, groans, and slaps it back down. "Aw fuck! Olives again. You know I can't stand that shit. Even if I pluck them off, the olive juice has already soaked in and tainted the entire pizza. The whole damn thing tastes like rotten vegetables." He throws the pizza back in the box and eats his beer for dinner.

Grabbing a piece of the pie for himself, picking off the olives, and taking a huge bite, Askew agrees through a mouthful of masticated pizza, "I know, it's pretty nasty. That taste don't go away. But then again, I do kind of like it, too. What's up with you tonight? You're being quite the whiny little bitch."

"I don't know. I'm just getting tired of the shit. I'm getting tired of the Fuckers."

"The Fuckers?" Askew asks, ingurgitating the greater part of the pizza slice in one gulp, and finishes the question with a raise of his eyebrows.

"Yeah. The Fuckers," answers Grundish. "The people that shit on me everyday. The punks who throw fruit[7] at me while I'm working my lousy job. Miss Velda eyeballing my fake dick. And did I tell you about my boss?"

"That fucker? What's his name again?"

"Exactly. That fucker. He is one of them – the Fuckers. And his name is Hayman." Grundish sneers. "He keeps telling me that I'm not enthusiastic enough with my arrow sign. He wants me to dance around and wave and smile at people. He'd probably like it if I wore those faggy short-shorts like him, too. Shit, for minimum wage I'm not gonna do anything other than stand there and be a sign post. He actually tried to give me lessons on how to spin my arrow and dance around. I was this far," he holds up his thumb and index finger exactly one centimeter apart, "from stabbing him in the face with my arrow. I don't know if I can stand to have this shit heaped on me everyday. Do you understand what I'm saying about the Fuckers?" Grundish crushes his aluminum can and throws it toward the kitchen area of the trailer. The can bounces off of the counter and lands beside a macramé framed picture of Askew's great aunt on top of a broken black and white television set.

---

[7]La Tomatina is a festival held on the last Wednesday of August each year in the streets of Buñol, Spain. Tens of thousands of participants come from all over the world to take part in a massive one-hour food fight involving more than one hundred metric tons of over-ripe tomatoes.

"Yeah, I get it." Askew starts in on another piece of pizza and Grundish opens another beer. "Did I tell you about the Buttwynns?"

"The butt winds? I got your butt winds," Grundish smiles and squeezes off a moist, reverberating bottom burp.

"No the Buttwynns," Askew shakes his head in disgust, flaring his nostrils at the olfactory assault. "I deliver two or three pizzas to their house every week. I'm always on time. The order is always right. Do you know what that fucker gives me for a tip?"

"Is his name really Buttwynn?" Grundish laughs.

"Yeah, it's Buttwynn. The fucker even has it on his vanity license plate – Buttwynn. But you're losing track of my story. Pay attention. Here's the thick of the plot: guess what he gives me for a tip every time?"

"I don't know, maybe a dollar," ventures Grundish.

"Hell, I wish," says Askew. "He gives me a quarter tip every time. The prick is the furthest house out on the delivery route, he always gets his shit on time, always, and he insults me with that tip. Acts like he just shit out a gold nugget and is doing me a favor when he places that quarter in my hand. And it's always really warm, like he's been squashing his fat mitt around it, not really wanting to hand it over to me. I'd rather he didn't even tip me, the bastard."

"Well, why don't you tell him you don't want his measly quarter next time?" Grundish asks.

"No way, man. I'm not giving up my quarter."

"Well why don't you spit on his pizza, or throw a couple of pubes on it? Do something to teach the fucker, ya know?"

"Yeah, maybe," Askew agrees.

"I mean, shit, I'd like to start striking out at the Fuckers. Fighting for the little people. The people like us. Maybe I should. Whatta ya think?" Grundish chugs the remainder of his cheap beer and feels the warm happies that only alcohol brings him.

"Yeah, maybe that's a good idea," Askew agrees and polishes off his beer. "Or maybe not. I don't know. I could see you going overboard. Taking things too far. Maybe it's not a good idea. But then again…"

"There you go again!" Grundish loses patience with his best friend. "Maybe. Maybe not. But on the other hand and yet again, maybe. I think you may be one of the Fuckers too."

"Well," Askew averts his eyes, "I do hate to be a fucker. But I've got some bad news that I have to share with you."

"Oh, sweet baby Jesus! What now?"

"It's my Aunt Turleen. Things have taken a bad turn for her?"

"That crazy little old lady?" Grundish smiles. "She's funny. I like the way she repeats everything she says. I like to give her wine and watch her get all wacky."

"She ain't crazy. She just gots *oldtimers* disease. So she forgets stuff sometimes and has bouts of *demention*."

"Well what's the problem? Does she have to get her other lung removed? Is she dying?"

"No. I think she's gonna live forever," answers Askew. "The problem is…I think she's going to have to live with us."

Turleen Rundle never was one for lasting relationships. In fact, her great-nephew Leroy Jenkem Askew wasn't really sure exactly what relationships linked him to his great aunt. For that matter, neither was the rest of the Askew family. Turleen was always around, though, and as best as any of the Askews could determine, she and Uncle Hank were both somehow related to them. Turleen was more of a parent to Askew than his biological mother or father. And Askew loved Turleen more than anybody else in his family.

Due to a fondness for hand-rolled filterless cigarettes, Turleen had one lung subtracted from her bodily equation at the age of eighty-five. Weakened and in need of recuperation, Turleen was unable to take care of herself and had to be institutionalized in the Emiction Lakes Nursing Home. At first Turleen enjoyed the company of the other patients at the home. Upon arriving at the facility, she formed a women's bowling team with other emphysema sufferers and named the team the Pink Puffers due to their frequent bouts of spastic hyperventilation that was necessary to maintain sufficient oxygen levels. There also was no shortage of gentlemen callers for Turleen or the Pink Puffers, as she and her lady friends had a reputation in the community for having a certain slackness in their morals.

There was one thing Turleen didn't like at Emiction Lake: Stubs the dog. Stubs the furuncle-covered, tick-infested, three-legged, flatulent dog. Aside from seemingly having the approximate intellect of the loose fecal matter that he littered about the facility, Stubs also had a golden mist of a urine stench that followed him about like a lovesick stalker. Stubs was brought to the home with the thought that he could be a companion to anybody who might be lonely. Animal Assisted Therapy, the staff called it. Turleen called it ridiculous. Stubs wasn't one to interact with any of the residents. After a while, though, the staff and residents noticed that Stubs sometimes wandered into the rooms of the sicklier patients and cuddled up at their feet. Almost invariably, when Stubs was affectionate with one of the residents, the patient would pass away shortly thereafter. People started calling Stubs an angel of mercy, saying that he was showing up to comfort the residents in their final hours, ushering them to the great hereafter. He would go his own way after tending to the infirm and keep his own company, only interacting with another person when it appeared that the person's time was close to being up. Whatever it was—maybe Stubs could smell impending death, maybe it was a psychic connection—nobody at the home doubted Stubs' ability to predict an imminent dirt nap.

And then, one morning, Turleen awoke to find Stubs in her bed gently licking her feet[8] and looking at her with smiling, soulful eyes…

---

[8]Licking feet is one form of foot fetishism, or podophilia. Some researchers hypothesize that foot fetishism rates rise in response to an increase in sexually transmitted diseases. An Ohio State University study noted an increased interest in feet as sexual objects during a gonorrhea epidemic in twelfth century Europe. Similar increases were noted during the European syphilis epidemics of the sixteenth and nineteenth centuries. Likewise, it has been noted by

"...and I snapped that mangy mongrel's neck right then and there, I'll tell ya," Turleen tells the boys, her arthritic fingers clenching the air in front of her and squeezing the imaginary dog. "That nasty little mutt was gonna kill me, he was. As I see it, it was either him or me. Angel of mercy, my wrinkled old ass. That hound was an angel of death. And I'm still here and he's the one that's pushing up little daisies, he is."

"And that's what got you kicked out of the home?" asks Grundish.

"Yeppers," snips Aunt Turleen. "You got a problem with it, do ya?"

"No, Ma'am," says Grundish, a look of calm satisfaction settles on his face. "I just wish I could'a helped you take that punk out."

"Good," says Turleen. "Now go get me a glass of wine, Boy."

---

some researchers that an increase in foot activity in pornographic movies has increased exponentially in correlation with the relatively recent outbreak of AIDS.

"Do you have a list for me?" Grundish asks Askew.

"Yeah. I got it," Askew says as he pulls out a folded yellow sheet of paper from under the cellophane of his Blue Llama cigarette pack and hands it to Grundish. "But are you sure you wanna do this? I know I said it was a good idea. And I have the *upmost* respect for your skills. But, then again, if you get caught, you're fucked." Askew draws out a smoke, lays it between the pointer and middle finger of his upturned palm, thrusts the cigarette-hand upward and smacks his forearm with the other hand, abruptly stopping any further motion of the cigarette-hand and sending the cigarette in an end-over-end trajectory that is halted by Askew's cracked and brownish prehensile lips, which grasp the Blue Llama and hold in place, waiting to be lit. The cigarette catapult, a move that Askew perfected after sitting on his couch for five hours straight, practicing again and again, was flawless. It was typical of his obsessive drive to accomplish meaningless things. Likewise, on a two day car trip with Aunt Turleen, a five-year-old Askew held onto his ears and manipulated them back and forth the entire time until, by the end of the journey, he could wiggle his ears.

"Well, I ain't gonna get caught. Not as long as you get me good information." Grundish grabs the Blue Llamas and taps out a cigarette for himself. "I thought you was gonna quit this shit. I would quit but you're always lighting up around me. A man can't quit smoking when his best friend keeps blowing smoke in his face."

"I am gonna quit. First of next month. I swear it," Askew says and smiles at his friend, the filter of the cigarette wedged into the gap of his front teeth, holding up his right hand in support of his promise.

"Yeah, that's what you say every month." Grundish lights his own smoke and reads the childish handwriting scrawled on the list, barely legible to most, perfectly clear to Grundish. He folds the list, nods to his friend and walks out of the trailer, leaving the barely-smoked Blue Llama smoldering on a dirty coffee saucer.

The list is smaller than expected, but not so lacking in possibilities as to disregard its potential. Outside of the trailer, Grundish checks his piecemeal mountain bike, stolen part by expensive part so as to have the best transportation available to a man with no driver's license. Peddling through the trailer park Grundish stares down the residents, mostly white males, mostly older than him, mostly sex-offenders who are prohibited from living in other areas of the city due to the proximity to bus stops, schools, daycares and public parks. They avert their eyes; some of them go inside, sensing he is different, not friendly to their kind. Grundish shivers with disgust at the perverse vibe given off by his degenerate neighbors. *The Fuckers*, he thinks, stopping in front of a pot-bellied slug of a man. Grundish stares him down. The man slinks into his trailer, both scared and aroused by the menacing tattooed bicycle-man, and zealously jacks off into a dirty sock.

The road winds its way along the river with no sidewalks for Grundish to ride on. Careless cars whizz by, close enough that he could easily kick them from his bike. Grundish peddles on, becoming one with the flow of traffic instead of shrinking from it. A full moon reflects the sun's light at Grundish, and he says to himself that it will be a good night.

The first address is a bust. Through the front picture window, a man, woman, and two children can be seen eating dinner, smiling at each other. They look happy. The house is too small. The one car, an old sedan, sits in the driveway slowly dripping oil and waiting for its opportunity to die just before the family's monthly mortgage payment comes due. Grundish sees no potential here. He peddles on, wondering if he should have worn a jockstrap. His balls dangle uncomfortably, one over each side of the hard bike seat, drooping lower than they used to, making Grundish ponder how far they will drop as his age advances.

The moon takes a more prominent position in the sky and witnesses Grundish's search. The mountain bike skids to a stop in front of the second house on the list. A blue octagonal sign stands sentry near the front door announcing that the residence is protected by an alarm service. And the owner appears to still be around. And the house is too big. *Why is he giving me these occupied houses?* Grundish wonders, making a note that he needs to school his friend on some of the finer points of casing a job.

The next address is perfect. The house is not too big, not too small. It's just right. Three bagged newspapers sit in the driveway. At least three days of the owners being gone. *And it's Friday*, thinks Grundish. *That means they will probably be gone until Sunday afternoon*. He rides his bike around to the side of the house and stashes it in the shrubs. Not one for using burglary tools, he circles around the back of the house, checking for an unlocked window as he goes. No lights on, no alarm, and an unlocked window in a back bedroom. Somewhere a clock strikes midnight. There's a full moon in the sky. He cracks the window and waits. Nothing. No sound. Grundish senses a lonely, empty feeling from the house as he climbs through the window. He sits still for five minutes, ten minutes, and nothing. No sounds. Just the feeling that the house wants him there. His stomach rumbles, evidence of a large lunch at the roadside *taqueria* working its way through his gut and looking for the exit.

Grundish cracks the bedroom door. It creaks as it moves. He cringes, stops, and waits again. Outside a fruit rat runs up an orange tree and a chill runs down Grundish's spine. He listens to the house. No sound. Through the door and relying on instinct, he creeps into the house. And then he knows. It's just a feeling, but that feeling is always right. Nobody is home. The calendar on the kitchen wall says *Cancun* and a line is drawn through an entire week, starting the Monday before. Grundish checks the refrigerator, left over pizza boxes, leftover restaurant food, imported beer, juice, and a giant bottle of hot sauce. The freezer is filled with frozen pizzas, frozen steaks, microwave burritos, frozen waffles, and Hot Pockets. Dirty dishes languish in the sink. Pictures on the counter show smiling children with a man – the father – but the mother is absent. Obviously divorced and living on his own, Grundish concludes correctly. He inspects the well-stocked liquor cabinet and decants a tumbler of scotch, a brand he has never heard of, and tosses back the entire tumbler like a shot of cheap tequila. He smiles and ethyl alcohol fumes waft from his mouth wavering in the air in front of his face, distorting his vision and warming his lips. Grundish thaws a steak and throws it on the grill portion of the custom stove. From a beer mug collection on display in what once was the china cabinet, Grundish takes a stein that came from Amsterdam. He studies the regal looking lions that book end a coat of arms with XXX running vertically down the front. Good enough for beer, he thinks and pours a dark German malt liquor into it.

The beer is good. The beer is strong. He eats his steak and cooks another. Before he realizes it, the beer is gone. Feeling the effects of the scotch and malt liquor more than he expected, Grundish lies down on the couch and orders a pay-per-view anal porn movie, *Stick it in the Rear Dear, IV.*[9] Gently sipping at another tumbler of scotch, Grundish drifts off to the sounds of sloppy, brutal ass-fucking.

The center of our universe strategically positions itself to shine a blistering ray of light through the picture window in the back of the house, and onto a face that covers the front portion of a throbbing head. A thick vein pulses on each side of the forehead, identical twitching worms pulsing to the same beat. Sweat beads gather and drip down the side of the face attached to the throbbing noggin. And Grundish stirs. He can feel that his pupils are

---

[9]Some funny porno names: *Buttman and Throbbin*, *Shitty Shitty Gangbang*, *Edward Penishands*, *Ass Pirates of the Caribbean: Curse of the Brown Eye*, and *Scrotal Recall.*

asymmetric, the vision in his left eye blurry, floaters dance in his vision, the harbinger of a debilitating migraine. Other parts of his body check in. A piss hard-on painfully throbs in time with the twitching worms in his forehead, demanding attention. The Mexican food from the day before knocks on the exit door and screams for freedom.

Stumbling through the master bedroom, Grundish throws open the door to the bathroom, his pants already unbuttoned and around his knees by the time he is halfway to the toilet. Grundish swings his ass around, trips over the pants that have dropped to his ankles and falls backwards onto the toilet seat, just in time to unleash the evil dwelling deep in his bowels. The release is sublime, almost as satisfying as sex. An unbroken rope of southern brown toilet snake coils itself into a perfect umber corkscrew, the point poking out of the water. He stands and examines it. Pride wells up in Grundish; he cannot bear to flush his masterpiece. Rather than ruin the presentation of the perfect dooty, Grundish leaves it unmolested and bunny-hops through the house with his pants around the ankles until he finds the other bathroom. Only then does he wipe. And he wipes. And wipes. And wipes. He wipes until he bleeds. Only then does he stop.

Still feeling the rush of endorphins from his glorious bowel movement, Grundish's pre-migraine throbbing ebbs, leaving him clear-headed enough to finish his mission. In an envelope in the underwear drawer he finds a stack of cash. In another drawer he discovers a stack of magazines with pornographic images of young children. His stomach churns, his head throbs, and the migraine feeling returns. Grundish spreads the magazines out on the kitchen counter and leaves a note on top of them that says, "Go ahead and call the cops. I dare you." In the medicine cabinet he finds the Xanax, Klonopin and a variety of other pharmaceuticals, all of which he grabs. Grundish takes a bottle of expensive cologne for Askew. He loads as much premium liquor as he can with the rest of the booty into a daypack that he finds in the front closet. Before leaving, Grundish orders an entire week's worth of vile pornography on pay-per-view and leaves the television running with the volume at full blast. He goes into the bathroom one last time and admires his work. Stopping once more at the liquor cabinet, he sucks hard at a bottle of Scotch to stave off the imminent hangover migraine that looms above him. And then he sneaks out the back door, grabs his bike, and peddles away unnoticed. First it's back to the trailer to unload the boosted goods, and then, off to work to maintain the appearance of an upstanding citizen contributing something of value to society.

The thought of spending another day as a human billboard chips away at Grundish's spirit, wears it down to a sensitive exposed nub. To go from the high of burgling the house of a Grade-A shithead and back to standing in the hot sun, hung over and waving at people in their cars who don't give a shit, it's like throwing himself at the wall. It ain't that pretty at all. Grundish dumps random pills from the pilfered prescription bottles and blister packs into his palm and thoughtlessly washes them down with a handful of warm water from the kitchen tap. He lies back in the recliner, rests his eyes, and waits for the sweet pharmaceutical numbness.

When Grundish opens his eyes again, Turleen is exiting the bathroom with a jelly jar of foamy amber liquid. She sets the jar on the counter. "There it is, fella. I filled it up and then some, I did. Why'd you say you want my pee again?" She sits down at her newly staked out position on the couch and removes her upper plate of dentures, setting them on the coffee table beside her.

"Thanks, Turleen," says Grundish. He grabs the jar; the outside of it is moist. He pours the warm liquid into the reservoir tank of the prosthetic strap-on penis. The urine smells like overly-ripe broccoli. "It's kind of embarrassing, but my parole officer randomly does pee tests on me. I don't feel like going back to prison just because I occasionally partake, if you know what I mean."

"I'm hip to the jive, I am. You do what you gotta do, Kiddo. You've always been a good egg. I don't mind helping. And, there's always more where that came from, there is." She nods at the jelly jar and smiles a big gummy grin at him. "Now, if you don't mind doing me a favor, could you light up a cigarette and blow some smoke my way? I'm not allowed to smoke, I'm not."

Grundish shrugs and says nothing. He grabs a Blue Llama from Askew's pack and lights it. The smoke wafts in Turleen's direction. She closes her eyes and inhales the second-hand cancer deeply, taking it into her mouth, down to her lung, and into the blood stream. She lies back into the couch, eyes still closed, and softly moans. Grundish notices that he can make out the outline of her nipples through her loose house dress. His member stirs and quickly swells into pulsing turgidity.

Taken aback by the ferocity of his sudden erection, Grundish rushes for the bathroom. He drops his pants to the bathroom floor and admires the harsh rigidity of his boner. A thick blue vein, fed by smaller boner-vein tributaries, courses blood to the angry purple dome. *Holy moly and great googly moogly*, thinks Grundish, *I ain't had a stiffy like this since I was fourteen*. Somewhere, maybe on a radio talk show, or maybe in a girly magazine, Grundish heard that one can get rid of a boner by squeezing tightly with the thumb and forefinger just below the head of the penis. Grundish tries to kill the boner with the two-fingered-headlock technique but it just makes his cock more engorged. He realizes that he cannot strap on the fake urine-filled schlong with his raging wurst in the way. He abuses and demeans himself to the point of release in an effort to get the erection to subside, only to find that it is still standing at full attention and refuses to go down.

Grundish leaves the urine-filled dildo on the sink and pulls his pants up. He adjusts the stiffy so that the angry head peeks out above the waistband of his pants. The prescription pills are still on the kitchen counter beside the sink. He examines them: Xanax (*fine*, he thinks), Vicodin (*even better*, he says to himself), and then the blister pack, soft-tab Sildenafil Citrate (*huh?* he wonders). The final medication, he learns, is a quick-acting male enhancement prescription. According to the warnings on the package, erections will occur almost immediately and can last up four hours or more.

Four hours? He thinks. *More?* Already late for work, Grundish decides to chance it for the day and head out without the strap-on piss-test insurance. The latex phallus remains on the counter, its large head hanging just over the edge of the sink, slowly weeping one golden, dejected, tear at a time as Grundish turns his back on it and heads out the door. *I can't wait four hours*, he thinks to himself and leaves the bathroom. He takes a hit off of the butt he left smoldering in the ashtray and tastes burning filter. Turleen is laid out asleep on the couch, her house dress hiked up enough to show the puckered, alabaster flesh of her inner thighs. Grundish's member pulses to indicate its interest.

The front door of the trailer slams shut behind Grundish and wakes Turleen from her catnap. She breathes in deeply, seeking out any remaining second-hand smoke.

Pedaling his bike as fast as he can, Grundish screams nonsense at the trailer park residents to take his mind off of the friction of his dick rubbing against his belly. Grundish's next door neighbor, Mr. Shirley, tries to avert his eyes as Grundish rides by. He shouts at Shirley: "WHO? WHAT? WHICH? WHY? WHO? WHEN DID YOU SAY THE EARTH WOULD STOP TURNING? WHEN DID YOU SAY WE WOULD ALL START BURNING? PUSH THE BUTTON. CONNECT THE GODDAMN DOTS. CONNECT THE GODDAMN DOTS." Shirley, clad in a t-shirt tucked into a lavender Speedo, averts his eyes, grips onto his walker, and scurries back to his trailer to avoid any trouble with his scary, buff, and severely tattooed neighbor.

"You should spin the arrow once in a while. And maybe dance around a little bit to get the motorists' attention," says Hayman to Grundish. "This is an important one for you today. They're counting on you to get people's interest in those two-for-one pepperoni pizzas. Now show me your moves with that arrow sign, Mister." Hayman steps back, hands resting on cocked hips, and nods at Grundish.

"Mr. Hayman," answers Grundish, "I don't dance, I've got a dirty whore of a hangover, and it's too hot out there to be moving around very much. How about I just hold the sign and wave?"

"Well, I don't have anybody else here to take your place right now, so you're going to have to do. But, and listen to me now and hear me later, you will not advance with this company with that poor attitude." Hayman, in his excitement, spills a little bit of his iced mocha latte on his hand. He wipes it on his tiny shorts. "Now get out there and use that arrow to turn people toward those delicious pizzas." Hayman walks toward the bathroom with his back turned to Grundish.

"You bet, boss. I'll do my best. And I might even try that dancing thing you want me to do," says Grundish as he slips three rapid-tab boner pills in Hayman's latte.

The humid Florida weather exhausts Grundish. But the boner remains. The thick exhaust from the buses, trucks, RV's and cars assaults his lungs. And the boner[10] remains. The mental exhaustion of mindlessly waving at people who look down on him erodes his soul. But the boner remains. Grundish stands on the corner with his *Two-fer-One Pizzas* sign and tries to entice passers-by to go into PollyEyes Pizza and take them up on their deal. Jess, the lazy-eyed owner of PollyEyes, brings Grundish a piece of cold pizza and lectures Grundish on how he should dance around with the arrow sign. The pizza has olives and makes him want to puke. Grundish doesn't know which of Jess's eyes to look at, the one pointed directly at him or the one staring off

---

[10]Priapus, a minor (Greek) fertility god, was the protector of livestock, fruit plants, gardens and male genitalia. He was known for his perpetually erect penis that grew so large that Priapus was eventually unable to move. Known as a watcher/protector of livestock and gardens, Priapus warned away thieves and transgressors, threatening to sodomize or to sexually penalize with his giant member whoever dared to steal the garden's greens and fruits.

toward traffic, as Jess tells him that when he was younger, he would have danced his ass off for $10.00 an hour. But still, the boner remains tucked in his pants, head peeking slyly out over the waistband, one eye surveying the scene and looking for something to spit on.

A rusty pickup truck blurts its horn as it drives past Grundish. The driver's kid, a freckle-splattered little girl with her front teeth missing, flashes a beautiful smile at Grundish. Momentarily, witnessing the unbridled mirth of the little girl, Grundish is touched by her innocence. For just that moment, joy stirs in his chest and begins to work its way up to his facial muscles, making his mouth twitch and form into something resembling a smile. And still his cock throbs. But, before Grundish breaks into a full-fledged grin...*SCHPLATTT*... something hits him from behind, splats on his neck, and oozes down his back.

"Hah-hah!" screams the pimply teenager hanging out of the window of the yellow minivan. "Loooooo-zerrrr!" shouts another voice from the vehicle as it speeds away before Grundish can try to catch them. He rubs his hand on his neck and studies the goo: rotten tomato. And still his erection persists.

"You really oughtta report those little hoodlums to somebody," says the raspy voice behind him. "It's ridiculous the way they taunt you."

Grundish turns around, shrugs his shoulders at Ms. Velda, and says nothing. His shoulders, having nothing else to say, droop. His arms hang limp at his sides. His back hunches up in deflated lump of defeat. His day is shot. He's been abused, humiliated, attacked, and generally beaten down. *And now*, he thinks, *ain't this great? I've gotta take a piss test with a bloodstream full of prescription meds. And I don't have my strap-on.* Yet still, his boner throbs.

"Come on, I need you to go whiz for me," says Velda, waving him in her direction as she turns and walks away. "The Git-n-Go is just around the corner. You know the drill." Grundish follows. As she walks away, he can't help but to study her form. Tight shirt stretched over her barrel-like upper body. The dirty jeans stretched over the wide, thick hindquarters, staying tight all the way down her tapered-off legs to mid-calf, where they stop. Her pigeon-toed feet clad in pointy, flat-footed shoes. The way her legs stay stiff while she walks with the points of the shoes veering off at forty-five degree angles from her forward direction gives her a waddle that a penguin would be proud of.

The Git-n-Go bathroom stinks like a bucket of rotten fish. Grundish towers over Ms. Velda, the top of his erection almost level with her sternum. He stalls: "Ms. Velda. Before I do my test, can I clean myself off? I have tomato all over my back, and it just hasn't been a good day."

"Turn around," she says, grabbing a paper towel from the rusty dispenser. "Squat down a little bit, and I'll help you clean your back off."

Still stalling for time to think, Grundish complies. Velda wipes down the back of his neck and tosses the used paper towel into the trash. She gets another towel to wipe him off and wets it in the sink. She cleans his back gently and then drops the towel. Grundish stares straight ahead, silent, not sure what to do next. Velda's hands start to gently rub his wide shoulders. Grundish shrugs his shoulders and says nothing, waiting to see what happens next. Whatever it is, he thinks, it's gotta be better than getting my parole violated and going back to prison.

"I've been trying to talk to you about something every time we meet," says Velda, soft and quiet into Grundish's ear as she slowly moves her hands down back, "and you always have to rush out and hurry back to work before we finish talking."

Grundish says nothing and in his head curses his throbbing knob. Still trying to figure a way out of giving a piss test or shagging Velda, Grundish stalls and allows her to slowly move her hands down his back.

"You know," she whispers in his ear, the not altogether disagreeable odor of corn chips on her breath, "I could recommend that your parole gets early terminated. Would that be something you would like?" Her hands pause at the crook of his back, just above his ass.

Grundish shrugs, noncommittal, while his cock twitches like a snake being crushed under a work boot. His back is still to Velda and his mind reels. A positive piss test means prison. On the other hand, sexing Velda means a loss of self-respect and perhaps an odor that will stick to him for days. *And*, he thinks, *God help me but I've gotta do something with this rod. Even Velda doesn't seem so bad right now*.

"You know what, Ms. Velda?" he says. "I think I know what you're getting at." Her hand slides down to his ass cheeks and kneads them. "And I've been thinking about this for a while now. I say, let's do it."

Before Velda can caress his gluteus maximus any further, Grundish unbuttons his pants and flips around, his rigid dong sticking out. Not as big as Velda was led to expect by his imposter penis, but still quite acceptable to her. Grundish stoops down to her level and buries his face in her neck in order to avoid kissing her corn-chip breath. His tongue flicks at a sweaty fold of her neck. He wraps his arms around her barrel-like figure.

Velda's entire body shudders. "*Yesss*," she moans in a voice not like that of a female. And still Grundish's erection stands firm. "I've been thinking about this, too. Ever since our first meeting. It's so right." Grundish struggles to unsnap her pants, the outward pressure of her girth stretching the denim taut, making it a difficult process. "Fuck me now! Fuck me here!" she grunts and reaches down to undo the pants herself.

Obeying Velda, obeying the primal urge in his groin, Grundish, in one fluid move, drops his own pants, and spins Velda toward the sink and away from his face so as not to have to kiss her. *You're going to hate yourself for doing this*, he tells himself as he jams his hand down between her legs from behind and feels the hair-matted, sloppy core of Velda. *You're going to hate yourself if you cum*, he tells himself as he bends his knees to get down to her level and slides into her from behind. *You're going to hate yourself*, he says as he pushes her forward, his hands gripping at the sides of her dimpled *steatopgia*[11], bending her further over the sink, taking in her wattled fundament. A fly flits about, buzzing in between them and alights on Velda's back, just at the top of her ass crack. Grundish notes the fly, notices

---

[11]An extreme accumulation of fat on and about the buttocks, esp. of women.

it resting on a soft tuft of hair growing from her crack and running inches above it onto her back.

Velda moans, "MM*mwaaaahhhh*," like an old man fiercely moving his bowels, and it just makes Grundish hotter.

You're going to hate yourself, he continues to tell himself as he slips his hands up under her shirt and pushes the bra up off of her breasts. He grabs onto the silky soft tits, pinches the nipples.

The smell in the bathroom is sickening – worse than when they entered. And still Grundish persists in slamming Velda from behind, balls-deep in self-loathing, gripping onto her sweater-meat like a rodeo champ trying not to get bucked off of a bull. The harder Grundish pounds, the more Velda grunts her senior-citizen-dropping-a-log sound. And nothing can make Grundish lose his erection. Not the thought that he isn't using a condom. Not the fact that scrogging Velda is like doing it to a man with jugs. Not the smell of ass, corn chips and urine in the bathroom. Not the flies buzzing about just above where he is vigorously penetrating his parole officer's baby hole. Not Velda's masculine moaning.

You're gonna fucking hate yourself, he thinks again as he buries his cock up to the base of the shaft and releases. She screeches in ecstasy, finally like a woman, as Grundish drives his hips into her so hard and collapses on her, ripping the sink off of the wall. They both momentarily deflate onto the bathroom floor, water spraying from the wall where the sink used to be, and relish the post-coital endorphins coursing through both of them.

"Holy shit," Grundish laughs and stands, quickly pulling up his pants, his erection just as firm as before. He holds out a hand to assist Velda. Her pants still down around her ankles, Velda accepts the hand and Grundish pulls her up. He notices a thick brown skid mark in her sizable panties and hates himself more for what he just did.

The spray from the sink soaks them. Velda leans down and twists off the water valve still connected to the wall. Still, Grundish's priapism persists. Still his hunger remains. He buttons up his pants. "I have to get back to work, Ms. Velda," he tells her, avoiding her eyes. He heads out the door, back to his just-above-minimum-wage-arrow-sign-hell. Velda remains and contemplates how she could allow herself to fall in love with one of her charges.

During the next week Grundish acts mostly on instinct. With Ms. Velda's recent visit, Grundish doesn't expect another visit from her for the next five or so days. He calls in sick to work, claiming the flu. And then he gets to work on the list. The rest of the houses on Askew's list are good. Grundish thinks to himself, during his more sober moments, that it is a good plan – having Askew case houses while he's delivering pizza. Grundish tells Askew what to watch for while he's driving around: front doors with notes for delivery men, days' worth of newspapers in the driveways, all but one light on in the house and all blinds or curtains closed, mailboxes overflowing with mail and flyers, un-mowed lawns. Askew makes a list. Grundish checks it out. Grundish sneaks in and out of the houses, a greedy grinch grabbing goods. At each house he gorges himself on the best food, drinks the best liquor. At each place he passes out. At each, he wakes the next day and leaves his new calling card, dropping a monster dooty log in the crapper, leaving it to wallow in the cool water, no soggy toilet paper to keep it company, waiting for the home owner to discover it upon his return. At each he snags the best goods, always thinking about what Askew and Turleen will like, and loads them into his newly-pilfered daypack. He retreats to the trailer and sleeps during the day, returning to the addresses on the list under the cover of the night to strike again.

At the final hit on the list, Grundish stuffs his daypack full of frozen meats: steaks, burgers, and pounds and pounds of kosher hotdogs. The migraine floaters threaten debilitation and are once again quelled with a huge snort of aged scotch. He goes into the bathroom one last time and leaves his steaming umber calling card. He admires his work. And then he sneaks out the back door, grabs his bike, and peddles away unnoticed, back to his trailer to sleep off the migraine for the rest of the weekend.

At the trailer, Turleen lounges on the couch in the front room, sleeping off her own bender from the burgled wine Grundish brought her. "Hi there, Honey," she says to Grundish as he flops down in a broken recliner. "Do you mind lighting up one of Leroy's cigarettes and smoking it? I can't smoke anymore, but I do like the smell of it, I do. Just blow it over in my direction." She cackles at her own cleverness in circumventing her doctor's orders. The cackle turns into a phlegmy cough. "Ah shucks," she smiles and wipes her mouth, "when I find out that I am dying of something, I'm gonna start smoking again, I am. I kind of look forward to it. Might as well at least enjoy my final days, eh?"

Grundish shrugs his shoulders and lights up a Blue Llama that he doesn't even want. They both drift off to sleep with wisps of smoke swirling around them in the trailer.

Instead of sleeping off a hangover, Askew works a split shift of pizza delivery. Sunday mornings during football season always require lots of prep work to have everything ready for the game-time rush. And Sunday mornings during football season always find Askew performing the necessary pizza prep.

The Sunday football rush is busy. If an order is fucked up, nobody cares. They still take the food. The customers are drinking and watching the Bucs' game and don't feel like waiting another hour for the right pizza. The bad news: no leftover pizza for Askew to take home for dinner. Due to the complete lack of leftover grub at the end of his first shift, Askew pulls into Barry's Big Beef Palace drive-through, orders the #5 combo meal and plumps it up for an additional fifty cents.

And the Fast Food Gods are watching over Askew. It's the type of thing people seem to say when something goes right: the (*fill in the blank*) gods were watching over me. The phrase is trite. It seems that every person attributes any given fortuitous result to a particular god or gods and the words lose all meaning and power. But, in Askew's case, the Fast Food Gods really were looking over him. Coniraya, once the Incan God of the Moon, and Zotz, the Mayan Bat God, temporarily share duties as the Fast Food Gods until they get bored or something better comes along. Times are hard for ancient gods. Down-on-their-luck deities tend to take odd jobs until perhaps they come back into style or give it up and retire. Both Coniraya and Zotz were once powerful but were later relegated to obscurity with the steep decline of their worshipers.

Coniraya was known for fashioning his sperm into a fruit which a mortal woman ate and was then impregnated. When she learned that the child was Coniraya's, she rejected him and fled, eventually turning herself into a rock. Potential worshipers are mostly turned off to worshiping him, as it is generally considered icky to eat his sperm. Given the choice, most people would elect the option of turning themselves into stone over guzzling a load of Coniraya's fruity jizz.

Zotz is a giant bat-like being. The cave god. Foamy candies are named after him. He commanded as little respect as Coniraya once his people's civilization disappeared.

After losing all potential worshipers, Coniraya mostly passed time by appearing to mortal women and having sex with them. He still liked to trick the ladies into eating his sperm and impregnating them. Zotz prefers straight up intercourse with mortals and is a prolific breeder. Occasionally his offspring are still discovered living in caves, malformed, demented and mentally impaired – the best known being the dolt-child known to most as *Bat Boy* who is widely considered to be a hoax created by a tabloid newspaper.

All clichés aside, the Fast Food Gods really were watching over Askew. The drive-through cashier at Barry's Big Beef Palace is a sickly-looking boy named Simon. His face is blighted with lumpy acne and a variety of pointy metal things stuck through the fleshier parts. He lisps to Askew, "that'll be four theventy-nine, Thir." Simon's lisp is not the stereotypical homosexual affectation. It is more the I-have-my-tongue-pierced-and-I-have-a-self-imposed-speech-impediment kind of lisp. The lingual barbell clicks against Simon's chipped front teeth as he talks, making Askew cringe.

Askew hands a twenty-dollar bill over to Simon and receives $55.21 in change. Before he can even begin to pocket the overpayment, Simon hands out a large bag packed to the top with burgers and fries and every kind of greasy deep-fried morsel Barry's Big Beef Palace has to offer. Flashing a big chipped smile and knocking tiny fragments off of his teeth with the barbell, Simon tells Askew, "thank you, Thir. Pleathe come back again."

Zotz and Coniraya look down on their work. And it is good. They smile upon Askew and wish him well. "Do you wanna make a grill cook hock a loogie on a cop's sandwich?" Coniraya asks his colleague.

"No. I think I'd prefer to go down to Earth to get some poontang," says Zotz. "You feel like tag-teaming a mortal hottie?"

"Yeah," smiles Coniraya, "I think we've done enough work for today. Let's do it."

"Groovy," says Zotz. He flashes his pointy bat-toothed smile and stretches, spreading his wings. "Please just don't try to get them to eat the sperm fruit again. I hate having to kiss them after they've had that in their mouths."

Askew studies the sanguineous meat juice seepage that has soaked into the carpeting around the daypack Grundish left sitting on the floor before falling asleep. "What the fuck? It smells like raw meat in here."

Grundish stirs, abruptly stands for a moment, his hand to his head, his vision tunnels down to a pinpoint and a load of head-rush dizziness kicks him right between the eyes. Gravity grabs onto the back of his shirt and yanks hard, dragging him back into his broken recliner. "*Ugghhhhh*," Grundish exclaims, his hand still slapped to his head, trying to push down the rhythmic throbbing in his temples.

"You better eat something. You can take care of the mess later," says Askew, evaluating his friend's condition. "I knew you'd be in bad shape so I stopped off and bought us a feast. Even used all my tips on it," he lies, handing Grundish a bag of unidentifiable fried nuggets. "I was thinking of you, Buddy. Have a bag of mystery nuggets."

Grundish stares at the greasy breaded morsels. The nuggets stare back at Grundish. Neither knows what to make of the other. In an effort to understand the fried lumps, Grundish bites one in half and studies the piece. "This one looks like sausage but tastes like ham," he says, still chewing his food, and pops the remaining fraction of a nugget into his mouth to reunite it with its masticated other half. Grundish holds the open end of the nugget bag toward Askew, offering him his friendship with a side of trans-fat-soaked, breaded mystery lumps.

"Naw," Askew shakes his head and peers into the Beef Palace bag. "I gots me some a' my own." He extracts two bags of mystery nuggets and sets one on the coffee table beside a still-sleeping Turleen. He pulls out one nugget and sets it on the pillow just under her nose. The old lady stirs, nostrils flaring. A light trickle of saliva runs out of the side of her mouth, hangs briefly on her cheek, then drops and soaks into the fabric of the couch. Studying his own mystery bag, Askew pulls out a lump half the size of his fist and bites into it like chomping on an apple. His face twists. Confusion dawns on the features. His thumb and pointer finger probe the inside of his mouth, searching through the mushy mass of fried mung and extract a beak. Askew holds the beak twelve inches before his eyes and examines the tooth marks scraped on the curious bird part.[12] "Dammmn," he smiles, "I got me fried chicken parts. And I thought I scored the jackpot with a giant corn-fritter." The smile is less complete than before biting into the parts-fritter – a fragment is absent from the right front tooth.

---

[12]In November of 2000, a woman in Newport News, Virginia, purchased an order of chicken wings from McDonald's. The wings were being tested in that market. When the woman got home she discovered a severed and fried chicken head in the package, beak and all. The absence of fried chicken heads on McDonald's menus would seem to indicate that they were not a big hit in the test market.

"Damn, dawg. It looks like you chipped your tooth," says Grundish. He pops a full nugget into his mouth. "Mmmm, corn."

Askew's tongue explores the rough edge of the chip, "Aww, it ain't that bad. *For all intensive purposes* it don't make no difference. So long as I can still hold a cigarette between my teeth, I can't get too upset about it. "

"I thought you were gonna quit smoking."

"I am. Next month. I can still puff away right now while I'm getting used to the idea, right?

"Yeah, I guess so." Grundish grabs a fried salad roll up from the bag and starts in on it. "You know, I've been thinking about that talk we had about the Fuckers."

"The Fuckers?"

"Yeah, the Fuckers." Grundish wads up the greasy paper from his fried salad wrap and throws it at Askew. The wad bounces off of Askew's forehead. "Are you daft, boy? The Fuckers. We talked about this two nights ago. The people that shit on us. The people that just don't belong in society. Ms. Velda. The Buttwynns. Remember? The Fuckers."

"Yep. I remember now." Askew gets up and grabs two beers, one for himself and one serving of hair of the dog for Grundish. "Matter of fact, I had a delivery to Buttwynn, today." He nods his head and smiles. "And I got the fucker."

"What'd you do?"

"I shook his pizza really hard so that the cheese would stick to the top of the box. That'll teach him to be such a shitty tipper."

"Yeah, Buddy. I applaud your efforts. You've got the right attitude. But you're pussing out. You need to do something more. Really show him he's a Fucker." Grundish chugs his malted brew. The throb of the hangover begins to back off. He dips a breaded frumunda cheese[13] stick in ranch dressing and shoves the whole stick in his mouth.

"Like what? I don't want to lose my job."

"You do two things for me and I'll tell you what to do. Number one, go get me another beer. And B, put another mystery nugget under Turleen's nose. That one you gave her is gone. She probably wants another."

Turleen's nugget is gone, even though neither Askew nor Grundish saw her eat it. And she is still asleep. Askew gently places another nugget under her nose. Again, the old lady stirs, nostrils flaring. Another trickle of saliva runs out of the side of her mouth, hangs briefly on her cheek, then adds more moistness to the already-stained upholstery.

"Well, here's another beer. Now, you tell me what to do."

"I can't give you specifics. I can only lead by example," Grundish says. "Like what I'm getting ready to do. Take notes if you like, and learn from the best."

"What are you gonna do?"

"I'm sick of the Fuckers in this trailer park. Every day I see those Fuckers out there, and they turn my stomach, you know?" Grundish stuffs two more frumunda cheese sticks in his mouth and chews, and thinks, and chews, and thinks some more. "We are probably the only ones in this trailer park that aren't registered sex offenders. These

[13]Frumunda cheese – frumunda my balls.

people are here because they are despicable. And society has told them that there are only a few places they are allowed to be. And we're hunkered down right in their midst because we can't afford to be anywhere nicer."

"So, what're you gonna do about it?"

Grundish places a cheese stick under Turleen's nose in the spot where the last nugget was. Turleen doesn't stir. Neither Grundish nor Askew saw her eat the second nugget. But, it is gone.

"I'm gonna strike fear into their hearts. I'm gonna get payback for the people they victimized. I know Fuckers like these people. I saw them in the joint all the time."

"You mean you saw people *simular* to these guys, right?" Askew asks. "I mean, you don't recognize any of these people from prison, do you?"

"Mostly, no. But, uh..." Grundish's nose wrinkles and his top lip twists up into a sneer. "You know that guy in Lot 49, right down at the end of our lane?"

Askew nods. "You mean the guy that stands out on the corner and tries to hand out balloon animals to kids?"

"Yeah, that's the guy. I know him from the big house. He was what we called a gunner. You know what that is?"

"Naw. I don't know that prison slang, man."

"A gunner[14]...well...he's a guy who stands in his cell playing with himself. He waits for people to walk by, mostly looking for women guards. But, it don't really matter who it is. Other inmates, guards, whoever. And when somebody walks by, he really start to jack it."

---

[14]Other fun prison slang: Diaper Sniper = child molester; family style = sodomy in missionary position; old lady = passive partner in homosexual prison relationship.

"That's a gunner?" Askew laughs, and a chunk of fried something-or-other falls from his mouth.

"That's a gunner," says Grundish. "And, then there's the snipers. They run up and try to shoot a load of spunk right on you. And that's really more what that fella down in Lot 49 was. I think his name in the joint was Bumpy D or something creepy like that."

"Damn, Dude. Did he ever shoot off a round at you?"

"Naah. No fucking way. I would'a split his wig. I'd still kind of like to, anyway. But I'm gonna do something a little different instead."

Grundish takes the half-full can of beer that Askew set on the floor and chugs it to chase the rest of his pre-migraine floaters away. He picks up the daypack and pulls out three large packages of semi-frozen hotdogs that he pilfered during his last burglary. In a plastic grocery bag, Grundish loads up the hotdogs and several more cans of beer. "I'm going for a bike ride around the park. You might want to step out and watch some of this."

Turleen sits cross-legged and her joints don't hurt. Between her fingers dangles an extra-long cancer stick capped with a burning ember. *Oh, good!* she thinks to herself, *I know it's a dream, but this is the only time I'm able to smoke*. She raises the cigarette to her face and notices that the hand is not wrinkled. The fingers are not bent into arthritic hag-claws. Instead of the liver spots she is used to, there are pinpoint freckles. She places the filter to her moist lips and pulls a deep drag from the smoke, inhaling it into both of her lungs. As she blows it out she doesn't cough. She smiles, and the back of her neck and her forearms tingle. *Damn, I love these dreams*, she thinks to herself. Turleen leans back and rests her back against the park bench. The sunlight warms her face. A cool breeze blows streamers of bluish vapors from the fireball of her cigarette. She closes her eyes and pulls another hit from the smoke – holding it long in her lungs, enjoying the nicotine rush.

"Hello," says the deep, warm voice that stirs Turleen from her tobacco bliss. "I've been waiting for you."

At Turleen's feet sit two dogs. One is a floppy basset hound with a wise face. The other looks familiar to Turleen, but she is unable to place it. She ponders the beast, searches her memory for evidence of the handsome animal regally posed before her.

"Pleased to meet you, ma'am," says the basset hound. "My name is Idjit Galoot. And this is my friend…well…you already know him, don't you?"

"You can talk?" Turleen leans back and looks sideways at the dog.

"Well, yes and no," answers Idjit. "You see, this isn't my first contact with a human in a dream. My first contact actually happened a few years in the future, and I tried speaking with a Scottish brogue. It was goofy and I've since just decided to go with the voice and delivery that you are hearing now."

"The future?" Turleen asks, still boggled by a talking dog and the concept of time travel, dream or not.

"Well, yes," says Idjit. "Time in this realm is not exactly linear. Sometimes I pop into people's dreams from years ago. Sometimes it's far into the future. It really isn't something that I have much control over. To me, it almost seems like some hack novelist's lame literary device used to fit a character from a previous book into a new book, thus preserving the conceptual continuity of the author's overall vision and giving a cameo appearance to a popular character. But I digress. Do you remember my friend?"

Turleen looks at the dogs, now over the initial shock that they can talk, and shakes her head. She studies Idjit's friend. "You look familiar, you do. Maybe younger than you're supposed to be. But my memory's horrible."

"You can't place me, huh? What's my motherfuckin' name?" says the dog.

Turleen swivels her head back and forth in a manner which indicates the negative and suddenly feels uncomfortable. She sucks hard at the cigarette. The smoke rapidly heats up the filter. The hot filter burns her lips.

"You know me," says the dog. "You killed me."

"Stubs?"

"Maybe. Or have you killed other dogs?"

"No, I haven't. Just you. And, I'm sure not going to apologize," huffs Turleen, placing a fresh unlit smoke in her mouth and lighting it with the ember from the almost-spent butt she had already been enjoying. "You were going to kill me, you were. All cuddled up at the bottom of my bed, you were. We know what that means, don't we, Mr. Stubs?"

"Um. I see your point," Stubs concedes. "The thing that really sucks about it for me was that I wasn't there to take you away," he chuckles at himself and shakes his head. "You weren't on my roster. I just liked your feet. They smell like meat."

"Ah, hooey! My feet do not smell like meat, they don't."

"They do. It's like that, and that's a matter-of-fact. That's why I licked them." Stubs licks his floppy, pink-and-black mottled dog lips. "They also tasted like meat, which shouldn't be so surprising. I mean, you are made out of meat, aren't you?"

"No, I'm not. And please get your friend away from my gams." Idjit, interested in feet that taste like meat, licks at Turleen's bare calf and slowly works his way down. She pushes the dog back with her other foot, strangely excited by the licking sensation. "Get back, you mongrel, or I'll give you what for, I will. I'm not going to have dead dogs licking my stilts, I'm not."

"I'm not dead, ma'am," says Idjit. "I'm just here with Stubs to give you some advice. But, I'll let Stubs fill you in on that. And by the way, your feet *do* taste like meat. Sort of like bologna with a hint of deviled eggs." Idjit wags his tail, thumping it happily on the ground.

"Well, your feet are not the reason we are visiting you right now," says Stubs. "I actually do have important business with you. But, uh, first," Stubs eyes sparkle, he pants heavily and slobbers a little, "is that a fried mystery nugget on your leg?"

"Ah, applesauce!" declares Turleen, waving her hand in the air as if brushing Stubs out of the way. "You must be addled, Doggy Dog. There is nothing on my lap but…" Turleen looks down and is surprised to discover a fried lump of breaded matter sitting in her lap. The peculiar breaded lump ignores the conversation and pretends it's elsewhere. "Why waddaya know? There is a mystery nugget on my lap, there is."

"I don't suppose you'd be willing to give me that tasty morsel as a peace offering. You know, for killing me and stuff?" Stubs raises his doggy eyebrows and wags his tail.

"And then we'll be Jake?" asks Turleen.

"If Jake is good, then yeah, we'll be Jake," says Stubs. Turleen grasps the oily nugget between her pointer finger and thumb and tosses it to Stubs. Stubs snatches the nugget mid-air and swallows it whole.

"And I'll promise not to lick your delicious feet again if you give me that other nugget on your lap," advises Idjit Galoot.

Turleen looks down to find another mystery nugget and a fried frumunda cheese stick lounging in her lap. "You have a deal, you do," she says and tosses the mystery nugget to Idjit. The nugget bounces off of Idjit's forehead and falls at his feet. He snatches it up and immediately swallows the nugget whole. Turleen jams the frumunda cheese into her mouth and does the same.

"The reason we're here," explains Stubs, "is to give you this." Idjit jumps onto the park bench and from his mouth drops a knife case onto Turleen's lap. The case is moist with basset saliva.

"A blade," says Turleen, as she grabs the black rubber handle and pulls the foot-long knife from its case. The weapon is perfectly balanced and honed to a razor sharp double-edged slicing surface. She puts a finger at the bottom of the handle and balances the knife there, and then flips it up, catches it, and wraps her hand tightly around the rubber grip. "I have to say that it feels good in my hand, it does. But, what am I gonna need a knife for?"

"It's not just any knife," explains Idjit. "Our friend Eshu wanted us to give it to you. He's kind of special. He said you will know when to use it and your aim will be true. That's what he said, and, that's all we know. So take it and keep it with you."

"Yeah," says Stubs, "go ahead and try it on."

"I don't mind if I do try on this little shiv," agrees Turleen. The case is made from black leather and has an elastic strap. Turleen hikes her dress up and straps the knife to her inner thigh. Realizing that she is not wearing underwear and that both dogs are staring intently up her skirt, she pulls her skirt down hastily and straightens it. "It feels good there, it does," she tells the dogs. It actually feels more than good to her. Having the powerful weapon strapped between her legs makes her tingle. Shivers shoot from her inner thigh, up her leg and gather all about her vulva. Momentarily she shudders with pleasure and then manages to refocus her attention. She addresses Stubs, changing the subject. "You look different...nice... not so..."

"Old and gross," smiles Stubs. "I know. I got pretty oogy there at the end. But now I appear as I did in my prime. Just call me Slim with the Tipton Brim. Not bad, huh?"

"Not bad at all. You even have all of your legs, you do. Why, if I were a lady poodle, I'd probably go into heat whenever you came around." She smiles and blushes at the realization that she is flirting with Stubs. "Anyway, I've no beef with you, I don't. And I'm sorry if I overreacted and kind of, you know, killed you."

"I do not hold it against you, Turleen," says Stubs. "As a matter of fact, I think I'm better off now. So in a way, I kind of owe you one. Maybe that's why I had to meet you here. I guess that's what the knife is all about. Anyway, Eshu says you must keep it with you at all times. Can you promise me that you'll do that?"

"Well, this is a dream, isn't it?" Turleen asks. Idjit nods his head in the affirmative. Turleen monkey-fuck lights another smoke with her old butt and considers the situation. "So, this is all a load of baloney anyway. So yeah, I'll keep the knife on me at all times, I will. I'll even make you another promise. If that knife ever actually comes in handy, I'll meet you both in another one of my dreams and let you lick my feet for as long as you desire."

"We'll be seeing you in your dreams," Idjit smiles.

"Can't wait," says Stubs, licking his chops.

Turleen awakens to the sounds of Grundish and Askew talking. Greasy spots from the nuggets mark the front of her oversized house dress. Beneath the dress, she feels a band tight on her leg. She reaches down and feels through her dress. She knows that it is a throwing knife without even looking.

Grundish straddles his bike; his eyes narrow with a look of grim determination. Grundish, the warrior readying himself for battle. He pounds on his chest, slaps himself in the face, claws at his own flesh, drawing bloody scrapes across his cheeks. The pockets of his cargo shorts are stuffed full with his weapon of choice: half-thawed, burgled hotdogs. Grundish chugs another beer and places a new one in the bottle holder on his bike. He looks at Askew and beams a mad grin. His migraine is all but forgotten. "If I don't make it back, tell Turleen I've always loved her."

"Get the fuck out of here and leave my aunt out of it," Askew laughs. "Let's see what you can do." Askew stands back, hands in his pants pockets, not knowing what to expect but thinking it will be good.

Grundish pumps hard on the bike pedals, pushing the machine as fast as he can around the park, screaming gibberish at the top of his lungs the entire time. "*YRARGHHH PIG SLOP MONKEY DOOTY DOLLY PARTON'S HOOTERS BLAAHHHHHHHH EEP OPP ORK MEANS MEET ME TONIGHT DING DING DING RUMPLE FUGLY BLOODY SHIT STAINS YEOWWWW...*"

And the residents of the park are drawn out of their double-wide dens of perversion to discover the source of the ruckus. Pot-bellied perverts roll their eyes and shrug their shoulders at each other. One man stands outside in only his yellowed boxer shorts. His matted body hair covers every square inch of his body up to his collar bone, the place where the man has decided to stop shaving his face and neck. His completely bald, shiny head tosses off rays of the Florida sun like a hideous flesh disco ball. Scrawny compulsive masturbators take time from their incessant monkey-spanking to witness the nonsense-spewing, raving lunatic speeding around their neighborhood on a bike. One buck-toothed miscreant stands with his hands in the opening for his pants pockets but the pockets have been cut out so that he can grope himself inconspicuously. He squeezes hard on his throbbing cock, aroused by all of the excitement but not sure why.

"*SPLIT PANTS SKANKY DONKEY MOTHERS IF YOU'RE GONNA DIE DIE WITH YOUR BOOTS ON I HAVE A LOVELY BUNCH OF COCONUTS BLEEEEEEEEE!*" Grundish continues to scream and rant and rave and pushes the bike around the small park until most of the residents are standing in their driveways witnessing the madness. When it seems that the whole park is watching, Grundish leaps off of his bike in front of a gathering of deviants and lets the bike crash into a white cargo van in front of one of the trailers. Before the crowd realizes what's happening, Grundish begins throwing semi-frozen hotdogs at the men.

Grundish sees it all as clear as day. In the middle of the battle he is singularly focused on striking fear into the hearts of the slugs[15] that inhabit his community. The hate

---

[15]The Great Gray Slug, *limax maximus*, has unusual mating practices. The hermaphrodite slugs will court each other for hours, circling

Grundish feels for the dirty, bad men steadies his hand and ensures that his aim is true. He reaches into his pocket, withdraws two hot dogs and flings them at the buck-toothed masturbator. The wieners fly directly at the poor excuse for a human. One bounces off of the side of his head, the other hits him in the neck. The man turns and flees for his trailer. Like a ninja with throwing stars, Grundish pulls frank after frank out of his pocket and pelts the congregation of rapscallions, deadbeats and degenerates about their heads and necks with partially frozen lips and assholes encased in intestines. His supply of wieners never seems to go down. After dispersing the crowd with a barrage of wieners, sending the gaggle of degenerates running for cover, Grundish mounts his bike and continues his jihad against the child molesters, peeping Toms, flashers and fondlers. He screams until his throat is raw and a bloody spray is exhaled with each yell, "*MONOCHROMATIC HALL AND OATES BOOGER SNOTS UH OH I BROKE IT TRAGLE TRAGLE OOO OOO HIGH AGA GAGA OOO OOO HIGH!*" With each logorrheic outburst Grundish flings another hotdog at the gawkers standing outside of their homes watching the

---

and licking each other. Then the slugs will climb to a high area and, whilst entwined together, lower themselves on a thick strand of mucus, entwine their sexual organs and exchange sperm. Sometimes their corkscrew shaped penises will become entangled in their mate's genitalia while exchanging sperm. When this occurs and they are unable to disentangle themselves, one or both slugs will chew each other's penises off. Once a slug's penis has been removed, it can still mate, but only using the female parts of the reproductive system.

carnage. At last his arsenal is almost spent. The final hotdog in his pocket is somehow still entirely frozen. Grundish launches it with all of his might at his next door neighbor. Mr. Shirley leans against his walker with his tattered bath robe partially open, exposing his tiny pecker and pendulous, hairy testicles. Grundish doesn't know what offense Shirley actually committed. He just knows that Shirley's name and picture are listed on the sexual offender poster tacked up on a rotting telephone pole near the front entrance of the park. Grundish doesn't care about the specifics of Shirley's proclivities. It matters not to Grundish that Shirley invites teenage boys into his trailer and trades his prescription medicines for the opportunity to suck the boys off. Grundish only cares that the final wiener hits its mark. The frankfurter hurtles through the air on a crash course with Shirley's face. The round frozen end of the dog strikes Shirley squarely on the eye, squishing the eyeball back into the skull. The wiener lodges in the eye socket and hangs there.

"*Blahhhhhhh!*" Shirley screams and runs for his front door. Blood streams down his cheek and onto his exposed chest. Only when he reaches the apparent safety of the inside of his trailer, with the door locked, does he pluck the hard frozen meat-stick from his eye socket. Blood trickles down the side of his nose, down his neck, and soaks into his dirty robe. Shirley drops into a shuddering mass of flesh on his couch, rolls up into fetal position, and weeps.

Outside of Shirley's trailer, Grundish doubles over in a hysterical fit of laughter.

"I think maybe you went a little bit far with this one, Pal," Askew says to Grundish. He laughs too, though. "I mean, aren't you afraid that the cops'll be out here and that Ms. Velda will violate your parole for this crazy fit you just threw?"

Gaining control of himself, Grundish stands erect again and laughs some more. "Hell, no! These guys want as little to do with the law as me. Nobody is gonna go and call the pigs out here. Hell, if the law comes out this way, they're gonna be looking to bust all of these guys for anything that they can. These old boys around us are sexual offenders, Son. They're a bigger target for the cops than one little old ex-con burglar who has been staying out of trouble."

"You may be right," Askew agrees. "But then again, you never know what's going to happen when you pull crazy shit like this. I guess the point is *mute* now. Next time though, please try to *appraise* me of your intentions to do crazy shit like this. I don't need to be involved in these kind of *incidences*."

In his peripheral vision Askew catches a blur of action. Before he has time to think about what is happening, Askew acts. And when the whole situation is done, and the blood is shed, and their lives are irreparably changed, it all plays back in his head like a bad movie.

Askew saw the man known as Bumpy D sprinting toward Grundish's back. Bumpy D's trousers were dropped to mid-thigh, the pervert's flag flying at half-mast, and he still displayed the swiftness of a track star. Even more amazing was that fact that the entire time he charged Grundish, Bumpy D was jerking his dick in large violent strokes.

Grundish had looked out for Askew almost all of their lives. If Askew was going to get caught for something illegal, Grundish gladly took the fall and never mentioned it again. If someone challenged Askew to a fight, Grundish jumped in and threw down before Askew ever had a chance to defend himself. If Askew needed money, Grundish would give him whatever little amount he could scrounge up or steal. Grundish, the ultimate big brother figure to Askew, always took care of his best friend. It was only natural that Askew's instincts would lead him to protect Grundish.

Bumpy D charged Grundish like a demented knight jousting with a crooked pork sword. Instinctively, Askew screamed "*NOOOOOoooooooooo.....*" and dived in Bumpy D's path, blocking Grundish from the masturbatory onslaught. At the same moment that Askew launched himself into the air, Bumpy D discharged a massive wad of spuz from his battered penis. The jism stretched into a pink-tinged pearlish strand, rounded on both ends and thin in the middle. The lustrous gob flew, end over end, seeking contact with Grundish. In mid air, Askew intersected the path of the projectile spunk. "*...oooooooooooooo*," continued Askew's scream until the warm load of Bumpy D's love went *SCHPLAAATTTT* across Askew's cheek and mouth.

The salty taste on his lips did something to Askew. Something awful. A switch was flipped in his brain. That switch turned off the self-control mechanism which had served to keep Askew out of trouble (in conjunction with intermittent interventions by Grundish) for so many years. The switch loosed a heap of crazy and sent violent pulses through Askew's body. His fat hands balled into tight fists, arms flailing. The muted *THUD, THUD, THUD* of bone-on-bone, fists crunching cheek bones and jaw and nose, did not register in Askew's head as he repeatedly pummeled away at what was once Bumpy D's face, turning the visage into a lump of ground meat. Askew mounted the prone figure, exacting a vicious ground-and-pound on the back of Bumpy D's head. Askew remembers being pulled off of the motionless heap that was once Mr. D. He remembers his arms still swinging, connecting with nothing but air and throwing off a crimson spray. He remembers his swollen hands flailing in front of him and Grundish lifting him off of Bumpy D, off of the ground. He remembers the deafening silence as the finality of his act dawned on him, and the complete loss of control faded. He remembers the shocking realization that his act forever changed his life. He remembers the awesome feeling of power and freedom. He remembers Grundish slapping his face and screaming: "We have to go! Now!"

"We have to go! Now!" Grundish shouts into Askew's crazed face. And Askew registers the urgent tone of his friend's voice. And a flurry of hectic activity follows. Still holding Askew off of the ground, Grundish carries him into the trailer and sets him down. "Get what you need and let's get out of here. Now!"

Without thinking, Askew grabs the keys to his El Camino and a carton of Blue Llamas from the freezer. Grundish tosses all of Turleen's belongings into her oversized suitcase and grabs his knapsack full of filched goods. "Get Turleen. She's coming with us," Grundish commands as he kicks the front door back, launches himself out the doorway and tosses the bags in the bed of the ridiculous truck-like car. The bags land in a pile of moldy work shirts, beer cans, and broken 8-track tapes. Grundish grabs his bike off of the ground and sets it in the back of the El Camino.

"Come on!" Grundish shouts into the trailer. The park residents slowly start peeking their heads out of their trailers once again. Slowly and awkwardly they lumber from their doorways, growing cautiously curious once again about what is happening outside. One neighbor, a lanky man with a head no bigger than a grapefruit, ventures from his retreat and approaches Bumpy D's fresh corpse, nudging it with his foot. Bumpy's form gives no more than a sack of potatoes. "We have to go, now," barks Grundish.

Inside the trailer, Askew hooks his hands under Turleen's arms and drags her backwards. In her efforts to get outside to see all of the commotion, Turleen twisted her ankle and fell in the bathroom. Unable to ambulate, Turleen allows herself to be dragged out of the trailer and set down in the middle position of the El Camino's bench seat. To Askew she says: "I need you to bring me my wine, I do, if we're gonna be cruising around."

Grundish, in the trailer, stuffs goods in a duffle bag. "Bring Turleen's wine," comes the shout from Askew, still outside. Grundish grabs a large bottle of Chianti from the refrigerator and throws it in the bag. The bottle, rounded at the bottom and tapering up toward the mouth, has a screw-on cap and is already half empty.

Outside, the crowd gathers around the pervert formerly known as Bumpy D. The lifeless exsanguinated corpse, he says nothing. The meaty unrecognizable knot-of-a-head gurgles a puddle of stinking blood, a slow-growing amorphous pool of Bumpy D's former life. The perverts stand and stare, confused doltish cows witnessing the end result of a slaughter, backing up little by little as the puddle of blood grows and advances on them. The man with the grapefruit head finally tears his eyes away from the gory display and points at the El Camino. Askew quickly cranks up his window and leans across Turleen to lock her door. An uneasy feeling about the crowd tugs at the base of Askew's scrotum. His testicles retract and his penis pulls back like a turtle under attack.

BLURRP…BLURRP…BLURRP. Askew, now too scared to leave the security of his locked car, honks the horn to get Grundish out of the trailer and to the car. *BLURRP… BLURRP…BLURRP.*

The gathering congregation of pimps, pederasts, pud-pullers, prostitutes and pickle-puffers collectively takes offense at the interlopers in their presence. The murderous, straight-laced, judgmental interlopers. Grapefruit-Head continues to point at the El Camino and belts out a piercing, multi-toned screech, incongruous high whines and deep bass notes clanging painfully off of each other. Moving in the manner of a provoked pack of attack dogs, the perverts charge, converging on the El Camino, banging on the hood, kicking the doors, pulling at the door handles, ripping off the windshield wipers and antenna. One man, a crooked-necked, squinty-eyed molester named Fester, pulls down the front of his sweat pants and smashes his smallish but semi-aroused genitals on the passenger side window. His bushy pubic mess envelopes the shriveled weenis, making his goods look like a tiny slab of fetid meat sinking into Easter basket hay. Pulling back, he leaves a greasy thumb-shaped smear on the window.

From the front door of the trailer, Grundish takes in the melee and formulates a plan. Not a great plan, but an effective one. He dashes back into the trailer and grabs more meat from the freezer – mostly boosted hotdogs – and dumps it into a pillow case. He sprints into the middle of the mob swinging the frozen meat in wide arcs with all of his might.

FWAAAPPPP! The pillow case connects with Grapefruit-Head's face, crushing his nose and knocking out his front teeth. Dropping to his knees, his hands held to his flattened and bloody face, Grapefruit-Head emits another discordant screech that throws the crowd into a frenzy. Grundish swings the frozen meat and connects with another head, immediately dropping the man to the ground. A circle forms around Grundish, just out of reach of the brutal weapon. One at a time, the perverts charge him and are felled by the mighty meat bag.

Crooked-necked, squinty-eyed Fester darts in and out of Grundish's striking zone, trying to get quick jabs in at Grundish. Pecking here and there, Fester delivers ineffectual strikes. With each successful poke or kick at Grundish, Fester grows more confident. He strikes out with a kick. His foot is caught in mid-air by Grundish's left hand. Swinging the meat bag at full force in a circle at his side with his free arm, Grundish brings the bag up, a power-packed meat product upper-cut, and slams the pillow case into Fester's chin, lifting the man's other foot off of the ground and throwing him back against the El Camino. Grundish swings the pillow case around his head and charges directly into the growing crowd, bellowing his own unintelligible screech, dropping all challengers with a face-full of frozen pain. A path to the El Camino clears and Grundish charges through, diving into the bed of the car. He slaps the top of the car with both hands and screams, "GO!"

With Grundish in the bed of the car, Askew drops the automatic gear selector into drive and mashes the accelerator to the floor. Twin streaks of smoking rubber tattoo the concrete as a wave of human perversion washes over the hood of the El Camino. The raw crunch of bones, the roar of the engine, and Grundish's battle cry fill the air as the bodies are thrown out of the way and off of the hood. Reaching into the pillow case, Grundish resumes his hot-dog massacre, flinging frozen wieners at the angry mob with precision, sapping the group of its mob bravery and dispersing the pathetic deviants. At the edge of the trailer park, just before turning onto the public street, Askew brakes and leans over to unlock the passenger door. Grabbing his backpack and Turleen's bottle of wine, Grundish jumps out of the truck's bed and lets himself into the passenger compartment. He smells of hotdogs, sweat, and victory.

"Where the fuck are we going to?" asks Askew in a panic. "What the fuck do we do?"

"Drive, Bro. Just drive us on out of here and don't stop for nothin'," answers Grundish. "We'll figure out where to go once you get us away from here." He uncaps the bottle of wine and chugs mouths full of the cheap grape squeezings. Wiping the mouth of the bottle on his shirt, Grundish passes the *vino* to Turleen. "Here you go, ma'am. Take a glug from the jug."

Grundish pushes an unmarked 8-track into the tape player. The opening notes of *Sweet Home Alabama* twang from the blown speakers: *Duh-da duh-duh, Da-Duh-da duh-duh, Da-Duh-da duh-duh, duh-da-duh-da-duh-da-da.* "Shit, Boy. Is that freedom rock?" asks Grundish.

Askew smiles, snaps out of his muddlement[16], and yells, "fuck yeah, man!"

---

[16]Yes, the author made up his own word. Muddlement. And it is a good word. Try using it in conversation and you will find it is quite satisfying. Make up your own words and challenge people to look

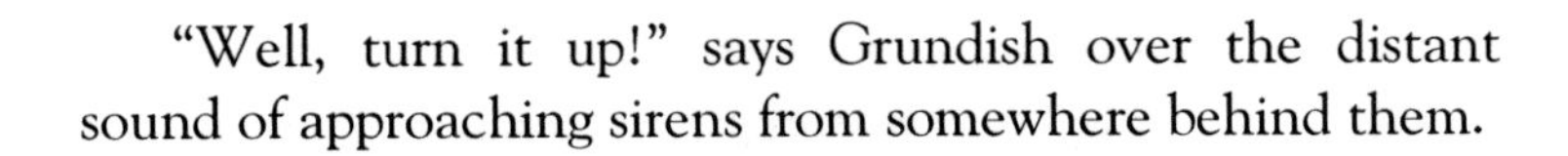

"Well, turn it up!" says Grundish over the distant sound of approaching sirens from somewhere behind them.

---

them up in the dictionary. When they can't find your words in their dictionary, tell them it's because they have a cheap, shitty, out-of-date dictionary. Challenge them to purchase the entire set of the Oxford English Dictionary and tell them that there they will find your fake words. When they don't, tell them they are stupid and that you made up your own words. If they have a problem with it, slap them in the face with a glove, demand satisfaction, and challenge them to a duel with the weapon of their choosing.

Turleen takes a glug from the jug and grows excited about the hullabaloo. Her throwing knife is still strapped to her thigh, and she wonders if the right time to use it has already passed. After the loss of her lung and her detention at Emiction Lakes, she had wondered if she would ever have any fun again. Seeing Grundish bludgeoning the scuzzy losers in the trailer park moved her in a way she never expected. And fleeing a gory crime scene was certainly a novel thing. Even listening to that rock and roll through the blown speakers of Askew's El Camino stirred something new in her. It all jammed a stick up her ass and stirred up her shit. Just when she was starting to feel her spark fading, Turleen Rundle was gaining a new zest for life. Chugging another glug from the jug and then passing the bottle back to Grundish, Turleen speaks: "I know where we can go, I do. But," she cups her hand in front of her nose and mouth and exhales, as if to check her breath, "I'm gonna need a day or two to line things up."

"Okay," says Grundish, panting heavily and taking another swig from the bottle. He grimaces at the sharp acid flavor of Turleen's wine. Warm fumes gather at the back of his mouth and gently ride out on a puff of stale breath. Grundish, still shaking from the major adrenaline dump into his system, takes another swig to calm himself and passes the bottle back to Turleen. "Okay," he repeats, "but we have to find somewhere to lay low for now. I think Bumpy D is worm food. Sex offender or not, when there's a dead body involved, the fuzz is gonna be looking to bust somebody. That somebody is gonna be us. You ever been picked up by the fuzz?" he asks Turleen.

"Heck yes, and it hurt like hell, it did," she answers, beating Grundish to the tired old punch line.[17]

Askew drives and stares straight ahead, following directions from Grundish but hearing nothing else that is said. He pushes the cigarette lighter in and waits. Turleen's and Grundish's voices are distant and muffled, as if coming to him through the water. The lighter pops out. Askew presses his knee against the steering wheel and catapults a Blue Llama up into his mouth. The cigarette finds itself wedged in the gap between his chipped and yellowed front teeth. Askew holds the lighter up and looks at the red hot metal coil. He touches the coil to the cigarette and inhales. Pulling the lighter back, Askew notes a small piece of tobacco is stuck to the red hot metal and is quickly reduced to ash.

Directing the unthinking driver out of the suburban sprawl, Grundish tells Askew to turn left, right, straight ahead, left again and leads them out onto slow country roads, away from what would now be designated a crime scene. "Over there," points Grundish, "pull over there, under that roof." Off to the left side of the road stands a deserted metal structure with no walls. The structure covers an area of ground equivalent to the size of a basketball court. Rusty I-beams, thirty feet high, are capped

---

[17]How many cops does it take to throw a suspect down the stairs? None, he fell.

off with a heavily oxidized metal roof. The structure, neglected and abandoned, is now a dumping ground – a depressing grave yard for dead refrigerators, dishwashers and other discarded household appliances. Littered about the overgrown ground are broken beer bottles, condoms, food wrappers, syringes and tires. A rusted old truck is turned on its side, the windows shattered. A discarded television set rests on a stump, its unbroken screen sadly blank, and its plug dangling impotently. A dry-rotted whitewall tire lies on the ground. It encircles a bushy growth of orange wildflowers, nature's beauty thriving in the midst of the obsolete and discarded manmade debris.

Grundish exits the car and Turleen follows. Turleen, an index finger looped through the ring of the jug, holds the wine out to Grundish again. The wine helps to slow his racing mind. Askew still sits in the El Camino, smoking. The ashes on the cigarette, unflicked since being lit, are gray and severe in their droopage[18].

"Hey there, Fuckstick!" Grundish addresses Askew, slapping the windshield to get his attention. Askew jumps and the cigarette ashes fall onto the front of his white tank-top shirt. Eyes blinking rapidly, a quick side to side shake of his head, and Askew is back in the moment. "You with us, Pal?" Grundish asks and gets a nod from Askew. "Good, then. Get out of the car, and let's put our heads together."

"Listen up, Sonny, I need my rheumatism medicine back while you boys figure out what to do next," says

---

[18]I know, I know, another made up word. But droopage is fun to say. Repeat it five times quickly and poke yourself in the eye with a pencil. Droopage seems to lose the meaning it never had in the first place when you do that, doesn't it?

Turleen, now sitting comfortably on a discarded toilet, her back leaned against the cracked tank.

"What do we do now? I think I done killed Bumpy D," says Askew with a look resembling something like satisfaction on his face. "I've never been in a fight in my life. I just fucking lost it when that guy splooged in my face. I mean," he stops and ruminates briefly, nods affirmatively as if agreeing with the voices in his head, "yeah. That mother fugger had it coming. And I'm glad I did it." Askew stops, smiles, and asks Grundish: "Ain't you gonna *land blast* me for getting us into this situation? I really kind of shit the bed, if you know what I mean."

"Hell no, Brother," Grundish shrugs his shoulders. "Bumpy D never would have come in gunnin' for me if I hadn'ta gone a little batshit myself there. This is as much my doing as it is yours. I ain't got no cause to go blaming you."

"That slimy piece of shit did have it coming to him, didn't he?"

"Yeah, I reckon he probably did."

"Well, I'm kinda proud of myself, then."

"Well, you can spank the dolphin over it later," says Grundish. "Right now we've gotta figure out where we can lay low. Do you have a new list for me?"

"Nope. No, I don't. But I think I know a house that's gonna be available for a couple of days. It's that Buttwynn fucker's place. I've been watching his house real close because I've wanted you to hit his joint for a while now. So far as I can tell, he's been gone for a couple of days. And I'd love to hunker down in his pad."

"Are you sure that the house is empty?" asks Grundish.

"As sure as I can be. I mean, his cars haven't been in the driveway, all of the lights in the house seem to be off, all of the curtains closed, the grass needs to be cut, *excetera, excetera...*"

"You sure about this place?" Grundish asks.

"As sure as I can be," Askew answers. "But then again, I'm no professional burglar. Maybe I'm sure, but I can't be certain. I've *appraised* you of all of the things I noticed. I mean, if you think that what I've seen doesn't *jive* with Buttwynn being gone, then we can try something else. But that's what I've got to suggest right now."

"Can you give me directions on how to get to his house?" Grundish asks.

"Well, fuck yes. I deliver pizza, don't I? I have to know my way around, you know."

With a map drawn on the back of a pizza shop menu and a belly full of sour wine, Grundish hefts his bike from the bed of the El Camino. "I need you to stay here while I check things out," Grundish tells Askew. "Don't go anywhere. I mean it. And, if you hear people coming, hide in the brush until I come for you. Okay?"

"Hide in the brush," says Askew slowly.

"That's it. Hide in the brush until I come for you. Can you remember that?"

"You got it, Grundish" smiles Askew, unexpectedly happy for just having snuffed out a human life with his bare and now-swollen hands. "Hide in the brush 'til you come."

"If I'm not back by two in the morning, head out of here and bring the car to Buttwynn's house. Otherwise, I'll be back before then and we'll come up with plan B."

"I need more wine, I do, if you find it necessary to come back," commands Turleen imperiously, and a bit slurred, from her porcelain throne. "Another jug of Chianti if you get a chance. And a fleet enema. And maybe some panty liners as long as you're at the store getting my wine. Big, thick, panty liners, fella. Oh yeah, and a can of feminine deodorant spray, extra strength."

Grundish and Askew cock their heads curiously at the request for feminine products for Turleen's superannuated plumbing. "Don't ask," she tells them. "You're better off not knowing about these things. A lady has to keep the mystery, she does."

Grundish salutes Turleen, clicks his heels at her request, and mounts his bike. "Don't go anywhere," he repeats to Askew. "Lay low and let me take care of this."

"I'm not going anywhere, Brother," answers Askew. "I'm sitting down on the hood of my car and I'm gonna teach myself what it would be like not to have hands. And I'm never going to use my hands again." He kicks his shoes off and wedges the big toe on his right foot into the top of the sock on his left foot and thus peels the cotton tube off without the aid of his hands. He then begins the same process on the other sock.

"Perfect," agrees Grundish before he pedals his bike away from the roof. "You can tell me all about it later."

Grundish takes the bike through fields, across backyards, through woods and scrubs of palmetto and over dry, hard ground that will become ponds and swamps when wet season bitch-slaps the drought with a sloppy moist backhand. Once back in town he pushes the bike through the undeveloped outskirts of the housing developments and into the Happy Rambler RV Resort Park. The center of the solar system already out of view, Grundish walks the bike through the campground in anonymity, waving to the occasional resident sitting on a porch, eyeing the trailers and RV's for vacancies, working out a Plan B, just in case.

At the community center, gray-skinned senior citizens float in the pool like sickly river otters, weakly paddling about to keep from sinking. *An appropriate metaphor for their golden years,* Grundish thinks to himself sadly. Actually, lacking the intellectual aptitude to think in terms of similes and metaphors, Grundish simply thinks to himself, *God damn, they look like a bunch of sick river otters trying to keep from sinking*. Irregardless[19], it strangely moves

---

[19]The word irregardless, believed to be a combination of irrespective and regardless, is often listed as nonstandard or improper in dictionaries due to its double negative use of *ir* (a prefix meaning not) and *less* (a suffix meaning without). However, it has become widely used and is slowly inching its way toward being a proper and accepted word. In the spirit of making up new words, I am throwing

him. At the side of an aluminum maintenance shed, Grundish spies a canoe. He drags the green, wide-bottomed Kevlar boat to the water and sets his bike in the front. Making note of the community center for later eventualities, Grundish wades the boat out into the Alafia river and climbs in once clear of the bank.

The river, flowing in a westerly direction, does not go out of its way to help move the canoe. Grundish paddles the boat, keeping her close to the bank. The river is an old friend to Grundish. As a child he sometimes spent summers at the Vagabond Village trailer park in Gibsonton with his Aunt Bernice. Bernice was nice but always seemed to drink too much. Mostly, Grundish remembers that she made something greasy, salty, and tasty that she called scrapple. Most of Grundish's Florida experience as a child, though, consisted of time spent canoeing and fishing on the river with a kind of surrogate father by the name of Lenny. Lenny was a black man who lived in the cab of a broken-down semi truck just off of Route 41, by the public docks, with his girlfriend, Melvetta, and their dog. Lenny told Grundish that he was from Chicago originally and was hauling a load of something or other when his truck broke down. Lenny always hung out on the shaded dock, fishing and smoking cigarillos. He would cuss, drink coffee, and sometimes reel in catfish or blue crabs on his line. *I'm gonna eat that mu'fugga tonight, cook 'im up in a pot and have me some seafood*, Lenny would say. *Don't talk so foul around the boy, he's just a baby*, Melvetta would chastise him. She

---

my support behind irregardless and attempting to help it move in the direction of standardization, if for no other reason than to irritate snooty vocabulary police.

was chunky white girl with stringy blond hair, and always cringed after she spoke to Lenny. *Woman, get off the dock, this ain't no place for a female to be peckin' at me*, Lenny would tell her. Usually she would obey. Sometimes she would yell at him a little more until Lenny would tell her, *Baby, God don't like ugly. Now get off this man's dock*. Lenny would apologize to Grundish, just a kid at the time, and explain that his lady was sad because she lost her babies in a car accident and she wasn't herself sometimes. *Really*, Lenny would say, *she used to be real sweet and funny. I love that girl more than a pig loves slop. Sometimes she makes me crazy. I'm gonna stick with her, though. Shee-it*, he'd laugh, *I ain't got nowheres better to go and neither does she*. Lenny would let Grundish use a canoe that he had somehow procured and Grundish would take that boat all up and down the river. Lenny and Melvetta lived in the truck for several years and were always around when Grundish came down for his summers with his aunt. One year, when Grundish came down, they were just gone. Years later he heard that Lenny shot Melvetta and their dog and then just disappeared. Paddling down the river now, Grundish momentarily thinks he senses the ghosts of Lenny, Melvetta and the dog. And then the feeling excuses itself and finds somewhere or someone else to haunt.

Off to the left, on the other bank of the river, a scuzzy looking band plays a Georgia Satellites tune at the Beer Shack. On the porch of the river bar, scurvy tattooed bikers laugh and yell and call each other nicknames like Snake or Knuckles or Stumpy. *It's Sunday, and that means fifty-cent malt liquor night at the Beer Shed*, thinks Grundish. A garbage can full of ice and 24-ounce cans of off-brand malt liquors sits on the dock. In order to get the cheap beer, the customers have to dig deep into the garbage can and pull out whatever can they grab. They pay fifty cents and take their poison. Aiming toward the opposite shore, Grundish paddles over and pulls the canoe up beside the dock. Climbing the steps up to the porch, Grundish heads for the malt liquor barrel. He pulls a handful of change from his pocket and counts it: three dimes, two nickels, and three pennies. The ice cold contents of the barrel freezes his hand as he gropes about and pulls out a steel white can that says *Malt Liquor* on it and nothing else. *When the hell did they stop making steel cans*, he wonders to himself as he walks over and slaps his handful of change down on the counter. "It's all I got," he tells the barmaid, Kimmie.

Kimmie looks down at the change, then up at Grundish again. "All right," she says, "but you don't want to be in here. Everybody knows about what you and your buddy done. Ain't nobody here gonna give you a hard time about it. But we don't need no trouble either. I just got my liquor license back. So do me a favor, Grundish. Just take your drink and slink on out of here. I never saw you here and neither did anybody else."

Grundish drains the generic can of malt liquor and returns to the canoe. He lies back on his seat and stares up at the full moon as the slight flow of the river gently urges the boat downstream. He stays on his back for a while in the canoe and allows her to drift. He drifts under an overpass and pulls the boat onto the northern side of the river under the bridge. Up above, on the bridge, traffic goes by and cares nothing about the tattooed man hiding underneath. Grundish extracts his bike from the canoe and commences to pedaling it again, heading north and west through backyards and on dimly lit streets, pulling off and hiding in the bushes when headlights approach. Eventually, based upon Askew's instructions, Grundish finds himself at the side of a darkened house in an upscale neighborhood.

The house is dark and quiet. Probably empty. No cars in the driveway, no noises from within. Grundish lays his hands on the aluminum siding and rests his forehead against the house. Like a phrenologist reading lumps on a skull, his fingers gently slide over the side of the house, pausing on notches in the siding, lightly tapping, divining the nature of the building. Nothing there to tell him that it is occupied. Following his strict protocol for entry, he finds an unlocked window and creeps in. Stealthy and slow, Grundish fluidly slinks through the unlit building, never bumping into anything, never tripping, never a noise, just effortlessly flowing through the house. He stops in a room, sits back in a leather home theater chair, pops out the footrest and reclines the back. He closes his eyes and opens his mind. Clearing his head of all thoughts, Grundish sends out energy and waits for it to bounce back. He concludes that house is clear and begins to ready the place for Askew and Turleen's arrival.

The doormat says *Welcome! The Buttwynns*, but Grundish can't read it in the dark. Motionless and silent, he waits for the rattle and hum of the El Camino. It appears to Grundish that the Buttwynns are gone for the next three to four days. In a long-winded, rambling, and occasionally incoherent message on the Buttwynn's answering machine, Grandma Buttwynn laid out the plans for the entire Buttwynn family's visit to Neenah, Wisconsin. Aside from a family reunion and taking everyone to a lutefisk[20] festival, Granny Buttwynn suggested that they take the whole family for a tour of the Neenah Foundry Company (*it's one of the nation's leading manhole cover manufacturers*, she said, *and, in fact, Grampa Buttwynn once had a job inspecting manholes*). Granny also suggested that she could drive the family to the airport on the ninth for their return flight.

Clad in silk boxer shorts, a silk robe, black stretchy dress socks held up by sock garters, and leather sandals, all compliments of Mr. Randy Buttwynn's closet, Grundish sits motionless on a metal bench beside the front door, smoking one of Buttwynn's cigars. Other than the glowing fireball of the cigar, Grundish is undetectable. Occasionally

---

[20]Lutefisk is a traditional Nordic dish of air-dried whitefish soaked in caustic soda lye, making the fish into a gelatinous stinky blob. Today more lutefisk is consumed in Wisconsin than in Norway.

he moves in order to dip the end of the cigar in a sniffer of Buttwynn's cognac. Grundish correctly guesses that with the absence of an identifying band on the cigar and the presence of a creamy, mellow flavor, the stogie must be a Cuban.

Off in the distance something sounding like a gunshot rings out. Grundish recognizes the backfiring of the El Camino. As it gets closer, he reverts into the house and hits the automatic garage door button. Having already unscrewed the light bulbs so as not to draw attention when Askew and Turleen arrive, the garage is dark. Askew's El Camino roars down the street, backfiring several times, with *Gimme Back My Bullets* blaring on the stereo. The headlights set on bright, Askew turns onto the driveway and into the garage. Grundish quickly shuts the garage door, pops open the driver side door and reaches into the car to turn off the ignition. The engine backfires one more time and spits out a puff of oily exhaust. The music stops.

"God damn!" snaps Grundish. "You trying to wake up the whole neighborhood? We've got four days in this house if you don't go screwing things up for us." And then he looks at Askew's face in the weak glow of the dome light. Half of his upper lip, ripped and glooping a bloody ooze, hangs from the left side of his face, exposing his front teeth and looking like a smooshed slug. A cut above his left eyebrow draws a straight line over the swollen orbit of the eye. The left side of Askew's face is inflamed and bulging. "God damn!" Grundish says again, shocked by the contrast between the perfectly intact right side of Askew's face and the pulpy mess on the left. "God damn!" he says again when he realizes that Askew's right leg is twisted up, knee against his chest, and his long, thin toes are wrapped around the steering wheel while his left foot is resting on the brake pedal. Askew sits uncomfortably with both of his hands in his pockets.

"Yessir," says Turleen, stepping out of the passenger side with a plastic bag full of feminine products, "he's powerful hurting, he is. That boy defended me against a whole gang of thugs ready to do me no good, he did. And he did it all with his feet."

"What did the thugs do to you, Turleen?"

"Well, it's not so much what they did as the way they were looking at me," she says. "They was giving me the up and down, they was. Looking at me the way a hungry dog eyes a piece of meat. And that boy weren't having no part of it. He just jumped out of the car and started putting the boots to them boys, he did. Seemed like he hurt them real bad. The boy's got moxie, he does."

Grundish studies his friend in astonishment. All of the time he has known him, Askew has been the one to walk away from conflict, the one to avoid physical confrontation, *a pussy*, Grundish thinks. And now he's dishing out a bucketful of mean at the drop of a hat. "Well, let's get inside, then," he says and helps Askew out of the car.

On the Buttwynn's kitchen table sits a spool of common thread, a needle, a lighter, a crusted tube of super glue, a bottle of single malt scotch whisky, two shot glasses and a pack of Blue Llamas. Grundish sits at the table, sipping at a tumbler of scotch on the rocks, waiting for Turleen to get Askew cleaned up. He takes a mouthful of the smoky liquid and lets it sit, warming and stinging his gums all at once. Leaning back into the chair and hanging his head over the back of the seat, he nods off and is awakened when Turleen and Askew return.

"Uh-uh," says Askew, holding a wash cloth and ice to his mouth. "Dyou er noth thewing my faithe," he tells Grundish, the words coming out mangled as they are filtered through his torn upper lip.

Grundish shrugs, fills both shot glasses with scotch, and slides one across the table. Askew, hands in pockets, stands on one leg and lifts the other. His long toes grip one of the legs of a seat at the table and pull it out. He sits and looks down at the shot glass and then back at Grundish. Grundish picks up his shot glass and gently clinks it on the top of the glass set out for his friend. Opening his bloodied mouth and leaning down over the shot glass, hands still in pockets, Askew grabs the top of the shot glass between his teeth and sits up quickly, tossing his head back and draining the contents down his throat.

"Ahhhh," they both grunt, as the warmth travels down their throats, spreads across their chests, and snuggles up in their bellies. Grundish pours two more shots and they repeat the ritual again. And again, and again, Grundish's serving getting smaller and smaller each time until he stops consuming his altogether and only refills Askew's glass.

"Now get up on the table, you big pussy," Grundish says, "and let me take care of that lip. We can't take you to a hospital looking like that. They will call the police and then you're...no...make that *we're* fucked. And this'll make you look tough, you little bitch."

Through the whisky haze, Askew tries to rethink the idea of getting stitches from Grundish. He nods toward the shot glass. Grundish shrugs, nods back, and fills up one more shot which is quickly downed via Askew's shot-glass-deep-throat technique. With a flick of the head the shot glass is thrown toward the sink and shatters on the floor. Askew stands on the chair, turns away from the table and sits down on it. Hands still in pockets, he wiggles himself fully onto the table, facing up, and tells his friend "Dyou vetther noth fuggup my faithe."

"I could do nothing to make your face any uglier," answers Grundish as the excessive alcohol consumption pulls the shades on Askew's consciousness.

Grundish never had one sewing lesson and never so much as bothered to stitch a patch to a pair of pants or a torn shirt. To him, Home Economics was a class in junior high for chicks and fairies. So what made him think that he was qualified to stitch up Askew's lip is anyone's guess. But stitch it he did. Luckily, Grundish did at least like watching surgery shows on the Health and Medicine Channel. He knew that it would be best to stitch up the skin so that the two torn pieces formed an outward ridge, and that they would heal up, tuck themselves back in and make for less of a scar. He also saw something, somewhere about super glue being used to mend minor wounds. Once the sewing was finished, culminating in a meaty, gashed seam running from mid-upper lip to just below Askew's puffy, rounded cheek pad, a heavy layer of glue was applied on top of the gash.

At mid-day, upon waking, Askew stumbles through the house, hands in pockets, and opening doors with his feet until he finds a bathroom. He looks in the mirror. An accident victim stares back. The super glue, being somewhat over-applied, adheres the torn lip to the gum line, exposing the teeth on the front left side, giving him a Presleyesque upturn of a lip (no fool Billy Idol lip either[21]).

---

[21]If you don't got Mojo Nixon, then your store could use some fixin'.

For the gash above his eye, Grundish had to shave the eyebrow in order to effectively seal it with more glue. For consistency, the other eyebrow was also shorn. In an effort to minimize the freakish browless appearance, surprised-looking and severely-arched brows were drawn in by Turleen with a brown El Marko permanent marker.

Reeling from a screaming headache and debilitating nausea, Askew leans against the counter and decides it is not worth it to try to pick at the wounds. He made a solemn oath to teach himself to use only his feet, and with the way he is feeling, it doesn't seem possible to twist himself up enough to prod his face with his toes. *Later*, he tells himself, *later I'll check it out*. He walks out of the bathroom, hands in pockets, and opens doors with his foot until he finds the master bedroom.

In the middle of the king-sized bed, snoring, dropping flatus, and drooling, is a lump of warm flesh known as Grundish. Lacking the energy and motivation to seek out another bed, Askew climbs in with the Grundish-lump, digs a knee into its back, and manages to clear himself enough room on one side of the bed.

Grundish and Askew sleep away the most part of the first day in the temporary hideout. But not Turleen. At sunrise, despite only having a few hours of sleep and a twisted ankle, she is up and about, working on plans for a safehouse for her and the boys. First it is half a dozen provocative squats. She takes a shower and squeezes her spots. Uses a brush on her teeth. Trims and deodorizes her twat. She looks at her house dress and says to herself, *a body can't expect to lure a man in a get up like this, it can't*. In the master bedroom, Turleen tears through Mrs. Buttwynn's wardrobe, being as loud as she wants and still doesn't wake the boys. The clothes look to be a close enough fit for her to make them work. She chooses a red dress and thinks to herself, *I would wear something like this if I were going to be on T.V.* She flings the dress over her shoulder and heads back into the bathroom.

The reflection in the mirror makes her happy. The fine red dress hangs on her slight frame just right. Mrs. Melba Buttwynn's pearl necklace and matching earrings are perfect. Turleen's hair, an unnaturally blinding shade of red, is pulled back and twisted up in a bun, a #2 pencil stuck through to hold it in place. She flashes a maloccluded grin, the lower jaw jutting out proudly past the ill-fitting upper plate of false teeth. A small foam of spittle nestles in the corners of her mouth. The make-up on her face is thick and garish, the rouge like berries smashed on each cheek, the eye liner thick and clumpy, the eye shadow a trashy aquamarine. Turleen takes in her reflection and feels young and vigorous again. She feels sexy.

While the boys sleep, unwittingly entangled in a tender spooning position, Turleen arranges the objects in the kitchen to her satisfaction. The way it was set up made no sense to her. Who puts the silverware in the cabinet when it should be in a drawer? Why would the dishes be under the counter when they should be in the cabinet where the silverware was placed? Shouldn't the dish rags and towels be in a drawer near the kitchen sink? What is the purpose of this dry-rotted rubber dildo hidden back under the sink, behind the Drano? These and many other ill-thought-out arrangements are remedied by Turleen. And the boys still sleep. Turleen decides to cook a pot of beef stew and have it ready for Grundish and Askew for when they awaken.

The sounds of moving bowels reverberate in the master bedroom. The booming flatulence bounces around from wall to wall until the noise finds its way out of the slightly ajar door of the bathroom and wends its way to Grundish's ears. He stirs, rolls over toward the middle of the bed and wonders why the mattress is warm in a spot where he was not lying. A smell tickles his senses – an awful, wonderful, sickening, delicious, vile and delightful aroma that disturbs Grundish. If the stink is from the evil goings-on in the bathroom, if Askew is turning the room into a bog of eternal stench, then the mephitis is one of the most disturbing and sickening olfactory assaults Grundish has experienced. On the other hand, the aroma is not unlike that of Turleen's famous beef stew. *If it is the beef stew I smell*, thinks Grundish, *then I'm ready to gorge myself*. His stomach rumbles in anticipation. *But if it's Askew's ass, then I'm never going to be able to eat Turleen's stew again.*

Rubbing away the eye-cheese, Grundish rolls out of bed, still attired in the silk robe and boxers along with the socks and garters, and removes himself from the bedroom. The lovely/awful aroma gets stronger as he navigates the hallway and tromps down the stairs. The fragrance of the stew hooks a finger in each of his nostrils and drags him through the house and into the kitchen.

"Well, hey there, sleepy head. I didn't think you boys would ever wake up," says Turleen to Grundish. She takes in his costume from the night before, and he takes in hers.

"What'cha all dolled up for?" he asks her.

"What? Can't a body pretty herself up once in a while?" Turleen asks, adjusting her dress, pulling down on the back in order to pull up the front and cover her exposed and pleated tit-hatch[22]. Her dried lips turn up subtly into a smile and a weak glow emanates under the make up and creased skin. Somewhere in that grin Grundish sees the vestiges of a young, sweet girl, one that he would have cut off his foot to be with were he alive sixty years prior. He blushes momentarily and looks away. "And, who are you to go pecking at my clothes? You look like Hugh Heffner's tetched little brother, you do, in your silk robe and sock garters. A real dandy, you are. Now go pour me a glass of wine, red please, while I get you a bowl of stew."

Grundish's stomach growls and he turns away, headed for the wine rack in the living room. Upstairs, Askew is performing intense stretching exercises in an effort to free himself from the use of his hands and arms. Downstairs Grundish uncorks a bottle of wine that is worth more than the trailer he and Askew shared. Grundish pours a large wineglass full of the maroon liquid. Turleen ladles steaming bowls full of chunky beef and vegetable sludge for the boys. For the moment, everybody feels safe.

[22]Cleavage.

"We have three days left here. That should give us some time to figure out what to do next," says Grundish to Askew. "Right now just sit back, relax, and clear your mind. We'll figure out what we're gonna do."

"I can't help but to worry," says Askew. A bowl of stew sloughs off steam in front of him on the coffee table. Between his big and second toes he grips a soup spoon and, with determination etched on his battered face, he scoops a spoonful and twists his foot up toward his face, slopping a warm helping of the stew into his mouth. "Ungggh," he drops the spoon and groans as a trickle of salty broth dribbles down his chin. The lip reattachment surgery makes it almost unbearable to eat the soup. But the thought of passing up a bowl of Turleen's stew seems even worse. In a pleasure versus pain evaluation, the stew wins out. He wipes his face on his shoulder. "I'm just a little freaked out. I don't know what happened with Bumpy D." The foot-spoon slops another load of stew into his crusted maw and more broth dribbles onto his shirt, "I just don't know. I kind of went crazy on him. I think I killed him…"

"I know you killed that sick fuck…"

"…and if I did kill him, I'm fucked. What am I saying, *if*? I know I killed him. The whole neighborhood saw it. And I just don't think beating somebody to death for cumming on your face qualifies as self-defense. I really shit the bed on this one."

Grundish sets his spoon in his empty bowl, picks at his teeth with a fingernail and says, "Listen, I don't know about self-defense. Actually, I do. And, that wasn't self-defense. Maybe temporary insanity. But not self-defense. The point is, we need to lay low for a little while and figure out our options. Let's not make any decisions about what to do just yet. We'll go see if there's anything on the local news about us and then reevaluate our situation. Right?"

The theater-style leather seats gently hum as they lean Grundish and Askew back into the optimal television viewing positions. Five different remote controls are laid out on the table between the chairs. Askew's drawn-on eyebrows furrow and his gnarled sneer intensifies as he shifts in his chair, kicks the controllers onto the floor, and punches at buttons on them with his toes, trying to turn on the Buttwynn's 50-inch rear projection television. "Fuck, I hate trying to turn on other people's TV's these days!" he gripes as his toes fumble with the buttons on the various remote controls. "It's different in everybody's house. It used to be you had a clicker with one button on it that said *On* and you pushed that fucking button and the fucking TV came on. Fuck!" A frenzy of toes pushing buttons, kicking controls about the room, and ripping and roaring about the good old days when there was an on/off button on the TV commences and endures for the next five minutes. Askew, entirely consumed by the need to turn on the television, is oblivious to Grundish or anything else around him. Grundish sits back and watches the fit with equal parts amusement and concern. With the completely random and fortuitous pressing of a series of buttons on the one remaining remote control, the boob tube powers up. And then Askew's storm passes.

"There we go," Grundish says in a mellow, rational tone. He shrugs his shoulders at his friend and smiles. "I don't know what you're getting all upset about. Let's just put on the BayNews Channel and see if they have anything about what happened."

"How about we put on some pay-per-view porn instead?" suggests Askew, his inked-in eyebrows wiggling suggestively.

Grundish shakes his head from side to side. "I don't want to sit here with you watching people fuck?"

"What? Don't you like seeing *baginas*? You queer or something, boy?" Askew taunts his friend.

"Nah. I'll tell you what's queer. A couple of guys sitting around alone in a room together getting all hot and bothered over a movie. I don't even want you sitting this close to me if you're gonna be sprouting a stiffy. Porn's for jacking off. I ain't gonna sit here burpin' the worm in front of you. And if you feel the need to do that, you sure as hell better excuse yourself to a private area of the house. I mean, gee whiz, just the thought of it makes me feel like a creep, Wally."

"Why you calling me Wally, Grundish?"

"It's a Leave it to Beaver thing," says Grundish. Askew's mangled face registers nothing akin to understanding. "Didn't you ever watch that shit when you was a kid? You know, Beaver, Wally, Eddie Haskell? Ah, never mind. Let's just check out the news."

"All right, fine. But I was really hoping to watch Fistfuckers 5. The first four of them were masterpieces and I have no reason to expect anything less out of number 5."

Grundish shakes his head and says nothing.

"Okay, whatever. Let's watch the news. Maybe we can get *appraised* of what the cops are doing about Bumpy D right now."

A pack of Blue Llamas and a Zippo lighter sit on the table. Grundish watches in awe as Askew grips the pack with the toes of his right foot, bumps it on the left ankle, taps out a smoke, grips it with the left-foot toes, and twists his leg up to bring the cigarette to his mouth. With the smoke wedged between his front teeth, Askew grabs the lighter with his right foot and flips the lid on the Zippo. The flint wheel drags against Askew's ankle and throws a shower of sparks at the wick, which smokes a little but fails to ignite. He drags it across his ankle again. This time a small orange flame fires up. Askew twists the foot and the lighter up to his face and finally lights the cigarette. The sweat beads on his brow as he lies back in the reclining chair to catch his breath from the whole effort.

"Hey, buddy," says Grundish, "do you think you could get me a smoke?" He sips on his scotch, smiling innocently at Askew.

"Go fuck yourself, ya rat bastard," says Askew and sucks at his smoke. His lips, unable to fully close over the cigarette make a faint, wet, sucking sound as he drags in air through the left side of his mouth along with the vapor from the burning leaves.

"All right, be that way," laughs Grundish. "I'll just have one of Buttwynn's Cubanos." He snips off the end of a ringless cigar and torches it up with Askew's lighter. They sit and smoke and wait for the day's top news stories.

"Good evening. I'm Sallest Holeinback," says the corpulent female news anchor of the BayNews Channel.

"And I'm Orlando Montenegro," says the co-anchor in a voice so deep and mellow that he could be hawking fine Corinthian leather.

"And we're BayNews 10 with your evening report," the both say simultaneously through blindingly white dental veneers that mask years-worth of coffee stains, tartar, and rot. A bright sparkle briefly flickers off of Sallest's cosmetically contoured front tooth facade and, almost imperceptibly, the sharp high-pitched chime of a tiny bell dings somewhere in the vicinity of her teeth.

Holeinback's face, a pool of soft, oozing, fishbelly-white skin with close-set eyes, a fleshy wide nose, and lips recently enhanced with collagen treatments, stares at the camera with the utmost seriousness and breaks into the top stories: "Stay tuned later, after our break, for a truly disturbing story. Our local investigator has uncovered information which may make you never want to eat in a restaurant ever again. The scenes which we will show you will be so shocking that you may vomit and possibly even have to call in sick to work tomorrow. Please make sure that children and the elderly are out of the room for this portion of our broadcast."

"But, first," says Orlando Montenegro, "our top stories. Police are seeking a pair of local men in connection with a murder which occurred in plain daylight as residents of the Knothole Mobile Home Park watched on in horror. A be-on-the-lookout-for order has been issued for these men, Leroy Jenkem Askew and a Mr. Grundish, first name currently unknown." The driver's license picture of Askew and a poorly-done and inaccurate artist's rendering of Grundish appear on the screen. "If you encounter either of these men, do not try to apprehend them. Find a safe place and call the police immediately."

"In other news," says Sallest Holeinback, "a rash of burglaries has occurred recently in Riverview and Brandon neighborhoods. The Hillsborough County Sheriff's Office believes the burglaries are all the work of one man and say that the burglar has a unique calling card."

The video cuts to a spokesperson for the Sheriff's Office who explains: "In each one of these cases, the families were gone from the home for several days and returned to find they had been burglarized. In each case, there does not appear to be any broken locks or windows. This man is clearly a professional. The perpetrator seems to like to take alcohol and frozen meats, among other things, from the houses. Finally, the person who is doing this leaves a distinctive calling card. We have dubbed the perpetrator the Turd Burglar because he defecates in the toilets of his victims and neglects to flush it."

The picture returns to Sallest Holeinback's grimacing fat face. "Oh my, what an animal," she gasps. "What is wrong with people, Orlando?"

"I don't know, Sallest. That is a pretty shitty story," laughs Orlando.

"Orlando, you can't say that. We're on live television," Sallest gasps again.

"Sure, I can," teases Orlando. "We're just fictional characters in some lame novel. I can say whatever I want. Watch this: Cuntlip, dogfucker, suck my balls and lick my asshole. Fistfuck. Bloody buttplug. And now watch this," Orlando looks straight at the camera and makes a peace sign with his fingers, places it up to his mouth, and wiggles his tongue around between the fingers in a vulgar simulation of cunnilingus.

"Well, Orlando," Sallest says, "if this is a novel, it seems to me that the author has just speckled it with bizarre characters, footnotes and profanity, hoping that the shock value will be enough to carry the story. But, the book's most painful flaw is its lack of any thoughtfully crafted deeper meaning or unifying theme. The characters are outright unlikable and the author fails to provide us with a point as to what, exactly, he is trying to accomplish. To be fair, it also cannot be said that this book is completely without any talent or redemption. The editing is not awful. But..."

"Would you shut your fat cake-hole, you morbidly obese bucket of diarrhea," shouts Orlando as he smashes his closed fist into the side of her head. "You are a pretentious, bloated, pompous bitch-hole and I've had enough of you. I should murder you!"

Before Orlando can do any further damage to Sallest's hideously bloated head, a man appears behind the rotund woman. The man, a rather tall, attractive fellow with a shaved head and goatee, slinks behind Sallest without a sound. In each of his hands is a wooden handle. A thin wire runs from one handle to the other. The tall fellow quickly wraps the wire of the garrote around Sallest's neck and pulls it tight, compressing the carotid arteries and jugular veins, while at the same time compressing Sallest's airways. Orlando Montenegro does nothing to stop the man as Sallest thrashes violently about, air-hunger making her oversized corpus flail and fight for her life. The tall man stands firm, holding the wire tight around her neck until her floppy hulking corpse collapses on the anchor desk. The television screen abruptly cuts to black and a *technical difficulties* sign appears onscreen.[23]

"Holy Shit," says Grundish. "Did you just see that shit?"

"Yeah, we're fucked. The police have a pick up order for us."

"No. I'm talking about the other story. How in the fuck can they call me the Turd Burglar? Why not something cool like The Nightstalker? I would have been okay with that. Or even just not naming me. But the fucking Turd Burglar? Man!" Grundish chugs the rest of his drink and groans at the indignity.

"Yeah," laughs Askew, "it does sound kind of gay. Maybe you could call the Sheriff's Office and get them to give you a new nickname. Maybe something tough sounding like The Rump-Ranger or The Ass Pirate."

---

[23]At this point the author must thank his readers for allowing this one self-indulgent passage. The fat, bloated, piece-of-shit anchor represents a reviewer of the author's first novel, *Smashed, Squashed, Splattered, Chewed, Chunked and Spewed.* The reviewer's name has been changed. But, the tall man's reaction is what the author felt like doing when he read the review. The author once again says thank you. Damn, that felt good!

Grundish and Askew

"Fuck you." Grundish grins at Askew.
"Fuck you, too, Buddy," answers Askew.
"You know we're fucked, don't you?" asks Grundish.

"Yeah, you're probably right. We're fucked. Definitely. But then again, maybe it's a blessing *in the skies*," says Askew.

"How so?"

"Well," says Askew, stroking his chin with his foot, "we trudge along through everyday, just trying to get by. We take everything for *granite*. Maybe all of this is a wake up call. Maybe it's time that we look at our lives and ask, 'what is it that we need to do to distinguish ourselves?' Maybe now we're truly free. I've been living my whole life doing everything I can to avoid going to prison. My heart has not always been my guide. I just made a promise to myself to break the family curse. And now I know that if we get caught, you know, we're both going to prison, probably for life. That is if they take me alive. But you already made me a promise about that. So, now none of society's laws apply to us. We've got nothing to lose. If I wanna rape somebody, I'll just go out and do it."

"You wanna go start raping people?"

"No. But you're missing the point. If I wanted to, I could. I'm fucking free, man. If I wanted to go out raping I could. I could rape somebody's dog, so long as my heart says it's okay. If somebody pisses me off, I can kill them. Like old Mr. Buttwynn. If he were here, and he gave me a twenty-five cent tip, I would bust his head wide open. And he'd deserve it."

A look of concern settles on Grundish's scruffy face. "Bro, let me stop you. I'm seeing a different side of you that don't seem quite right. All this violence, it ain't you. It kinda' worries me."

"You're being *hypocratical*, man. You just went and attacked an entire community of people with frozen meat and you're worried about me being violent. Come on, Bro."

"You know I can be a nutcase," says Grundish. He puts his cigar in the ashtray and turns it with his fingers to knock the ashes off to a tapered burning tip. "But, I ain't never seen you talk the way you're talkin' about busting heads. It don't sit right with me. And, tell me," Grundish looks Askew in the eyes and holds the stare, "what happened when you got your face all messed up?"

Askew giggles and doesn't know how to answer. He just giggles and looks at Grundish. "I don't know what to say."

"Well, what happened that you needed to fight several people without the use of your hands?"

"Well," says Askew, "I didn't really have words to explain it at the time. It was really just more of a feeling. But, uh, you know how you've been talking about the Fuckers?"

"Yeah. I know all about the Fuckers."

"Well. These guys was them. They was the Fuckers. I mean," he grits his teeth and clenches his fists, "if you could've seen them, you'd agree that they's the Fuckers. You should'a seen the way they was eying Turleen. She's an old lady and they was looking at her in a way that wasn't right."

"So what'd they say?"

"They didn't *say* nothing," says Askew. "It wasn't about what they said. It was the way they was looking at her. They was Fuckers all right."

"Okay," say Grundish, "so they started giving you a hard time and you kicked the shit out of 'em."

"Yeah, kind of. I could just tell that they was trouble so I guess I kind of cut out the middle man, so to speak, and didn't wait for them to say something. I just took care of them. I kicked the shit out of them because they had it coming."

"How many were there?"

"Three that stood their ground, a couple backed off. But, three that came at me."

"And who won?"

"I look bad, but they gotta look worse. One of 'em was out cold on the ground when we split."

Grundish sighs, starts to say something, and then stops again.

"What?" asks Askew.

Grundish shrugs his shoulders and says nothing.

"What?"

"I just want you to chill out a little bit," says Grundish finally. "You never been in a fight in your life, and now you're all ready to start tearing people up. It's like you got a taste for blood or something. Just chill out a little bit. We've gotta lay low and don't need no more trouble. I need to figure out our next step."

"I'll try. I'm just saying to you that now I'm not worried about losing my job or getting evicted or anything else at this point. There is nothing worse they can do to us when we're caught unless we're executed. And that ain't gonna happen. And you made me your promise, so, well, I guess I ain't gonna go to jail or prison either. We're free, man, that's all I'm saying."

"Aw," scowls Grundish, "don't go talking about that stupid promise I made to you back in high school. We was just kids. You don't wanna hold me to that now."

"Damn straight I do," Askew's volume increases. "I wasn't kidding then, and I ain't kidding now. You promised."

"Yeah, but..."

"But nothing. You promised. You swore."

"I know..."

"My god you're *flustrating* the shit out of me. I don't mean to get all loud and *voicesterous*, but, you gotta keep that promise. You gotta renew your vow. Say it."

"All right. All right."

"All right what?"

"I promise."

"Good. Now you've got me all worked up. Can you get me a drink?" Askew sighs as he grabs his Blue Llamas with his feet and extracts another cigarette. The first cigarette is broken. When it's broken by the filter there's a trick Askew found. He just breaks it all apart and turns it around. He slides it in easy and twists it in tight and then he gives it a light. But with his vow to master his feet, the cigarette-fix trick is out of the question. He shakes out another smoke, this one unbroken, grasps it with his toes, and brings it to his mouth with ease.

"I should make you do it with your feet," scowls Grundish, still sore at being badgered. "What do you want?"

"Just a beer," says Askew. He struggles with his feet on the Zippo and finally manages to light his smoke.

"Here," says Grundish, returning with a frothy mug of darkish beer. A fluorescent pink bendy straw leans against the rim of the mug.

"You're not gonna let me go to prison, right, Pal?" asks Askew again.

"I'm not gonna. I promised you. But, you just gotta chill out a little. Now, will you drop it?" snaps Grundish.

"And you ain't never going back are you?"

"I've already told you," explains Grundish, "I'm never going back. No matter what. I made a promise to myself last time I got out. I gave myself my word, just like I done with you, that I ain't going back. I can't go back."

"Why not?" asks Askew. "What's so different for you this time?"

Grundish just shrugs his shoulders and says nothing.

"Come on. Just tell me what it was that changed in you the last time," prods Askew.

"All right. One time." Grundish holds up an index finger and stares Askew down. "One time I talk about this and then you don't ask me about it no more. Agreed?"

"Yeah, Buddy, agreed."

Grundish mutes the television and refills his tumbler with scotch. No water. No ice. Only room-temperature scotch to just above the top of the glass. The surface tension holds a slight bubble of the liquid just above the top of the rim. He takes the lighter from the coffee table and relights his neglected cigar. The scotch is sipped at, lowering the level of the fluid to just below the rim. The cigar is smoked. Grundish says nothing. Askew waits, smoking the cigarette that is wedged between his front teeth.

Just when Askew is about ready to say something, when the silence is killing him, Grundish speaks. "There's a saying in the joint. The guys in there say that you ain't in prison when you're sleeping. Does that make sense to you?"

"Uhhh, not really," says Askew as he bends down to sip from his pink straw. "I'm not like, you know, a *neucular* scientist or something. Just tell me without asking me to think too hard."

"Well, let me put it this way. Whenever I was down, I slept a lot. Because when I slept, I dreamed. And I always had dreams about getting pussy and smoking weed and driving fast cars. Sometimes I just dreamt about sitting out on the beach at night, maybe fishing for catfish that I'd just throw back, but fishing for 'em anyway. I'd catch some big ugly bastards in those dreams. And it was nice. Real nice. Sometimes I'd dream about having a dog and just walking him or taking him to a park to play Frisbee. Other times I dreamt that I was somebody special. Not necessarily famous or anything. Maybe just a successful guy with a hot wife and a couple of kids. You know, a guy that took a different path in life than us. A guy that other guys would like to be."

"Yeah. Yeah. I get it now. You ain't in prison when you're sleeping because it's like you go somewhere else in your head."

"Right." Grundish nods. He sips at the scotch and stares at his fuming cigar. "Well, the more I was down, the more I slept. And I guess I kind of got to the point where I could control what happened in my dreams. I was flying and looking through walls with x-ray vision. Every damn night I was having a threesome with a set of identical twin babes that had three boobs[24] apiece. That's six boobs in my face at one time. I didn't care that I was in prison because my dream life was better than my real life. But this last time I was sent up, it was like I used up all of my good dreams. I started losing control of them and having bad ones."

"Like fucked up nightmares?" Askew grunts. "I hate that shit. I have a *reoccurring* one where there's this little female goblin thing in my closet and I open the door and go in. And she's there. And, I can't explain it, but she scares the shit out of me. For some reason, I start fucking her mouth. And then I wake up all freaked out. You mean shit like that?"

"No, you little fruit," scoffs Grundish. "I don't mean anything like that. It started off with just stupid stuff. I would dream that I was at home and my alarm would go off. I would drag myself out of bed and go through my

---

[24]Polymastia is the condition of having an extra breast (or accessory breast). Accessory breasts may occur with or without nipples and areolae. Some can lactate. The extra breasts can appear, in rare cases, on the neck, face, shoulder, back, buttocks, thighs or even on a foot.

morning rituals, and you know how I hate to get up in the morning. And then they would wake me up for real and I'd have to go through waking up all over again. This time in prison. And my dreams all were in black and white, mostly shades of gray. They say that everybody dreams in black and white, but not me. I always dreamed in color. But when I started losing control of the dreams, they just got all gray and staticky, like watching old shows on a TV with bad reception. And they started getting worse."

"Like the goblin?"

"Ab-so-fucking-lutely not like your fruity little goblin. I really don't know what the hell you're talking about there, so let that shit go." Grundish shakes his head in disbelief and sips down several fingers of scotch. "The thing that got to me, I mean really shook me, was when I started dreaming that I was in prison. I mean, I was dreaming about having to line up for count. I was dreaming about guards hurrying me in the mess hall to finish my meals and about having to be aware of what each and every person around me was up to. My entire existence, even in my sleep, was incarceration. I was becoming institutionalized. Something in me finally clicked and I realized that I had to make some changes or I would get to the point where I couldn't remember what it was like on the outside. And that scared me. Worse than any sissy dream about knob-gobbling closet goblins. I promised myself then that I would never go back. And here we are in this fine mess now."

"Excuse me, boys," shouts Turleen from the kitchen. "Is anybody hungry for some steak? I'm cooking up some meals in here, I am. I can bring some out if anybody wants it."

"Yes, ma'am," Grundish and Askew shout back.

"Anyway," says Grundish, "that's that. And I don't wanna talk about it no more."

Turleen brings in a wooden cutting board with a T-bone steak on it, cooked to the point where it's brown on the outside and still bloody in the middle. She clunks down a half-full bottle of steak sauce and two plates. Grundish and Askew sit back in their chairs and watch as Turleen cuts the steak into tens of little pieces for them with an impressive rubber-handled knife, slicing back and forth, cutting the meat with the top and bottom of the blade. Turleen, her red dress covered with an apron, expertly separates the fat and bone from the meat and slides the mouth-sized chunks onto the plates she set on the table for the boys. Askew sits back and ponders what Grundish just shared. Grundish sips at his scotch and admires Turleen's knife skills. Without a word, Turleen wipes the blade on her apron and slips the knife under her dress, up by her thigh. She returns to the kitchen to cook more food. Grundish and askew sit without talking, staring at the muted television screen. Askew drowns his plate in the rust-colored steak sauce and uses his foot to fork pieces of dead cow into his mouth. Grundish sits still and silent, off somewhere in his own head. Askew finishes the meat on his plate. Like a statue, Grundish does not move a muscle nor does he speak.

"Tell me, Grundish," says Askew, "like you done before."

"Tell you about what?"

"About the ladies."

Grundish snapped, "You ain't gonna put nothing over on me. Come on, Bro, I'm thinking here."

Askew pleads, "Aw, you come on, Grundish. Please. Tell me like you done before."

"You really dig that shit, don't you? All right, I'll tell you," Grundish gives in. "And then we fucking party."

Grundish drops his voice to a soothing, mesmerizing tone. His eyes close and the words flow freely from his mouth, almost like he's said them a thousand times before. "Guys like us, you know, the ones that work the shit jobs and scrape by, are the loneliest guys in the world. Can't keep jobs. Don't fit in. They work for a couple of weeks at some minimum wage job for a paycheck, then they go out on the town and blow their wad, forgetting about obligations, bills, shit like that. Next thing you know, they're working another shit job and will prob'ly fuck that one up too. They ain't got nothing to look forward to."

Askew is delighted. "Fuck yes. That's it, that's it. Now tell how it is with us."

Grundish continues. "It ain't like that with us. We're different. We still got a future. We got somebody to talk to that gives a damn about us, you for me and me for you, Buddy. We don't have to sit in some shitty bar, bitching and moaning just because we got no other place to go. Those other fellas get thrown in jail. They can rot there for all anybody gives a damn. But not us. Not anymore for me and never for you…"

Askew breaks in, "…yeah, not us. And why? Because I got you to watch my back, and you got me to watch yours. And that's why." He giggles like a little kid. "Go on now, Grundish."

"You know it by heart, you can do it yourself."

"Naahh. I forget some of the shit. Tell about how it's gonna be."

"Okay. Someday we're gonna get the loot saved up and we're gonna buy a boat."

"A real big boat," interrupts Askew. "Like a yacht."

"That's right. Maybe bigger," says Grundish. "And we're gonna get a stable of hookers, and maybe some hydroponic equipment to grow weed."

"And tell me what we're gonna do, Grundish." Askew's tone grows more excited. "Go on. Tell me about the hookers again. About the international waters. And the hookers, like how they'll all have big fake titties, and they'll never say no to us, 'lessen they're on the rag or something. Tell me about how I get to take care of the ladies. Tell me about that Grundish."

"Why don't you do it yourself? You know about all of it."

"Nahh. You tell it. It just ain't the same the way I tell it. Go on, Grundish, tell about how I get to tend the ladies."

"Well," says Grundish, "we're gonna anchor that boat out in international waters, where we ain't violating no U.S. laws. Just like those cheesy gambling cruises like to do. We'll keep a stable of girls out on the boat and they'll sell their asses, bringing in money for us. We'll get rich."

"Yeah, Grundish. We'll live off the fat of their asses. Go on and tell it."

"Well, we'll grow weed, have hookers, maybe some other shit that ain't legal here. Our clientele will be brought out to our yacht by boat or helicopter or something sweet like that. Then they'll pay us to do all the shit that they want to do here but can't. And we don't have to do shit except for rake the money in, and maybe protect our girls once in a while. Mostly, though, we just party, have a different lady every night, maybe we fish, whatever we want. And you can take care of the ladies if you want. Damn." He stops, picks up his fork and steak knife. "I ain't got time for no more of this shit." He scrapes half of his steak chunks onto Askew's plate and keeps the other half for himself. They sit for awhile; the only sound is the open-mouthed chewing of Askew, a big, happy goofus grin on his face.

Grundish samples the steak and becomes silent again, staring at the muted TV. As he drifts off to sleep, Grundish smiles and thinks to himself, *life ain't so bad when I got Askew around. No, it really ain't.*

"Wake up! Wake up!" Askew jumps about the room, bouncing off of the furniture and shouting at Grundish. "The goat of day is butting dawn! No ifs or buts! Bang! Come on you girl! Pimp! Punk! Hangman! Run with Me! Let's run!" Askew, drunk from sitting all night sipping at dark beer with a straw while Grundish slept, dances in front of the television in an outfit from Buttwynn's closet not unlike the threads sported by Grundish. The red silk robe, too small and tight around Askew's thick chest is left untied and open, revealing B-cup man-boobs and a hairy, rounded belly. The black dress socks are stretched over the thick calves, the elastic in the cheap socks pulled to the point of breaking, tiny white strands of snapped elastic thread sticks out randomly from the fabric. The socks, irreparably misshapen, only remain held up through the use of a pair of Buttwynn's sock garters. The garters, a size too small for Askew, press deep on the skin of his leg, just below the knee, leaving a white ring of bloodless flesh just around the edge of the band.

"Wha? What the fuck?" His back, neck and shoulders ache from sleeping in an awkwardly twisted position in the chair all night. The fog of a fresh awakening clouds his thoughts. Grundish rubs his eyes and slaps himself lightly on the cheeks. "What time is it?"

"It's time to dump your lumpy ass out of bed, Monkey Head!" shouts Askew, still leaping about, a grotesque rotund gnome of a man, scantily clad and jiggling obscenely. His chest heaves out and retracts quickly in a spastic fit of hyperventilation, nostrils opening and closing like gills. He rips and roars and grits his teeth. "It's morning. It's light out. It's time to get up." Askew grabs a half-full mug of beer with his hand and chugs it.

Grundish eyes Askew suspiciously, watching him set the beer down and use his hands to catapult a Blue Llama up into his mouth. "I thought you were never going to use your hands again."

"I never said I'd never use them again," snaps Askew, still breathing heavily. "I said I wouldn't use them until I mastered the use of my feet. Or something like that anyway. Besides, I took a shit this morning and I couldn't for the life of me figure out how to wipe my ass. I tried unrolling toilet paper onto my heel and then squatting down on it and wiggling around but I just made a nasty mess. So, at that point, I decided I had mastered the use of my feet enough to begin using my hands again."

"Good enough. I hope you washed your feet off."

"Naah. I didn't feel like it.[25] I'll shower tonight."

---

[25]95% of adults say they wash their hands after using public restrooms but observational studies have shown that the actual number of hand washers is far lower. Hand-washing behavior increases when an observer is present. A person is more likely to wash his hands in a public restroom if he knows the behavior is being watched by another. This has been explained by the theory of objective self-awareness. It is theorized that attending to one's self increases adherence to social norms. Self-awareness is enhanced by

Askew draws in a large drag off of his Blue Llama and inhales deeply. He tilts his head back and exhales a thick plume of smoke and laughs. The laugh, that of a madman, continues and mutates into a raspy, jagged, coughing spasm. Askew, his hands clamped over his mouth, hacks and chokes and gags almost to the point of vomiting when he finally settles into deep congested breathing and sits down into his seat to catch his breath. "Damn," he says, looking down into his hand, "I ain't never seen one that big."

"What is it?" Grundish asks, half-afraid to find out.

"Look." Askew holds out his hand. In his palm is an off-whitish lump, looking like an oversized yogurt-covered raisin drizzled with spittle. "They ain't even usually half this big. I'm almost tempted to save this one and put it in a jar or something. Maybe call Ripley's Believe it or Not, I don't know."

"I see it, but I still don't know what it is."

"It's a lump of throat cheese[26], Bro. Ain't you never coughed one of these up?"

---

being watched by others. Thus, having an observer present in the restroom may remind a user of the social norm to wash his hands.

[26]The technical/medical term for Askew's throat cheese is tonsillolith, commonly referred to as tonsil stones. Tonsilloliths are irregularly shaped, whitish/yellow, foul-smelling globs of mucous and bacteria that get caught in the back of the throat. They form in the tonsil crypts which are small pockets or divots that appear in the tonsils. Why do people smell them? Who knows? But talk to anybody who has coughed one up and, if they are honest, they will tell you they took a whiff of it and regretted it.

"I ain't never seen anything like that. It don't seem right. You really ought to get that checked out. And like I told you before, you need to quit smoking."

"Nah. Fuck that noise. It's just throat cheese. I hork 'em up all the time. Ain't nothing wrong with throat cheese except that if you smash it, it lets off a stench that'll knock a buzzard off a shit wagon. Here, check it out." Askew smashes the firm, slick nugget between his thumb and middle finger and waves it in the direction of Grundish.

The smell, like blood, halitosis, and fish, finds its way to Grundish, sticks its stinky finger into his mouth and touches the back of his throat, triggering a forceful gag reflex. "Urrrp!" The acid bile makes it just into the back of his mouth and Grundish manages to swallow it back down. "Get that fucking thing away from me or when I puke, I'll make sure to do it on you."

A hurt look washes over Askew's mug. "Yeah. I'm sorry, Bro. I just got kind of wound up." He flicks his hand toward the wall opposite him. The mucilaginous tonsillolith splats on the Buttwynn family portrait, a direct hit on Mr. Buttwynn's face, and leisurely makes its way down the portrait, finding a comfortable final resting place at the point where the non-glare glass cover meets the frame. "Seriously, I don't know what came over me. I guess I'm kind of delirious from the dark beer and lack of sleep."

"It's all right, Bro. Just keep your fucking throat cheese to yourself from now on."

"You got it, Pal." Askew smiles a moronic gap-toothed grin, relieved to be forgiven so quickly. "I've got something

I gotta show you. It's bad ass. Wait right here. All right? Don't go anywhere."

Askew leaves the room. Askew returns. Grundish is bent over with his legs straight and his hands flat on the floor. He returns to an upright stance, grabs his chin and the back of his head and twists it to crack the neck, making a sound like somebody stepping on bubble wrap.

"Check this baby out." In Askew's hands is a two-foot long flintlock rifle. The gun's stock is cut off just inches below the trigger, leaving just enough reddish wood for Askew to wrap his hand around it. A thick barrel, flared at the end, is held to the ornately-carved wood stock and points in the general direction of Grundish. "It's called a blunderbuss."

"Where'd you get that fucked up gun? How do you know what it's called? And stop pointing the fucking thing at me." Grundish steps to the side of the gun.

"I found it in Buttwynn's den. It was mounted above the fireplace. And chill out. It can't be loaded if it was mounted on the wall, right?"

"I don't know," says Grundish. "Probably not. Just don't point it at me though. Or I'll take it away and beat you with it."

Askew laughs and points the gun away from Grundish. "This here blunderbuss is bad ass. It had a little plaque beneath it on the wall that told all about it. This one was used by sailors and pirates. It was *exspecially* supposed to be used to clear the deck when the pirates would board another ship. They'd load it with rocks and broken glass and nails. The blunderbuss'll fuck you up, *Bee-yatch.*"

"Put that thing down, Askew. You ain't never held a gun in your life, and now you're holding a fucking sawed-off shotgun on steroids. Give me that thing."

"I do, too, know how to handle this bad-boy. You just pull the cocking thing back." He half-cocks the flintlock mechanism, points it at the wall, and shouts "*Blam! Blam! Blam!*" He pulls the trigger, releasing the half-cocked hammer. The hammer gently clicks against the flash pan lid and does nothing more. "See, I told you it ain't loaded."

"You don't know shit. Acting like you fired it three times in a row. It ain't no fucking semi-automatic handgun. It's like a muzzle loader. You have to reload it after each shot. Give me that thing. You freak me out with it."

"Here you go, ya' party pooper." Askew lobs the blunderbuss at Grundish, who catches it in front of himself with both hands. "Come on, I got more to show you before I crash." Grundish notices that Askew's words are becoming more and more slurred.

In the front of the Buttwynn residence is a formal sitting room with an oversized picture window facing the street. Askew pulls back the curtains. Grundish looks out and growls softly.

"Does that look familiar to you?" Askew asks, a cloud of his beer and cigarette breath enveloping him. A devilish grin forms on his face.

Out the picture window, Grundish feasts his eyes on a yellow minivan. The Tampa Bay Buccaneers vanity license plate reads *2GUD4U*. "That's the van," Grundish mutters. He growls low, like an animal. "That's the fucking van. The one with the kids who throw shit at me." His teeth grind, making a sickening scraping sound. His hands clench and unclench, fingernails leaving pale crescent imprints in the palms of his hands. "That's the fucking van."

From the front door of the house across the street exits a teenage boy. He shouts back over his shoulder into the house: "I know, Mom. Do you think I'm a flippin' retard?...I know!...Jeez, don't you trust me?...Don't be stupid, mom!" He slams the door and walks to the minivan. Inside the house, the mother counts the days until her son reaches the age of majority. She secretly hopes that her son ends up learning a little lesson about disrespecting people. She doesn't want him to get hurt, but maybe just scared by somebody that isn't going to put up with his shit.

Grundish stares out the window, staying mostly behind a curtain, and watches as the yellow van pulls out of the driveway and then squeals its tires in front of the Buttwynn's house. The van is gone but Grundish glares at the space that it occupied, his hands still clenching and releasing, his teeth grinding off enamel. Minutes pass and he silently simmers.

"All right, Buddy," says Askew, putting his hands on Grundish's tensed shoulders. "It's time to move it along. Nothing to see here anymore. Let's go in and eat some of the breakfast that Old Turleen's been cooking."

Slowly, with the guidance of Askew, Grundish moves from the picture window and allows himself to be guided into the kitchen. In the kitchen, a feast of breakfast foods covers the counter. Turleen limps around the kitchen in her red dress, stirring pots on the oven, sprinkling spices on the various dishes and sampling the food here and there.

"Well, good morning," she says to Grundish. "I wondered if you were ever gonna wake up, I did."

For Grundish the morning is spent eating the smorgasbord cooked by Turleen. She had been mixing and stirring and blanching and grilling and parboiling and chopping and mincing, frying and cooking, stuffing, stewing and searing, infusing and basting and fricasseeing in the kitchen almost the entire time at the house, only taking a brief period of time to doll herself up in Mrs. Buttwynn's clothes and stopping now and again for a catnap or a glass of wine. On the counter, beside a mostly-empty wine glass, a lit Romeo y Julieta cigar is spiked on a meat thermometer. A trail of smoke wafts from the stogie and mingles with the scents from the foods, giving the room a comforting aroma.

"Turleen," says Grundish, "not that I don't appreciate it, but, why are you making all of this food? It's not like we're gonna be staying here for more than a day or so." He cuts a thick chunk of country ham away from the round ring of bone and crams the salty meat into his mouth.

"I'll tell you something, I will," says Turleen, pointing a wooden spoon dripping with batter at Grundish. A trail of smoke blows Turleen's way and stings her eyes. She rubs the incipient tears with her forearm and inhales deeply through her nose. "I ain't had the opportunity to cook up a decent meal for a hungry man since Uncle Hank was kicked in the head by a pony and his brain swelled up too big for his skull."

"He was kicked in the head by a pony?" Confused ridges of skin ripple above Grundish's eyebrows.

"And how. A right short little feller, he was," says Turleen, alternating between stirring the batter and shaking the spoon in Grundish's direction for emphasis. "He was short. But, he was a big man, Uncle Hank was. Big on the inside. And big in the pants. And he could eat like a man three times his size. Mostly he just liked Sloppy Joes, he did. But he'd let me cook him anything I wanted to. He couldn't really taste what I made for him anyway since he bit off his tongue when he was a young 'un. He just had a little nub of a tongue that couldn't taste most flavors. But for some reason he could really taste those Sloppy Joes, he could. Here, have some pancakes." She limps over to the table and sets a plate of flapjacks buried in snozzberries in front of Grundish. "Where'd Leroy go?"

"Leroy?" Grundish laughs. In the entire time he had known Askew, he almost never heard anybody refer to him by his first name. He had always been Askew to Grundish, to friends, to teachers and even to other Askews. Sometimes Grundish called him Douche-nozzle, Fucknuts, or just plain old Scrotum, but never Leroy. Only Turleen ever called him Leroy, and it never failed to make Grundish chuckle. "Oh, yeah. *Askew*. I don't know, I guess he finally went to sleep."

"Well, it's about time. That boy's been up all night going through these people's stuff, messing around on their computer and ranting and raving about them. Something about a quarter, or no quarter, or something, it is, that he was raving about. I'm kind of getting worried about that boy, I am. He don't seem quite right, you know? Kinda tetched, and I haven't seen him like this before."

"Well, maybe he just needs some sleep," says Grundish through a mouthful of some of the best pancakes he ever tasted. "What happened with him when got his face so messed up anyway?"

"Well, I been thinking about that, I have," says Turleen. She grabs her wine glass to take a sip and realizes it's nearly empty. She turns it up anyway and drains the few remaining drops into her mouth. "At first I thought those boys was looking me up and down with the bedroom eyes, I did. Like they were ready to start pitching woo with me. But the more I think about it, I think Leroy just kinda went loopy. I think I was trying to excuse that boy's actions, I do. He just jumped outta the car and started hurting people real bad, calling 'em Fuckers and kicking at 'em. Just kicking 'em real hard and not stopping. Maybe I kinda made it up in my head a little bit that he was protecting me, I did. Maybe. Because when I think about it, I don't know how they could have even seen me very well, me being in the car and it being dark out and all."

"Yeah, it ain't like him. We gotta keep an eye on him. Maybe he just needs a little bit of sleep. This is a pretty stressful situation and maybe he just needs to chill out, reflect on things a little. Let's let him sleep for now." Grundish stands and fills his plate from edge to edge with food from the counter. He sits again at the table. The waistband of Buttwynn's silk boxers constricts uncomfortably around his expanding stomach. Grundish pulls the elastic band up over his stomach, over the navel, to a place where it doesn't have to stretch so much. Chunks of egg and pancake stick to the thick bearded area around his lips. Grundish doesn't care. He stuffs a sausage into his mouth and goes to check on Askew.

Damn. He looks so comfortable. I don't wanna bother him, Grundish thinks to himself about Askew. Laid out, spread-eagle on his back on the Buttwynn's bed, Askew sleeps the REM-deprived sleep of the overweight, of the sleep apnea afflicted. His snores are gentle. His round, uncovered belly rises and falls, rises and falls, rises and falls, and then the snoring stops, followed tens of seconds later with the abrupt choking sound of his body trying to start breathing again. The intermittent snoring and choking are a gentle lullaby to Grundish, a sound he finds it hard to sleep without. Some people need relaxation tapes of classical music and rainstorms. Some need white noise. Grundish needs Askew's snores to fall asleep. In the trailer, Grundish could always hear Askew snoring. Like an infectious yawn, the snores always seemed to affect Grundish likewise, making him want to snooze, too. Despite having just slept the night away, and largely due to the breakfast gorging he had done, Grundish decides to try for more sleep. The Buttwynn's bed is far more comfortable than the theater chair Grundish slept on so he pushes Askew out of the middle of the bed, over to one side, and closes his eyes himself. Flashes of light glimmer on the backdrop of his closed eyelids, streaks of color appear and then evaporate; his inner voice speaks nonsense in a derailed train of thought, consecutive sentences having no connection to each other, phrases and concepts melting with no concern for their meaning. And then: Grundish sleeps.

And then: Grundish awakens. He is roused late in the day, just after dusk, by a bare-chested, partially robe-covered, dirty boxers-wearing Askew. The short, overweight man has climbed atop the slumbering Grundish[27], and dangles his mangled red face right above his friend's. Breathing the labored and congested rattle of the heavy smoker, Askew wheezes his stale bum-breath in Grundish's face.

"Come on," says Askew, shaking Grundish by the shoulders. "Wake up. You gonna sleep the entire time we're here? I've got some shit I wanna show you. Shit you're gonna be proud of."

"Get off'a me you filthy animal," grumps Grundish. "Your breath stinks like you haven't brushed your teeth in a week. Your face is crusty and you're getting some kind of greenish tint around the areas where I stitched you. And something on you stinks like death. Go take a shower and get yourself cleaned up and then come back to wake me up."

The round little man lets himself go limp on top of the big man. "I just wanna cuddle, Honey Bear. Will you give

---

[27]By the way, Slumbering Grundish would be a very cool band name, and I am willing to sell the rights to it at a very reasonable price.

me a back rub?" Askew nuzzles his muzzle up against Grundish's neck.

"Get the fuck off me, you homo, and let me sleep!" The tight muscular arms push quickly, launching a flabby ball of Askew into the air and away from the bed. A wild guffaw trails Askew as he arcs through the air, his silk robe flapping behind him like a cape. Gravity's pull on Askew is abruptly halted as his mass meets the floor and both refuse to budge for the other.

"God damn, Grundish! I was just playing. You don't have to get all mean. Does this mean you don't love me no more?" Askew stands up, places his hands on his sides and cocks his hip.

"Go!" Grundish shouts and pulls a pillow over his head to block out Askew.

Askew leaves. Askew showers. Grundish sleeps. Askew returns. Grundish arises.

"Come on," urges Askew. With the blunderbuss gripped in his hand, slung recklessly backwards over his shoulder, he leads his best friend down the hall. "I know it ain't your birthday, but I got you a little present."

"Hey. Don't point that fucking thing back at me. I don't ever like having a gun pointed at me."

"All right, ya big wuss," says Askew, letting the gun hang, its flared barrel now threatening the floor. The two men, similarly dressed in robes and sock garters, wear the clothes so differently. Grundish, with his tattoos, thick beard and large frame carries the look of a deranged and dangerous loner, one who lives in a cabin stacked wall to wall with useless clutter and perhaps an arsenal of guns.

Askew's appearance, on the other hand, is more that of an innocuous village idiot or that of an overly medicated and brainsick mental patient who has perhaps just recently shat himself. "Close your eyes," Askew says. "I want this to be a surprise."

His hand on Grundish's elbow, Askew opens a bedroom door and leads the way into the room.

"Okay, is everybody in?" Askew asks in a wavering, spooky voice. "The ceremony is about to begin. Go ahead an open your eyes and feast them on this." A look of pride flashes on Askew's face, the look of a cat leaving dead rat on its owner's doormat. He almost purrs at Grundish.

Before the men, strapped to a rolling office chair with leather belts, is a teenage boy who used to have stringy blond hair and a skeevy little mustache. The belts are cinched tight around his chest, making it difficult for the boy to breathe. His hands are pulled behind him and secured to the chair with electrical tape. The mustache remains but is crusted with dried blood and snot, looking like an afflicted caterpillar. The blond hair is haphazardly cut off in uneven patches and scattered about, some of it dried to coagulated smudges of blood on the floor. Some of it still kicked about by Askew's feet as he circles the boy.

"You want to talk about a Fucker," sneers Askew, his own face twisted and mangled, but not looking as bad as the boy's. Askew, dressed in the silk robe, boxers, and sock garters, circles the teen. There is now a sense of danger to his aura; a distinct change from the harmless mental patient now into a keen predator. A disconcerting air of madness drips from Askew and puts Grundish on edge. Askew balls his fist and hits the boy in the ear. The boy screams. Not with his mouth. The mouth is covered with electrical tape that is wrapped around his head again and again. The boy's cheeks are bulging with a pair of Mrs. Buttwynn's underwear that Askew stuffed in his mouth before the taping. The boy doesn't scream with his mouth. His eyes, though, silently shriek in terror.

"Askew," Grundish says, trying to shake Askew from his spell, but to no avail. "Askew," he barks. The sharp tone of Grundish's voice breaks the trance and Askew looks at him.

"What?" His eyes unfocused, his heart visually palpitating in his chest. "What?" He steps back from the boy.

"What did you do to this kid?"

"He's the one." Askew smiles. He slows his voice and says it again. "Heeee's…thhhhe…onnnne. He's The Fucker you been telling me about. The punk that throws *fecus* at you while you work. The one that shouts *despairishing* things at you. Well, we finally got him. And I've been working him over for you. I wanna show you something." Askew turns the chair to allow Grundish to see the other side of the boy's face. Where his ear is supposed to be, there is nothing. The spot where the ear once was is now a jagged bloody circle of lacerated skin, thick and meaty at the edges, looking like under-cooked ham.[28] Seeping from the wound is a sticky mess of rust-

---

[28]Vincent Van Gogh did not cut of his entire ear as many believe, only the earlobe. He cut the earlobe off with a razor and delivered it to a prostitute named Rachel, telling her: "Guard this object carefully." Many attempts have been made to diagnose Van Gogh's madness, attributing his mental problems to, among other things,

colored discharge. "I did him like that movie that we always watch. Cut his fucking ear right off. And he cried like a little bitch while I did it." He digs in his pocket and extracts a pale floppy piece of skin that, at one point, helped to catch sound waves and direct them into the boy's auditory canal.

His hand on Askew's chest, Grundish eases his friend back from the boy. "Stand back and let me talk to this kid." Askew first allows himself to be nudged back and then stands firm. Grundish locks eyes with him, pushes slightly on his chest, and speaks again, slowly and deliberately. "Please let me have a word with this kid. Go eat something. Go have a cigarette. Go take a shit. Just go. Okay?"

Askew eases up and walks backwards toward the door. "All right," he says, "but don't finish him off without me, Brother."

The smile on Askew's face as he exits doesn't sit right with Grundish. The goofy, good-natured Askew that he has known for so long doesn't seem to be anywhere behind the smile. The malignity in Askew's eyes, something Grundish had never witnessed in all of their years as friends, slams Grundish like a kick in the balls. *Don't finish him off without me*, thinks Grundish, *what the fuck does he think I'm gonna do?*

A warm circle of moisture spreads across the crotch of the boy's pants as Grundish approaches him and walks behind the chair. Leaning in close to the still-attached ear, Grundish speaks softly. "Do you recognize me?"

---

lead poisoning, absinthe ingestion, syphilis, schizophrenia, bipolar disorder, and temporal lobe epilepsy.

The boy shakes his head from side to side and whimpers beneath the tape.

"Are you sure?"

He continues to shake his head *no*, not stopping until Grundish places his hand atop the boy's head. "Well. I'm the guy with the sign. The loser that stands out on the side of the road with the arrow sign waving people in to get pizza deals and directing people to condo sales. Do you know what I'm talking about?"

The boy doesn't move his head, but the rest of his body trembles violently.

"You've had so much fun at my expense, haven't you?" Grundish spins the boy around and gets in his face. "Do you recognize me now?"

The boy shakes his head *no* again.

"I think you do. I think you know exactly who I am. It's really funny to throw things at me and shout shit when you know I can't catch you, isn't it?" The boy's bloodied eyes strain to escape the sockets. Sweat streams down his face. "Don't bother shaking your head at me again. Don't bother denying it. I want you to be a man now." He gets inches away from the boy's face. "You know who I am, don't you?"

Finally, the boy shakes his head in the affirmative.

Grundish's words come at the boy like an enraged pit bull barely restrained by a thin leash. The tendons on his neck pop; his teeth clench as he speaks. "I've thought every day about what I would do if I ever catch you and your little punk friends. I've fantasized about this day. My life is shit. And to have some rich little punks rubbing salt in the wounds, smashing my face in the shit that is my life, it's a mighty hurtful thing. To have you throw things at me from your car has made me wish for the opportunity to snap your neck. I've found myself really wanting to hurt you. Wanting to hurt you bad. And now here we are, my prayers answered." He squats down in front of the boy and stares him in the eye. "Should I let you up from that chair? Maybe take the tape off of your mouth? I can let you stand up and you can call me names. Call me a loser. I'll bring a whole bowl of fruit in here for you to throw at me. Would you like that?"

The boy shakes his head and shudders. Tears course down his cheeks. His sweaty body convulses with fear.

"Then," Grundish says. "Then we can see what a big man you really are. What do you think of that?" Standing again, he walks several circles around the chair, saying nothing, pausing behind the boy. Time stretches and contracts. Elsewhere, people are being born and people are dying. The only sound in the room is the low breath of Grundish and the muted whimpering of the boy. Grundish leans in close and speaks into the excised circle on the side of the boy's head. "Can you hear me?" he says into the bloody mess of an ear hole. The boy remains still. "Can you hear me?" Grundish says, louder this time.

The boy nods.

"It's your lucky day. I ain't gonna kill you. I ain't even gonna hurt you. I won't let my friend hurt you neither. I'm not a killer, and I'm not about to start down that path now. Although if I were, you would be as good a starting point as any."

Grundish spins the weeping boy around again to face him. "I can't let you go yet, though. So you're gonna have to sit here for a day or two. I'll get you some water and a little something to eat in the meantime, as long as you can promise me not to make any noise when I take that gag out."

The boy nods in agreement.

"So while you're sitting here, I want you to think about your life. About your future. You're being given another shot at becoming a human being and not some shitty abusive little puke. When you get out of here, I think you need to go thank your mother for everything she has ever done for you. Tell her you're sorry for being disrespectful, that you know you've been a problem, and that you're going to be different. Maybe come up with a list of people who you've tormented, and then plan to make things right with them. You think you can do that?"

The boy nods in the affirmative again.

"Because if you can't, then I can just let my friend come back in here and hang out with you. But I don't think we want that, do we?" Grundish and the boy both shake their heads side to side together. "So, you just sit here and think about these things we been talking about, and I'll get back with you later. And don't try to escape or anything or I will have my friend have a little talk with you."

In the center of the kitchen table is a silver serving dish heaped with juicy roast pork marinated in mojo sauce. Askew scoops a serving spoon of meat on top of the black beans and rice on his plate. He stares across the table at Grundish and says nothing. Grundish stares back, trying to read Askew's eyes, trying to interpret his blank face.

"I don't know why you boys are so quiet, I don't," says Turleen. She dumps a heavy load of hot sauce on her food. "But, I done cooked up one heck of a swell meal, I did. I wish I had some real Cuban bread to go with it, but this crappy French bread from frozen dough will have to do. It would be real nice to have some dinner conversation, though, it would. I've been cooking in here the whole time and haven't had anybody to talk to. So, if you boys ain't saying nothing, I'm just gonna monopolize the conversation, I am." She reaches up under her dress and pulls out the throwing knife to slice up the baguette. The knife is lifted and brought down like a cleaver on the loaf again and again. It makes a solid chop on the wooden cutting board each time she lowers it and cleaves off a piece of the crusty bread. Normally either Grundish, Askew, or both would have commented on the impressive blade, not to mention the fact that Turleen was pulling it out from under her dress. Askew is oblivious to the knife; his thoughts are elsewhere. Grundish focuses his attention on trying to figure out what is going on with Askew and barely gives a second thought to the weapon. "Well, anyways," continues Turleen, "I got things worked out for us to get to a safe place where we can lie low. But we can't go there until tomorrow night, we can't. I'm gonna tell you fellas all about it..."

...*Wah waaa wa wahhh wa wahhhhh*, is what the boys hear from Turleen as they cram their mouths with the tangy, moist, pig meat. Instead of hearing a word from the old lady, the boys stare silently at one another. *Wah waaa wa wahhh wa wahhhhh*, Turleen explains and Grundish nods automatically, paying no attention.

Wah waaa wa wahhh wa wahhhhh. Askew continues to stare and stuff himself with food, not even acknowledging Turleen.

Grundish sops up the pork juices with a piece of the French bread, wiping the plate clean. He jams the soggy bread into his talk-hole, and, with his mouth full, says to Askew: "We need to talk."

"I know," answers Askew blankly.

"*Wah waaa wa wahhh wa wahhhhh*," says Turleen.

"I don't wanna play pool," Askew whines. "My hands hurt, and we've got more important things to do." He flips a Blue Llama into his mouth, catching it with his teeth since his lip is still partially adhered to the gums.

"Well, we're gonna play," says Grundish. "We've got a custom-built eight-foot slate table that's better than anything we've ever seen in the places we hang out. Look, there ain't no stains on the felt. You ain't gotta put no coins in it to play. Ain't gotta put no coins down to wait for your turn. The balls roll straight." He rolls the cue ball slowly down the table. It goes forth deliberately and does not stray from its course. The white ball bounces off the rail at the other end of the table and rolls to a stop half a foot from the cushion. "And check out these cues. Hand made. Perfectly balanced. And not warped." Grundish sets a cue stick on the table and pushes it. The stick rolls smoothly, not like the chipped and bowed cues Grundish and Askew have come to know in the smoky bars where they play Eight-Ball. "Now rack 'em, bitch." Grundish rubs his hands on the dusty white cone of chalk attached to the wall, and then smacks his hands together, making a small cloud of dust.

Grundish circles the table and pulls balls from the leather pockets. He rolls them down the table to Askew, who places them in the rack and looks miserable in the process.

Behind Askew, on the wall, hangs an original oil painting of dogs playing pool. A gruff-looking bulldog holds a rolled cigarette between his teeth and concentrates on lining up his shot while the rest of the canine crew watches intently. A drunken German Shepherd-mix hefts a mug of beer and pants excitedly. Next to him a Cocker Spaniel goofus in a bowtie and bowler's hat leers lasciviously at the bulldog bent over the table. A foxy-looking Finnish Spitz chomps on a cigar and waits for his opponent to finally miss a shot so that he can have a turn on the table. Off to the right a Great Dane smokes a pipe and crosses his arms. He realizes that his friend is being hustled by the bulldog and doesn't care. Instead, he finds himself thinking about the tasty roadkill he feasted on earlier in the day. In the middle of the crowd sits the smiling basset hound named Idjit Galoot, who doesn't really fit in with the rest of the group. Idjit seems to be looking out past his canine friends, paying attention to something outside of the realm of the painting. Grundish notices that, as he walks around the room, the Basset Hound's eyes seem to follow him. Askew tightens up the balls in the rack, rolling it back and forth on the table, and sets the tip of the rack over the dot on his end of the table.

"Well, are you gonna talk to me, or are you just gonna stare at that painting?" Askew asks as he gently lifts the rack from the triangle of balls on the table.

"Let's play some pool first." A square of blue chalk is rubbed on the tip of the cue stick. Grundish blows off the excess chalk and leans over the table. The cue sits on the arched bridge of his left hand while the right hand grips the back of the stick and strokes it backward and forward, stopping the stroke just short of the waiting cue ball. With the last stroke, Grundish leans into it and sends the cue ball hurtling toward the hapless cluster of balls at the other end of the table.

The white ball smacks, just off-center of the lead ball in the rack, bounces back into the air, and lands again on the table. The rest of the balls, shocked by the audacity of the white ball, abruptly scramble for safety. The eight-ball makes a beeline for the left corner, drops in, and cowers in the leather woven pocket, out of sight of the rest of the surprised orbs.

"God damn!" Askew shakes his head. "I hate it when you do that."

"Rack 'em again, bitch." A smile forms on Grundish's face. In his life, he has not been good at much, but he could always shoot some mean pool. Full of confidence from dropping the eight-ball, he shouts out: "Hey Turleen. Hows about you bring us a couple of beers in here?"

"I'm busy cooking, I am," comes the voice from the kitchen. "Hows about you bring me a glass of wine?"

"Aww, shit. I'll be right back." He lights a cigar and starts out of the room. "Go ahead and rack those balls up nice and tight. When I come back we can talk. Oh, yeah," he grins, "and I'll kick your ass again."

Grundish's simultaneous swagger and submissiveness brings a genuine, albeit battered, smile to Askew's face and he starts to warm up to the idea of discussing recent events. The balls are gathered and forcefully placed in the wooden triangle, the rack is perfectly set on the center dot and the balls are tightened. He lifts the rack so as not to disturb the balls and admires his work. "Damn, that's a perty rack," he says to himself as he sits on a stool and smokes his cigarette, waiting for Grundish.

Two tumblers filled with ice and Scotch enter the room, leading the way for the two hands carrying them. The two arms attached to the hands follow in their wake. The thick arms are stuck to the torso that trails behind. Atop the torso sits a bearded grinning face chomping on a fuming cigar. "That's gotta be one of the shittiest racks I ever seen," says Grundish. "Rack it again and do it right this time."

"Fuck that. And fuck you. And give me that drink." Askew lets out a warm laugh that calms Grundish's nerves.

He's acting like his self again, Grundish thinks. *Maybe he just needed to blow some steam off.*

They clink their tumblers together and throw back healthy snorts of the whisky. Grundish sets the drink down and lines up his break, this time scattering balls all over the table and dropping two solids. But the eight-ball remains on the table. Next he drops the three-ball, then sinks a perfect bank shot on the five. An attempt at jumping the cue ball over the thirteen fails, and, in the process, the felt gets slightly torn.

"Hey, no jumping," scoffs Askew.

"House rules allow it," says Grundish.

"How do you know the house rules?"

"Just made 'em up." Grundish steps back from the table, still feeling the watchful eyes of the Basset Hound from the painting following him. He sips at his drink and starts to feel okay, like things are getting back to normal with Askew. "Go ahead, it's your shot."

"I know. I know. Don't rush me." Askew drops his cigarette on the carpet and smashes it out with his foot. "I gotta check out my options, come up with a game plan. We both know that I have to think not just about this shot, but setting myself up for the next shot, and even the shot after that. I gotta be strategic. You can't rush me on this. I play this *simular* to the way some people play chess." He stalks around the table, checking the lines and angles, plotting the order in which he will drop the balls. "All right. I'm ready to run the table on you." He bends over the table and lines up his shot. The tip of the stick pokes at the cue ball. The tip scuffs off of the side of the white ball, ruining the shot; the cue ball careens off of the six-ball and drops into the side pocket.

"Fuck!" Askew slams the butt of the stick on the ground.

"You might wanna put some chalk on that." Grundish smirks and throws the square of billiards chalk over the table to Askew. Grundish fishes the cue ball from the pocket and sets it down on the table. "So, you wanna talk about what's been going on with you?" He looks up at his friend while he shoots at the four-ball, still making a perfect shot and giving himself a proper leave.

"I don't know what to say." Askew's eyes drop and stare at the drink in his hand, refusing to make eye contact with Grundish. "I know I fucked up. I've been fucking up here. I thought you'd be happy that I brought that kid in here for you. And then, when you kicked me out of the room, I could tell you weren't happy. I started thinking about what I did and realized that it was probably pretty stupid."

"I ain't gonna argue with you there." Grundish lines up his shot and drops the six-ball in a corner pocket. The backspin on the cue ball drags it back and to the left, leaving an easy shot on the seven-ball. "I mean, shit, I appreciate the thought. Hell, I been fantasizing about fucking that kid up for months now."

"I know. I know. That's why when you were sleeping, and I saw the opportunity, I snagged that little Fucker and dragged him over here." Askew downs the rest of his drink and swirls the ice in the bottom of the cup in a circle. "And then I started thinking that it would do your heart good to see that I already worked the kid over for you a little bit."

"A little bit? A little bit?" He stares at Askew. "You cut the kid's ear off." Askew does not stare back.

"I got carried away. I don't know. I just…" He stops and watches Grundish line up his next shot. "You're gonna fuck this one up. Ain't no way you'll make it. Plus, you'll prob'ly scratch."

Grundish ignores the taunts and lines up his shot on the eight ball. The cue ball knocks the eight into the end cushion. The eight springs back and barrels down the table and clean into the left corner pocket. "Now rack 'em, bitch. And we'll talk more about this in a minute." He leaves the room to refill their glasses and returns with two more Scotches on the rocks. Askew sets up the balls on the table again.

Askew takes the glass from Grundish when he returns and they clink the tumblers. "You know," says Askew, "when you was sleeping, I got to thinking about all the things we been talking about lately. First you tell me that we gotta get the Fuckers. Then you tell me that the shit that I'm doing ain't enough. So I kick it up a notch and then you start telling me that I'm getting out of hand…"

"Well," interrupts Grundish, "within the last couple of days, you beat a man to death, you took on a group of guys with your feet, and you cut a kid's ear off. That seems a little out of hand to me. Especially considering that you ain't never been in so much as a wrestling match in your life." Grundish stands with the pool cue vertical before him, the butt on the floor, both hands gripping the stick. He stares at his friend, challenging him to explain.

"You're right. I don't disagree. I was getting out of hand. And then again, my *enragement* served a purpose for me. It was *catharsic* for me to get all of that out. That's stuff that's been building up in me my whole life. I ain't never been smart enough, good looking, tall enough. I've been a disappointment to my family and my lovers. I've fallen short on every measurement of my usefulness in my life. I've taken a lot of abuse. Been looked down upon. Passed over for the better jobs. Shit, I've been working at Pizza Brothers for five years, and they won't even make me a shift manager. I didn't even know how much shit I had bottled up until I let it all out on Bumpy D, and those other guys, and that kid upstairs. And then I get to thinking about our plans, and the fact that you're the only person that's ever stuck by me and not talked down to me. And I think about what you been saying about the Fuckers. And I get all confused. I wanna lay low, get out of here, maybe go live in Mexico for a while until we can get our floating whore house up and running. And then on the other hand, I get so pissed off and I wanna hurt people. I wanna hurt them bad. I ain't never felt like that before, and it's been a real rush for me."

Grundish remains in the same spot, his hands still gripped on the pool cue in front of him. "Yeah, but do you have that out of your system now? 'Cuz if you're gonna run around and start killing and maiming people, we ain't got no future with the brothel idea. So the question is: what's it gonna be, Boy? Yes or no. You gonna turn cuckoo for Cocoa Puffs, or are we gonna lay low and get out from under all this shit hanging over us?"

"I got it out of my system," Askew smiles. The super glue on his lip cracks and exposes the stitched area to stinging air. He grimaces but continues, "you're right. We need to lay low and follow through with our plans." He sits back on the stool and sips at his drink.

"Good," Grundish sits down on his stool, still feeling as if the eyes of the basset hound in the picture are watching him, judging him. "Now promise me you ain't gonna do nothing more to that kid upstairs."

Askew mumbles, "I promise."

Grundish nods, satisfied, and grows silent. He fixes his eyes on the dog painting and feels as if he is having a staring contest with the hound.

"Tell me, Grundish," says Askew, breaking his friend's trance. "Tell me like you done before."

"Tell you about what?"

"About the ladies."

Grundish snaps, "Again! Come on, Bro. We're talking serious shit here. And you want me to tell you the same shit that I tell you every time things get tough. I don't feel like it right now." Despite the charade, Grundish welcomes the opportunity to rehash the scheme for his friend. It's an old standby, a comfort conversation they fall into whenever things get tough. And to have Askew ask about it makes Grundish feel like his friend isn't so far gone that he can't come back.

Askew pleads, "Aw, you come on, Grundish. Please. Tell me like you done before."

"You really dig that shit, don't you? All right, I'll tell you," Grundish gives in. "And then I need to sleep again."

Grundish smoothes himself out and starts his well-worn rap. "Guys like us, you know, the ones that work the shit jobs and scrape by, are the loneliest guys in the world...."

The cold tile floor on his feverish face is comforting, like a tall glass of ice water, like a swim in a mountain stream. Everything else on his body is sore from sleeping on the bathroom floor. How he ended up in such a condition, Grundish does not know. He suspects it may have had something to do with excessive Scotch consumption and the vomit that he smells. He is contorted, with an arm up under his ribs and twisted behind his back, bottom half turned so that the groin is flat on the floor and the legs sprawled out, and head wedged between the toilet and the wall. Nothing else about the position is comfortable. But the tile, the cool tile, feels so good on his cheek that the rest of the discomfort is bearable. The thought of moving is out of the question. The arm pinned beneath his side is numb, his neck aches and refuses to budge, and his legs are like concrete. Stuck to the floor like a bug on flypaper. His temples throb. He focuses his attention on the small patch of facial flesh in contact with the tile and everything else is relegated to the junk drawer of his mind. Only the disconnected sounds of shouting, conflict, and some sort of explosion from elsewhere in the house forces Grundish to peel his cheek from that heavenly patch of tile.

Before Askew could comprehend what was happening, he found himself playing the role of the bad dog getting his nose rubbed in another turd on the floor of life. When it was all over, and the smoke cleared from the barrel of the blunderbuss, when the blood had already begun to coagulate on the wall, when the only sound was the ringing in his ears, Askew stepped back and took account of what he had done and saw that it amounted to something very bad.

"Shit," Askew mumbles with no trace of emotion. "Shit. Shit. Shit. Shit. Shit. Shit. Fuck. Shit. Fuck." In front of him, crumpled on the floor, is the husk of the man known as Randy Buttwynn, with a hole in his body where his life had been. On the wall behind his remains, a chunky Rorschach splotch of gore, blood, and gristle presents a pattern that to some might look like a goat's head and to others the female reproductive system. To Askew it looks like trouble.

Dangling from Askew's hand is the still-warm blunderbuss. Around his ankles is a pair of Buttwynn's silk boxers. His dick hangs limply between his legs. After the long talk with Grundish the night before, after Grundish started heaving up his dinner and passed out on the bathroom floor, after Askew ran about the house seeking petty revenge on Buttwynn's belongings, after checking in on the kid in the guest bedroom, after tolerating the inexplicable, painful and insistent erection for hours, Askew sat down alone in the theater room and put a blanket over his lap in case Turleen should walk in on him. With the blunderbuss on the chair at his side and remote control in hand, Askew searched the adult channels on the television until he found a promising movie entitled *Ouch! That's My Asshole!*, to which he unsuccessfully and repeatedly attempted to rid himself of the aching stiffness in his loins. He wondered how he could keep such a strong erection for four hours.

Askew was right about Randy Buttwynn. He is a Fucker. After spending part of the planned vacation with his family in Wisconsin, Buttwynn claimed to have a work emergency that required him to return home early. "Oh no," he told his wife and children, "I don't want to ruin everybody's trip. You all need to stay here and take advantage of the time with Grandma. I'll be okay. It breaks my heart to have to leave you guys halfway through our only vacation this year. My boss just won't budge on this, though. He insists that I'm at the meeting tomorrow." Kissing his wife and children and wiping a tear from his eye, Randy Buttwynn walked out on his family so that he could have several days free of them to spend instead with Dora, his part-time whore.

When Randy Buttwynn would think about the things he would do to Dora, the things she let him do because he paid her, it excited him to the point of frustration. Even the fact that he paid her made him excited. Dora, a rail-thin kid, met Buttwynn as a customer at the Scrub-N-Rub massage parlor where she worked in Tampa. A quick handjob and a courtesy rubbing of the nubs where her tits should be was enough to make Buttwynn become obsessed with her. All he could think about was the eighteen-year-old girl with crooked teeth who looked to him like she was thirteen. And the thought of fucking a girl that looked the same age as the cute little friends his daughter brought home made him hot. Really hot. So Buttwynn regularly met with Dora at the Crosstown Inn and paid her the money he was supposed to be setting aside for the Buttwynn children's college funds. The wide-bored nostrils on his upturned porcine nose flared and contracted as he fantasized about her. His tiny teeth had a funny way of sitting in his swollen pink gums, and he sucked at them nervously, making a wet clicking sound whenever he would think of the things he would do to her. In the airplane seat beside Buttwynn, an older woman—one with bluish-gray hair and the menthol aroma of a topical pain reliever—was disturbed by the odd teeth sucking and subtle hip thrusts of Buttwynn. The woman moved seats and later told her husband that there was something about the man in the seat next to her that made her skin crawl. Something in his strange mannerisms reeked of perversion, something rotten just below the surface.

Cheating on his wife thrilled Buttwynn. And with her gone in Wisconsin, the biggest rush would be to have his way with Dora in the bed he and his wife shared every night. Mister and Missus rarely had sex, and when they did it was merely for the purpose of procreation. There was nothing exciting to Randy Buttwynn about turning the lights off and fucking his homely wife through a hole in a sheet that covered the rest of her body. That's what she insisted on – a hole in a sheet with just her bushy slit exposed. With the family gone, Buttwynn saw the opportunity of a lifetime to show the marriage bed what was really supposed to happen between a man and a woman. Thoughts of filling Dora's various orificial openings with body parts and inanimate objects consumed Buttwynn as he parked his car in the driveway and briskly ushered her through the front door of his house. Greeting the couple was the welcoming fragrance of meatloaf and freshly baked bread.

"What the dickens is going on?" says Buttwynn to his lady friend, his nostrils flaring and twitching like an annoyed pig. "It smells as if someone is cooking. But nobody is here."

"Don't know," answered Dora in the clipped tone she liked to use with Buttwynn. For the money he was paying her, she was willing to let him violate her however he wished. But that didn't mean that she had to have a conversation with the creepy pig-faced man. "Don't care. I wanna drink."

Placing his hand on her bony back and sliding it down to grab her ass and nudge her forward at the same time, Buttwynn leads Dora to the theater room to fix them a drink.

"Now, what the dickens is this?" Buttwynn shouts when they enter the theater room and see the bulbous, hirsute little man passed out in the reclining chair, his boxers down around the ankles and the robe wide open and freely displaying wilted and reddened genitals. "I said, hey there fella! What the dickens is this?" Buttwynn kicks Askew's foot to wake him. "I'm calling the police." He turns and walks away from Askew with the intention of getting to a phone.

Askew is shaken from sleep by the irate Buttwynn. The man who always tipped him a quarter. The man who never said *thank you*. The Fucker who figuratively and invariably spits a big loogie in the face of pizza delivery guys. The Fucker who is kicking him in the foot and yelling at him.

Askew leaps from his chair, boxers still around his ankles, and screams: "Hold it right there, Buttwynn!" Buttwynn continues to walk away. "Hold it right there, you Fucker, or I'll fucking shoot you."

Buttwynn stops in his tracks and turns to face Askew. He eyes him and then flashes a look of recognition. "Say," says Buttwynn. "I know you, don't I? Where do I know you from?"

"Shut up, Fucker! Shut up!" Askew, his voice rising in pitch, levels the blunderbuss at Buttwynn and yells at him, "Don't you fucking worry about where you know me from! It don't matter! And if you know what's good for ya, you'll keep your mouth shut and let me *condemplate* this situation!"

"I know where I know you from," Buttwynn smiles and shakes his pointer finger at Askew. "You're that funny-looking little pizza guy. The one who's always late. The one who gave me my pizza with the cheese stuck to the top of the box last week. Always have something smart to say. I don't even know why I'm so generous to you with my tips."

"I said shut up or I'll shoot!" Askew yells. Dora backs away from Buttwynn, away from the area where the odd-looking gun is pointed, and finds herself backed against a wall but well out of Buttwynn's vicinity. "Just shut up!"

"Listen, Sonny," condescends Buttwynn, "that blunderbuss that you're holding is an antique. It's for display purposes. It's only been shot a few times, and it's not loaded now, I can tell you that. So stop threatening to shoot me. Why don't you just hand me that toy, and let me get on with calling the police?" Buttwynn sucks at his rat-like teeth, making a moist, squeaky sound, and starts in Askew's direction.

"I said stay back, you Fucker!" screams Askew. He pulls the hammer from half to full-cock position. Buttwynn stops again.

"Come now. You must be kidding, Sir. I am confident that my gun is not loaded. And I'm sure that if you did find my shot and powder, you would have no idea how to properly load the gun and pack the barrel. Heck, you can't even get my order right when I call for pizza." Buttwynn starts again in the direction of Askew under the assumption that the gun is not loaded. Buttwynn is wrong.

BLAMMMMO!

A flash explodes from the end of the blunderbuss and propels a fiery load of metal shot and nails toward Buttwynn. The blast of debris hits him in the gut and knocks him backward; metal balls and nails chew a massive chunk of flesh from his torso. The shot exits his back and splatters the wall with bloody nails, fluids and bits and pieces of Randy Buttwynn. As he lies on the ground, the remainder of his life quickly seeping into the carpeting, he looks at the bloody splotch on the wall. In the pattern, he sees the face of his father, a face he had forgotten long ago.

Grundish takes in the scene without speaking. The beanpole-of-a-girl, in her cut-off shorts and pink t-shirt, cowers and whimpers in the corner, her face in her hands, her body shivering. On the floor is an overweight hunk of bloody pig-faced cadaver. The missing puzzle piece of the corpse is splattered on the wall in a shape that reminds Grundish of a prison transport van. Standing in front of the dead man is Askew, mumbling blankly to himself. “Shit. Fucking shit. Shit. Shit. Shit.” His hand still grips the wooden stock of the mighty blunderbuss, his finger still on the trigger.

Without a word, Grundish moves about the room and evaluates the situation. *Dead guy splattered on the wall*, he notes to himself, *not good*. He grabs the crusty blanket from the floor in front of Askew and covers the corpse sprawled out in front of him. *Askew with a cannon in his hands and another homicide to answer for. Not good*. Grundish grabs the barrel of the gun with one hand and grabs Askew's wrist down near where he is gripping the gun. Askew allows the blunderbuss to be pulled from his grip. Grundish tosses the gun in the corner opposite the cowering girl. *Skeletal girl going into shock in the corner. Tiny little pants. Chain around her boot. Shaking in the corner. She's a teenage prostitute.*[29] With a hand on her elbow and one hooked under her other arm, Grundish helps the girl stand. He walks her over to a reclining chair and sits her down.

Grabbing the pack of Blue Llamas from atop the pool table, Grundish extracts three cigarettes and lights them all

---

[29]Rock-n-Roll mythology provides that during a concert, Alice Cooper once shat on the stage and Frank Zappa ate the shit. Some versions have Zappa shitting and Alice Cooper eating it. Other versions have Alice Cooper stomping baby chickens to death and then Zappa shitting on the stage. Responding to the allegations, Frank Zappa denied the rumors, saying that he never shit on stage and the closest that he ever came to eating shit was at a Holiday Inn in Fayetteville, North Carolina, in 1973.

at the same time, handing one to Askew, one to Dora, and keeping one for himself. Dora accepts the smoke and drags hard on it, her hand still shaking as she holds the cigarette up to her mouth. Askew jams his smoke in the gap between his front teeth and lets it dangle. Grundish sucks on his cigarette and gives Askew the hairy eyeball. "God damn, I wish you would quit smoking. I can't quit if you keep doing it in front of me."

"I know. I'm gonna quit at the end of the month," Askew answers. He is happy that they are not talking about the single, solitary, thing that everybody in the room is thinking about: the fat dead guy on the floor.

"So, that must be Buttwynn," says Grundish.

"Yeah. That's him. He was coming at me, and he was gonna call the cops on us. And then he started talking about how generous he was with his tips. He was a real Fucker right to the end. So I shot him," says Askew matter-of-factly, as if explaining why he took a right turn at a red light.

"Obviously," says Grundish. He ashes his cigarette on the floor and takes another hit off of it. "So, what we've got here is what we call a situation. And if it ain't a bona fide situation, it'll do until the real thing comes along."

"Uh-huh." Askew nods and waits for his friend to figure out what to do.

"We have a dead body. We're already wanted for the Bumpy D situation. We have a hostage upstairs. Now we have another person that we can't let go. I have one mean bastard-of-a-hangover. And we don't know when the rest of the Buttwynn family will be showing up here."

"The family won't be here for two more days," says the girl under her breath.

"What's that, Sweetheart?" Grundish asks. "Speak up. I can't hear you."

She takes a long drag off of her smoke, burning the remainder of the tobacco, and says again, "I said, the family won't be here for two more days."

"Well, that's good news. Now, what's your name, Sweetheart?"

"Dora," she answers and looks down at her hands.

"Well, Dora, first off, let me tell you this. We ain't gonna hurt you or nothing. But we can't let you leave here right now either. You're gonna stay here while I figure out what to do. Okay?

"I guess I don't got no choice, do I?" she says.

"No, you don't. Now, I need to know how you are so sure that the family won't be here for two more days."

"Well, if you haven't figured it out yet, I'm, like, an escort, so to speak. That man," she looks at Buttwynn, "paid me for two days of services. And we was planning on staying here in his house and partying while the family was gone."

"And he told you that?"

"Yep."

"And he brought you to his house while his wife and kids are gone?"

"Yep."

"What a Fucker!"

"I told ya," says Askew. "I told ya! The man is a Fucker!"

"Well, we need to be out of here within a day. And the sooner the better." Grundish drops his butt on the carpet and smashes it out. "Where the hell is Turleen anyway?"

"I haven't the slightest idea," answers Askew as he crushes his cigarette out on Buttwynn's head.

Turleen is sleeping the sleep of a one-lunged octogenarian who has been awake for several days straight, cooking, drinking wine, and breathing in as much second-hand smoke as she can manage. Laid out spread-eagle on the Buttwynn guest bed, one arm curled around an empty, wicker-wrapped Chianti bottle like it's a teddy bear, and twitching the minor spasms of one in deep REM mode, Turleen soundly sleeps through screams and gunshots. Instead she finds herself in a smoky pool hall leaning up against a table and surrounded by dogs.

"Hello, Darlin'," says a low, gravely voice behind her. "Nice to see you. It's been a long time."

She turns around to discover Stubs standing behind her, leaning on a pool stick with one paw, holding a frothy mug of ale in the other. "Stubs," she says, happy to see him. "Why, I must be dreaming again, I must. Give me one of your fags, please." Stubs reaches into his shirt pocket and shakes a cigarette halfway out of the pack and holds it out toward Turleen. She takes the cigarette, rips the filter off of the end, and puts it to her mouth, waiting for one of the crowd to offer a light. Stubs, the Spitz, and the Great Dane all scramble for their lighters. Stubs wins the honor of giving the lady a light. "Where's your friend? The hound dog."

"I don't know." Stubs looks around the room. "He was just here."

Turleen feels a cold wet sensation on her foot. "All right, Mr. Galoot. I can feel you down there, I can. And you promised to never lick my feet again."

Idjit Galoot pops up from under the table and flashes a sheepish grin. "I wasn't licking them, Ma'am. Just getting a nice little sniff. Sorry if my nose is a bit cold." Turleen stares at him with one eyebrow cocked. "I assure you," says Idjit, "it won't happen again."

Turleen looks down and sees that she's wearing the red dress, but her cleavage is full and firm and wrinkle-free. She tugs this way and that at the shoulders of her dress to re-adjust the way her breasts hang. The room about her is a seedy dive of a bar. "Kind of a rough crowd here," she says to Stubs. "I like it."

Stubs nods in agreement. "It feels like home, doesn't it?"

"Well I don't know about that. But it sure looks like an interesting time, it does." She nods toward the front door where a beagle drags his ass on the welcome mat.

"Yes, well, ah-hum," Stubs clears his throat. "We're here to show you something. Take a look past the billiards table. Toward the other side of the room."

Turleen looks and the area on the other side of the pool table is a swirling gray and brown mass, like a vortex to another realm. "I cain't see nothing but a gray cloudy mess. What am I supposed to be looking at?"

"Just focus your eyes on one point," say Idjit. "Don't blink. Don't look away. It'll come to you."

"What'll I see? Because it all looks like a big shit cloud to me, it does."

"Just keep staring, please."

Just when she's about to blink, when her eyeballs go dry and scratchy, just when she's ready to give up and look for a newspaper to roll up and start swatting dogs with, it comes to her. The haze clears. In front of them, on the pool table, the bulldog sinks the eight-ball and smiles. The Finnish spitz throws a fifty-dollar bill on the table in disgust and walks away. Turleen doesn't notice. Instead, she looks just past the action with the dogs and it is as if she is gazing through a two-way mirror into the Buttwynn's billiards room. But the room looks different. On the wall is a red splatter that, to Turleen, looks like a giant human heart. Not the romantic Valentine's Day heart symbol, but like a throbbing human heart. In front of the splotch on the wall is an oversized wild boar, slit open down the middle with its entrails spilling out onto the floor. Hanging on one wall is a three-by-five painted portrait of Mrs. Buttwynn. Her face is smeared with heavy make up, her mouth twisted into a malignant grin as she looks down at the boar. Standing over the bore are Grundish and Askew, in their robes and sock garters, with blood smeared on their faces and arms. They smoke and talk, but Turleen cannot hear what they say. Turleen's peripheral vision catches movement in the corner of the room. She directs her attention toward the movement, toward the battered blond angel hovering in the corner. The angel's arms are bruised, her hair tangled. She wears a poncho. A real poncho. A Mexican one. Not a Sears poncho.

"Those boys mucked things up again, they did," says Turleen.

"A-yup," agrees Stubs.

"What's all that light and fog forming around their heads?"

All around the heads and shoulders of Grundish and Askew is a fog. Grundish is enveloped by a glowing apple-green mist. Askew's head throws off coils of black with reddish streaks.

"I don't know, Turleen. I'm just a dog[30]," answers Stubs. "But if I were to guess, I'd say those are probably their auras. The big bearded fellow there looks healthy. But, uh, that funny looking little guy seems almost like he's polluted or something."

"It does look that way, it does. Why are you showing me this?"

"Because one of those boys needs your help."

"How am I supposed to help him?"

"That's for you to figure out," says Stubs. "I think they need you now, though."

The vision on the other side of the pool table returns to a swirling vortex. The image of the Buttwynn billiards room fades.

"Well, I better get going then, I better." Turleen starts for the front door of the bar and stops again. "How about one more cigarette before I go, and an extra for the road, Mr. Stubs?"

---

[30]Cordozar Calvin Broadus, Jr., is the given name of rapper, actor, certified football coach, and creator of the Pig-Latin-like suffix *-izzle*, Snoop Dogg.

Stubs shakes two more smokes free from his pack and hands them to Turleen. He lights one for her and she tucks the other behind her ear. "Thanks, boy," says Turleen as she scratches him on the back, just between the shoulder blades.

"You're quite welcome, Turleen. Anytime." Stubs thumps his foot on the floor in response to the back scratching. "Hopefully, we'll meet again soon."

Turleen turns away from the pack of beer-swilling, pool-playing dogs and walks out the front door of the bar. Once out of the bar she turns and looks at the building. A blinking green neon sign hangs above the front door, announcing the simple but powerful sounding name of the bar, *THE HUB*.

"Where the hell is Turleen anyway?"

"I haven't the slightest idea," answers Askew as he crushes his cigarette butt out on Buttwynn's head.

"I'm right here, I am." Turleen walks through the doorway, a cigarette tucked behind her ear. "And you're right, Grundish. We need to get out of here now, we do."

"Well, we have to figure out where to go." Grundish scratches at the thick pelt of hair on his head, trying to stimulate his brain into coming up with an idea.

"I've got that figured out, I do. It's all taken care of. You just figure out the best time for us to leave, how we're going to travel, all of that crap, and I'll take care of the rest, I will. I have the perfect place for us all to lay low and for however long we need to."

"All right, Turleen, tell me what you've got planned for us." Grundish grabs another of Askew's Blue Llamas and torches it up. Turleen inches closer to Grundish.

"Well, the way I see it, we need to put some distance between us and this mess, we do. And I've got just the place." Turleen inhales as deeply as her one lung allows, relishing the second-hand smoke. "So I set up what they call a safe house for us a little ways away from here, over in Polk County. It will at least buy you boys a little time to figure things out, it will."

"Well, who's gonna be willing to put us up?"

"An old flame of mine. He's crazy about me. The old boy'll do anything I ask, he will. I mean, talk about being dizzy with a dame."

"Well, I don't see that we've got much choice 'cause I ain't got no friends other than Askew, and he ain't got no one but me. But now we've got this young lady that we can't really let go. And we've got a kid duct taped to a chair upstairs. The smart thing to do would be to knock the kid off so he can't identify us."

Askew abruptly rotates 180-degrees on his heels and starts out of the room.

"Askew, get back here."

Askew stops and turns. "I'm just going to get me a sodee pop. I wasn't going to do anything to the kid." But, just under the tattered flesh of Askew's face, Grundish recognizes a hint of disappointment.

"I ain't got it in me to take that kid's life. And neither does Askew. So I guess we're gonna have to leave the kid upstairs, maybe just give him some food and water before we go. Buttwynn's family will find him and let him loose. And, yeah, he can identify us. But we'll be long gone by then. And I don't see no other way around it 'lessen we want to kill the boy. And we don't wanna do that. Right, Askew?"

"Yeah," grumbles Askew, his tone flat and unenthusiastic.

Turleen pulls an unlit cigarette from behind her ear and rolls it around in her hand. It's not a Blue Llama. It's not a Red Apple. It's a brand called Sordes Pilosus.[31] *Hmmm*, Turleen thinks to herself, *that doggie gave me some fancy French fags. Next time I see Stubs, I'll have to do something nice for him, I will.* Turleen decides that now when she goes to sleep, she'll always make sure to keep a baggy of chopped meat with her for her canine dream-friends. The urge to light the cigarette almost overwhelms her, but Turleen maintains control, merely relishing the feel of the Sordes Pilosus between her fingers. She breathes in another whiff of Grundish's second hand-smoke and secretly wishes to be stricken with a terminal illness so that she can justify taking up smoking again. "Well," Turleen says, "I'm gonna take this young lady into the kitchen and give her a nice meal, I am. Then I'm gonna freeze all the

---

[31]Sordes Pilosus is a small pterosaur that lived during the late Jurassic period of the Mesozoic Era. It's name literally means hairy devil.

leftovers for this here dead fellow's family because they're probably not going to feel up to cooking when they get home. Now, come on along with me, honey," she says to Dora.

Cautiously rising from the chair, Dora stands and allows herself to be led to the kitchen by Turleen. She looks to Grundish to see if he'll allow her to exit the room. Grundish waves her away with his hand, confident that Turleen will be able to handle the fragile-looking girl if she tries to make a break.

"You boys do whatever it is that you need to in order to wrap up your business here," says Turleen. "This young 'un and I'll be ready to go when you are, we will."

"There ain't much use in cleaning this mess up," says Grundish to Askew. "We ain't got the time. Why don't you go take a plate of food to that kid upstairs? Give him some water. Don't let him up, though. He can shit and piss himself until somebody comes along and releases him. Speaking of which, I gotta go take a dump, myself."

"God damn! God damn! God damn!" Grundish can't believe the torpedo in the commode. Turleen has been stuffing him with mounds of meat the past couple of days, so it only makes sense. Grundish still cannot fathom that the monstrosity in the toilet bowl came from his body. The colossal ass-baby spans the widest part of the bowl and dares somebody to try to flush it. *Come on*, it says. *Don't be a pussy. Go ahead and try to get rid of me. What? Are you afraid of a talking turd? You disgust me. Yeah. How does that make you feel? You make a turd feel queasy.*

"Well," Grundish says to himself (and the turd), "we're already wanted for murder, and they're bound to realize that we were involved here. I'm going away for good if they catch us. Why not leave my mark?" He walks away from the porcelain throne. He walks away from a blue-ribbon, first-prize-winning log of solid waste. The Turd Burglar strikes again.

"Did you feed the boy?"

"Yep."

"Water him?"

"Yep."

"And he's still alive?"

"I told you I wouldn't kill him," Askew takes umbrage at the question. He pulls his robe around his pot belly, barely managing to tie the belt to keep the robe in place. Fumbling with his pack of Blue Llamas, he finally manages to shake one out and light it. "You gotta cut me some slack, Grundish. I already told you that I know I fucked up with some of the shit I done. But you gotta recognize that some of that stuff happened in the *mist* of some chaotic shit."

"Give me that thing," says Grundish, snagging Askew's freshly-lit smoke. "You just keep smoking these fucking things in front of me so that I will too." He takes a hit off of the cigarette and hands it back to Askew. "I know you've been a little confused here. So, I am trying to cut you some slack. Just try…please just try not to kill anybody else."

"Hey. I'm not a cold-blooded killer, *per se*, you know." He looks to Grundish for confirmation. "Bumpy D, for example. He was literally asking me to kill him for what he did. And Buttwynn. He charged me. What could I do?"

"What about that kid's ear?"

"That was excessive and uncalled for, *granite*. But I recognize that now, and it won't happen again. I'm making a *three-hundred-and-sixty-degree* turnabout. Heck, I even apologized to the kid the last time I was up there."

Grundish thinks about going to check on the kid and then decides to take his friend's word for it. Askew seems sincere, and Grundish gives him the benefit of the doubt. "Let's go check on Turleen and the girl."

In the kitchen, Turleen sips at an oversized glass of Chianti. She and Dora pick at a plate of fava beans and an unidentifiable cut of meat. Dora sips at her own glass of wine and looks as comfortable as if she were dining with her grandmother.

"Everything going all right, Turleen?" Grundish asks.

"It's hunky dory, it is," Turleen smiles at the girl. "This young lady here has nowhere to go and no problem with coming along with us. Ain't that right, Dura?"

"Yep," says Dora. She forks several more fava beans into her mouth and nods.

"Her name's *Dora*, Turleen," corrects Askew. "It ain't Dura. You're *mispronounciating* it. Her name is Dora."

"That's what I said, it is," answers Turleen. "*Dura*."

"Okay, whatever," interrupts Grundish. "We can call her Dora, Dura, Darla or Dharma. Shit, you can call me Ray, you can call me Jay. It don't matter right now. What matters is that we get out of here before Buttwynn's family shows up. Right?"

Everybody, including Dora, nods their heads in agreement.

"All right then. What do you need to do before we go, Turleen?"

"I just need to bag up and freeze the rest of my food and I'm ready to scram, I am."

"Good," says Grundish. "When we're all ready to go, I'm gonna have you go out in the driveway and bring Buttwynn's car into the garage. Can you do that for me, Turleen?"

Turleen pulls the Sordes Pilosus from behind her ear and holds it between her fingers. She daydreams about what the fancy cigarette would taste like. Lost in the smoky reverie, Turleen forgets about Grundish's request.

"Turleen!" snaps Grundish. "Can you do that for me? Can you bring the car into the garage when we're ready to go?"

"Of course I can, Sonny. Why you getting so snippy?" She tucks the cigarette back behind her ear and starts filling a freezer bag with chopped steak.

"Askew, do you need to do anything before we go?

"I probably oughta go to the little boys' room," says Askew, trying to be cute for Dora. He winks at her and she offers a slight smile in return. "And maybe we both should get back into our old clothes."

"Yeah," agrees Grundish. "We don't want to draw too much attention when we're in the open. But I've grown to like these sock garters. And, have you tried on the sandals in Buttwynn's closet? Incredible. I think I'm taking some garters and sandals with me."

"Fuckin-A right," says Askew. "There's something comforting about wearing both the garters and the sandals, isn't there?"

"You need anything, darling?" Grundish asks Dora.

"Nah." She half-grins a snaggle-toothed smile. Her teeth crowd and cross each other, a random jumble of chipped ivory bits that are otherwise well-maintained, not stained. "Just don't hurt me or nothing."

"Fair enough. Let's plan on being out of here within the hour then." Grundish leaves the room to begin filling a duffle bag with necessities.

And they are on the road again.[32] Turleen drives the van with Dora at her side in the passenger seat. The boys stay out of sight on the floor in the back of the vehicle. Turleen hands Dora a cigarette from one of Askew's half-empty packs. Dora kicks her bare feet up on the dashboard and lights up.

"Did we really have to leave the El Camino?" Askew asks, sticking his whack-a-mole of a head over the back of the middle-row seats in Buttwynn's Toyota Sienna van. Grundish's fist is the mallet that pounds the head back down. It pauses, hovering near the top of the seat, waiting for the next pop of the head

"Get your fucking head down," says Grundish from his crouched position in the middle row of minivan seats. "We need to stay out of sight. Do you wanna get us busted on the way to our safe-house? "

"No, I don't wanna get us busted," answers Askew. "I just don't see why we had to leave my car behind. We

[32]On September 13, 1980, Willie Nelson performed on the south lawn of the White House for President Jimmy Carter. First Lady Rosalyn Carter joined Nelson for a duet of *Up Against the Wall Redneck Mother*. Later that night, Nelson retired to the roof of the White House to smoke a joint. In his biography, Nelson admitted that whenever he stayed at the White House, he would smoke a "big fat Austin Torpedo."

could still go back and get it. I fucking love that car." The El Camino sits abandoned in the Buttwynn garage. Grundish already explained to Askew that the sheriff's office will have an all-points bulletin for the car, which is registered in Askew's name and in which an entire trailer park full of witnesses saw them flee. "By the way," continues Askew, "you're virtually assuring that they can pin Buttwynn's death on us by leaving the car there."

"I already thought about that," says Grundish. Crouching in the back of the van is awkward for the large man. The frustration born of the discomfort makes him itch with prickly heat. He readjusts his position and straightens his legs. Despite his growing frustration, he speaks to Askew in a calm voice. "Like I told you already, there were things I had to weigh. For example: was it more important for us to clean up the mess at the house or get out of there before somebody else showed up? We can't take any chances with being caught. Another example: should we kill the kid or leave a witness alive who will undoubtedly be able to identify us? My conscience won that one easily. So, you see, we're leaving a dead body, our fingerprints and DNA all over the house, and an eyewitness who can identify us, to boot. Oh yeah, and I left a big Turd Burglar calling card in the toilet. We're already wanted for murder. At this point, it don't make a bit of difference if we left the El Camino there or not. They're gonna know it was us in that house. The smart money says take Buttwynn's car, which, of course, will not be reported stolen until his family returns and sees the mess in their house. So you see, telling me that you have a sentimental attachment to your car is a futile argument."

"It is not *feudal*. I love that car more than I love most people. If you weren't such an asshole sometimes, you would realize how important it is to me." Askew pops his head up over the seat again and casts a demented, popeyed glare at Grundish. The closed-hand mallet whacks the mole back into its hole.

"The question is this: is your car worth us all getting arrested?" Grundish readjusts his position again, trying to discover a more comfortable manner in which to twist himself. He presses his mouth against the tiny gap between the middle and the passenger side seat and speaks into the crack. "Because if we were to go driving around in that car, we'd be busted before the second track of your *Gimme Back My Bullets* eight-track tape is over. They'd take your car. They'd take your Skynyrd tape. And they'd take you, me, and probably even Turleen to jail. Is that what you want? 'Cause if it is, then let's have Turleen turn around, and we'll just go back to the house. Is that what we should do? God damn, Askew! I'm always having to watch out for you and clean up your messes. And now you're wanting to go back and get us all caught. You are always trying to fuck up my shit. Man, it would be so much easier if I didn't have to deal with all this nonsense sometimes. Do you want us all to go back so you can have your car, even if it means getting everybody thrown in prison?"

"No," Askew's voice trembles. "It ain't what we should do. I'm just saying that you ain't being sensitive to my feelings about that car. I love that fucking car. And I just wish you wouldn't blow me so much shit about it. You want I should go away and just leave you alone?"

"Where in the fuck would you go, anyway?"

"Well, I could find my way south and live in the swamps. Build myself a little chickee hut or something."

"Yeah, and how'd you eat? You ain't got sense enough to find anything to feed yourself."

"I'd find things," says Askew, his voice hitching. "I'd hunt. I don't need no nice food with ketchup. Nobody'd bother me. And if I wanted to keep a car, nobody would try to take it away from me."

Grundish hesitates, breathes deep. "Fuck," he sighs. "I been mean, haven't I? Hey, I'm sorry we have to leave it there." His tone softens into vocal putty. "It's just that it's the only choice we really had, ya know. I know it was a sacrifice[33] on your part. And I appreciate it, Bro."

Askew, sensing an advantage, tells Grundish, "Well if you don't want me, you just have to say so. I'll go off into the swamps right now. I'll go live down there all by myself. And I won't get no more cars taken away from me."

"I said I was sorry," says Grundish, and meaning it. "Jesus Christ, Askew. Out in the swamps, you'd starve. You'd get eaten by gators. Somebody'd shoot you. Nope. You stay with me."

"Well, you could be more considerate of my feelings. Why couldn't you just explain it to me in the first place why we had to leave my car, instead of just dragging me off and not telling me your reasons. I mean, I get it now. But, yeah, you was just being mean there for a while."

---

[33]The Aztecs are said to have sacrificed at least one person per day to aid the sun in rising. A good portion of the humans sacrificed were war captives. It was said that those who were sacrificed would become helpers of the sun and could return as humming birds and butterflies.

"Well," Grundish's tone hardens again. "I done said I was sorry. Are you gonna keep grumbling about it, or, are you gonna let it go?"

"I told you, I'm letting it go."

"Good. 'Cause you're the only friend I got." Grundish cocks his hip up and jams his hand under his waistband to peel his sweat-moistened nutsack from his thigh and readjust the equipment. "Now shut your pie-hole, and let me take a nap. And stay out of sight until we get to wherever it is that Turleen is taking us." Grundish closes his eyes and lays his face on the floor. His cheek rests on a cool strip of metal track for one of the seats. He pretends it is the tile floor that provided him with so much relief earlier. With nothing better to do, Grundish effortlessly transitions into napping mode.

Askew lies on his side in the row behind Grundish, glaring at the back of the seats in front of him. The ebb and flow of his emotions drag him from warm appreciation for having a friend like Grundish to childish resentment about leaving the El Camino behind. The tender feeling for his best friend overpowers the resentment, smothers it. Askew, too, closes his eyes and drifts off to sleep, smiling and thinking to himself, *Grundish always watches out for me. I ain't never had a brother, but I bet that this is what they's like with each other. Pissing each other off sometimes but mostly feeling good about each other.*

In the far southeast corner of the United States is Florida, a peninsula dangling limply from the rest of the country. Florida is sometimes referred to as the nation's genitals. In the center of the nation's dong is a largish, ruptured varicose vein known as Polk County. Sitting right smack in the middle of the burst vein is an infected carbuncle, a little pus-filled town by the name of Bartow. State Route 60 funnels drivers out of Bartow and sends them on their way to the east coast of Florida. Just east of Bartow, on a small side road running off of Route 60 is Jerry Mathers' Foreign Car Parts and Service. It is really more of a junkyard than an auto garage or service station. Just beside the front gate is a rusted metal sign that says "Jerry Mathers' Foreign Car Parts and Service." On the left side of the sign is a buck-toothed beaver with two of his paws giving the thumbs up[34]. Two dilapidated Corvairs sitting on concrete blocks flank the front gate. An eight-foot tall cement wall encloses the yard, all five acres of it. The wall is covered with moss and kudzu vines and has holes chipped into it in places. Small trees grow from some of the holes. But the wall stands sturdy against the

[34]In the seventeenth century, the Roman Catholic Church ruled that beaver was a fish for purposes of dietary law. Therefore, the Church's general prohibition on the consumption of meat on Fridays during Lent does not apply to beaver meat.

elements and intruders. Densely packed about the property are countless sickly Volkswagen vans in various states of decrepitude and a motley collection of other broken down vehicles.

Inside the junkyard's concrete walls, Randy Buttwynn's van sits next to a large metal building. Randy Buttwynn has nothing to do with the van any more. Buttwynn is a bloody mass of putrescible flesh patiently waiting for the rest of the Buttwynn clan to return home and discover his cadaverous condition. The *de facto* owners of the van, Grundish and Askew, are in their own way dead to the world, sleeping the coma-like, dreamless sleep that sets upon those who reach a point of complete exhaustion.

A sore-covered donkey uses his mouth to pull weeds from the ground around Buttwynn's van. His few remaining teeth mash the vegetation into a pulpy meal. He tries to swallow it. Instead, he suffers a bout of retro-peristalsis and regurgitates a compact, shit-brown lump of waste product from his stomach. The ground around his feet is littered with the brownish lumps. The donkey wheezes. His breathing is labored and his sides suck in, looking like they are trying to meet at the beast's core and touch each other. His brown hide stretches tight across the harshly-defined ribs. He has lived for a long time and his years are kicking the hell out of him. The name of the donkey: Alf the Sacred Burro.

Alf the Sacred Burro was tethered to the large metal building in the center of the junkyard complex. He had been tethered there for years. Providing shade and a constant source of food for Alf is a Dwarf Fuji Red Apple tree. While sitting under the apple tree and contemplating the flies buzzing about and landing on his snout, an idea struck Alf. He usually doesn't like ideas. Ideas mean thinking, and sometimes physical effort. And it was always easier for Alf to just hang out under the apple tree and eat the fruit that fell to the ground. But this day he said to himself, *maybe I should go check out the rest of this place. All I ever see is this little patch of land that I am tied to.* With his remaining teeth, Alf gnawed through the rope that restricted his freedom and he set out to learn more about the property around him. And then he regurgitated some of the hemp rope that he swallowed. Alf left the safety and comfort of his designated area and explored the property. Staying close to the side of the building, Alf ventured around the corner, settling on the spot just outside of Buttwynn's van as the place most interesting to a sick donkey. The remainder of his tether dangles from the metal building, its end frayed and moist with stinking donkey slobber.

Inside the metal building, Turleen is giving Jerry Mathers a firm hug and breathing her hot breath into his ear. Jerry has to stoop his emaciated body to accept the embrace. Tall, lanky, and skeletal are all words that apply to his appearance but still fail to adequately describe the man. The skin on his face is stretched taut like a thin protective barrier over the bone. Buck-teeth jut out from the skull, just barely anchored in bloody gums. Sunken eyes smolder in the sockets; the eyes are given the appearance of even greater depth by the purplish-black bags beneath them. The hunched over wisp of a man is hideous in his appearance. But his face radiates a peace and happiness in reaction to Turleen's presence. The unadulterated joy he experiences transforms his appearance from concentration camp survivor to that of a child waking up on Christmas morning. Jerry wears a knit Peruvian beanie cap with tassels dangling from the side. He pulls the hat off and shivers even though it is 95-degrees outside.

"Look at you," he says, stepping back to give Turleen the up and down, "always forever young. Always a beauty." He pulls back and straightens up to his full height of six feet and seven inches. The sweater he wears dangles from his shoulders in the same manner it would from a wire hanger. "Well, how does it feel?" he asks. "How does it feel to see ole' Jerry Mathers after all these years?"

"It feels real nice, it does, Jer Bear." Turleen's cheeks flush, and sweat forms on the back of her neck. She touches her hair and smiles at Jerry. Instead of talking, they gaze into each other's eyes.

Jerry tears himself from the gaze and looks toward Dora. "And what's your name, young lady?"

"Her name's Dora, it is," Turleen answers for Dora. Dora nods at Jerry and winks. "She don't talk much, but she's sweet. Poor thing got messed up in my boys' problems, she did, and got dragged right along with us."

"Well, it's a pleasure to meet you, Dora." Jerry grabs her hand and bows down to her level.

"Hi," says Dora. She winks at him again.

The wink makes Jerry smile and look away. *You've still got it, Ole' Jer Bear*, he thinks to himself.

Dora actually does not usually wink at anybody. On the rare occasions that she does wink, it is with her right eye. When she is nervous, the left side of her face cramps up and causes the eye on that side to involuntarily blink. The blink is not a disturbing facial tic that makes people look away. Instead, it is quite appealing. Most people assume that she is winking at them. Women who talk to Dora usually feel like there is some sort of inside joke that they share with her. It makes them feel superior. Men assume she is flirting with them. In her early teens, the boys all figured Dora was easy because she was always winking at them. She was cute in an undernourished, troubled-kid sort of way, and friendly, and she seemed to wink a lot. So the boys were nice to her. While the other girls in junior high were having innocent crushes on the boys their age, Dora was getting rides from high school boys and doing the things that proved to make her popular with the guys. The rumors that she was easy made her a pariah amongst the girls in her school. The rumors also acted as a self-fulfilling prophesy. Dora realized that she could use her body to control boys. And then she realized it worked on men. And then her abusive alcoholic stepfather kicked her out of the house, and her mother didn't stand up for her. Dora started hooking at fifteen and somehow managed to avoid the drug addictions that most of the other girls on the street fell prey to. The day she reached the age of majority, Dora took on employment at the *Scrub and Rub Massage Parlor*, the place where she met Randy Buttwynn.

"So these are the boys you been talking about, huh?" says Jerry to Turleen. He nudges Alf the Sacred Burro out of the way and clears the area of the donkey's vomit-shitballs with his feet.

"Those are they boys, they are," answers Turleen.

Jerry stoops down to peer into the open sliding door of the van and catches a snoot-full of sour body odor. He recoils and takes several steps back. Looking up at the sky, he drinks in the fresh air and notes the smell of rain. "Well, we better get them up. That long black cloud up there is coming down. Before you know it, it'll be dark, too dark to see."

The chewed-up hemp rope dangles from Alf's neck. Grabbing the rope, Jerry leads the odd-toed ungulate to the side of the van, its hindquarters facing the vehicle. "Watch this," he says and winks at Turleen and Dora. He smiles when Dora winks back. "Kick! Alf! Kick!" he shouts at the donkey.

Alf bends down to pull more weeds and ignores the towering beanpole shouting in his face.

"Come on you jackass! Kick the van!"

Alf grinds the weeds and swallows, finding the greens to be slightly bitter but not unpleasant. He looks away from the crazed bucktoothed man barking orders in his face.

"Watch me, you obstinate burro!" yells Jerry as he bends down and places his hands flat on the ground. Bending his knees and launching his rear half in the air, Jerry abruptly straightens out his legs and kicks both feet into the side of the van. "Izzat so hard, you danged numbskull!?" He launches his hindquarters again and again, kicking at the side of the van, all the while spewing obscenities at Alf.

Alf looks the other way and regurgitates a donkey poop-ball. He wonders to himself if he should return to his favorite spot under the apple tree or if he should wait until the tall man regains his sanity. He decides to wait it out.

Awakened by the banging and retching donkey noises, Grundish hangs his head out of the side of the van. His face glistens with sweat. His shirt is soaked. The inside of the van is sweltering. "What the fuck?"

"Well, there's one of em," says Turleen. She gently elbows Dora and smiles at her. "Come on out, Grundish. I want you to meet Jerry, I do."

A sluggish Grundish extracts himself from the backseat of the vehicle as Jerry continues to do his best impression of a demented burro, bucking and kicking at the side of the van. Alf stands to the side, feeling embarrassed for Jerry and his undignified display. The donkey looks the other way and pretends he doesn't see what his owner is doing. Askew drags himself from the van and stands beside Grundish. They watch Jerry wind down.

With one last kick to the side of the van, Jerry straightens up to his full height and puts his hands on his hips. Between deep raspy breaths, he introduces himself. "Hiya, boys. I'd shake your hands, but, uh, I got the donkey vomit-shits on my hands right now. My name's Jerry. Jerry Mathers."

"Hi," Grundish and Askew say.

"Well," says Jerry, pointing at Grundish, "you're the big one. So you must be Grundish. And," he points at Askew, "you're the little feller, so you must be Askew."

"Yep," the boys answer.

"Well, follow me inside. We've got plenty to talk about."

Grundish, Askew, Dora and Turleen follow the gaunt, gangling man into his building. When they are out of sight, Alf leans forward and lets loose with a powerful kick of his rear legs at the van. Two hoof prints dot the door and the side-view mirror falls off. Alf decides that maybe Jerry was onto something and kicks at the car several more times before returning to the apple tree.

With his shoulders hunched and his head slung low so as to avoid banging it on doorways and low-hung rafters, Jerry leads the group through the cluttered maze of stacked boxes and deep into the metal warehouse. Electromagnetic radiation spills into the dimly lit building from skylights above while burnt out florescent light fixtures droop uselessly from the ceiling. Green eyes glare out from behind boxes as they pass. A cat-piss-ammonia-fog clouds the air. "You might not believe it," says Jerry, "but I've got thirty or more cats living with me here."

"Yeah," says Askew, "who would'a guessed?" His eyes water from the caustic cat stench. At regular intervals in the labyrinth of useless junk are litter boxes spilling over with stale litter and cat turds. A greasy tomcat with nicked ears and a respectable collection of battle scars mews and rubs against Askew's leg.

"Look at that," laughs Turleen. "You've already made a new friend, you have."

"That's Beaumont," explains Jerry. "He doesn't like anybody. Doesn't usually even come out. Usually mean as hell. But he seems to like you, Leroy."

"Lucky me," Askew says. "And please, Mr. Mathers, just call me Askew. Nobody but Turleen calls me Leroy and I don't even like her doing it." Askew pushes the cat away with his foot. Beaumont takes it as an act of affection and circles Askew's legs in a figure eight, rubbing his face and sides against his calves.

Dora squats down to Beaumont's level and reaches out to pet him.

"I wouldn't do that if I were you, young lady," Jerry says.

Dora ignores the advice and moves closer to pet the cat. "Aw, he's kinda cute for such a grimy old guy." Before she can try to rub the back of Beaumont's head, he takes offense at her interest. His brain stem receives a garbled message that the girl is a threat and tells his suprarenal glands to dump an overload of adrenalin into his system. Beaumont's pupils dilate, his hair stands on end, chicken skin forms on his bald spots. He lets out a sickening yowl. Fight is chosen over flight. Beaumont launches himself at Dora's face, a psychotic flying furball, missing Dora's head and instead digging his claws into her shoulder and clamping his jaws down on her earlobe. He changes his attack and locks his front claws onto her cheek as she tries to shake him off.

Dora doesn't scream. She remains completely silent, her mouth forming shapes of words but failing to give birth to them. Only a slight hissing sound escapes her mouth as she tries to run from the cat ripping into her head. A storage box sits in the aisle minding its own business. The flailing teenage prostitute with a feline stuck to the side of her face interrupts the box's quiet time, tripping over it, and lands on top of Beaumont as she falls. The cat yowls and growls in pain and frantically tears at her face. Without thinking, Askew jumps into the fracas and plucks the cat off of the young girl. He steps back and squeezes on the cat. Beaumont's struggles subside. Askew holds Beaumont in his arms. The feline calms and begins to purr. Jerry and Grundish both offer hands to Dora. She grabs onto each of the offerings and allows herself to be pulled to her feet.

"Oh, sweetie," says Turleen, wiping at the bloody slashes on Dora's face with a used tissue plucked from her bra. "You're bleeding, you are. Let me get that for you."

Shaking off the damage and wiping at the blood with her forearm, Dora fixes her gaze on Askew. "You saved me," she says softly, wiping again at her face and leaving a bloody streak across her cheek. "Thank you." She winks at him with her right eye. A slight crooked-toothed smile forms and she turns her head away quickly. Dora's left eye involuntarily blinks out the Morse code for S.O.S. to Jerry. *Dot Dot Dot...Dash Dash Dash...Dot Dot Dot* says her eyelid, unintentionally.

Jerry flashes a grin at the girl and feels a stirring in his holy undergarments[35]. "Well, come on, people," he says. "Let's go have a sit down and talk about your situation." He leads them through the narrow aisle, around corners, through doorways, past dirty cats and overused litter boxes.

---

[35]Some members of the Church of Latter-day Saints wear what is known as temple garments (or holy undergarments). The white, sleeved undergarments come in a one-piece suit or a shirt and shorts. The design covers the torso and extends to the knee. Men's shirts feature scoop necks. Women's shirts often have cap sleeves and lace trimming and are to be worn under bras. The temple garments are viewed as an either symbolic or literal source of protection from the evils of the world. Jerry is not Mormon, he just likes the idea of undergarments that protect him from evil.

Turleen follows close behind Jerry, walking with a slight limp and savoring the feeling of the throwing knife rubbing against her inner thigh. Askew is next in line. Beaumont remains at his ankles, rubbing against them when he gets the opportunity, and occasionally turns back to hiss at Dora. Dora trails Askew, watching him walk, staying out of range of the hostile feline. She feels drawn to the stout waddling man in front of her. He protected her. Something nobody had ever done for her before. Grundish lags behind the group.

Grundish senses something happening between Dora and Askew and is happy for his friend. He sees that the embers of Jerry's soul still burn for Dora. He finds himself thinking about Velda. His thoughts turn to their coupling in the Git 'n Go bathroom and he is surprised by the longing that grips him.

"Well, this is the inner sanctum," says Jerry, his arms wide open, inviting his guests into his living quarters within the metal building. A scroungy cat lounges on each piece of furniture in the large room. Papering the walls are centerfolds from pornographic magazines depicting females with wide open beavers. Pushed against the walls are more waist-high stacks of storage boxes. Against one wall is an oversized waterbed with a purple velvet comforter and sheets. Grundish and Askew stand in the doorway with Dora and Turleen looking into the room from behind them. "Well, don't stand in the doorway. Don't block up the hall. Come on in here, boys and girls. Have a sit down and let's talk."

They file into the room and look around. Beaumont, in Askew's arms again, leaps down and runs to hide behind some of the storage boxes. Dora is relieved and moves in to wrap her hands around Askew's flabby bicep. She tugs at his arm and smiles at him. Turleen approaches Jerry and eyes him curiously.

"Jer Bear," says Turleen, "What's become of you? You used to be such a thick, sturdy man, you did. Now you look to be wasting away. I hope you're okay, I do."

"I'm just fine, little lady," smiles Jerry with his hideous, jutting buck teeth. "I've lost a ton of weight because I barely eat anymore."

"Well, I'm gonna fix that, I am. Where's your refrigerator?"

"I don't have one and don't need one. I get everything I need from that food machine over there."

Turleen looks in the direction that Jerry is pointing and sees a vending machine stuffed with sandwiches, rotten apples, and other foodstuffs. Beside the vending machine is a tiny microwave oven. "Well, how in tarnation do you keep your belly full just eating out of that there vending machine?" asks Turleen.

"I don't keep it full, and I don't want to. I'm on a starvation diet. I restrict my calories to keep myself just above the starvation threshold. It's the key to my longevity. By staying just above the starvation level, my body focuses on survival. Studies have shown that the starvation diet can increase life spans by seven percent or more. Hell," he laughs, "I'm eighty-nine and feel great." Jerry looks at Grundish, "You wanna wrestle me, big boy? 'Cause I'll whip you if you do."

Grundish shakes his head side to side and says nothing. He notices that Dora and Askew have vanished and wonders where they are.

"Yeah, Jer Bear," says Turleen, "But there has to be negative side effects to a diet like that, there does."

"Well, I take four or five naps a day. But who's gonna complain about something like that?" he asks in Grundish's direction again.

Grundish shrugs his shoulders, scratches at his beard and remains silent.

"And I'm always hungry and cold. I shiver when it's a hundred degrees out. That's why I wear sweaters, caps and even mittens sometimes." He tugs at his baggy sweater and smiles. "And I have bouts of what my doctor calls Micturition Syncope, but you don't want to know about that."

"I do want to know about it, I do."

"It just means that sometimes I faint when I take a whizz. It's nothing big. Something I don't mind putting up with in order to significantly extend my life."

"Speaking of which," interrupts Grundish, "where's the john? I've gotta take a leak."

"My boy," laughs Jerry, "where I come from that means you're going to steal a mirror. We call mirrors leaks."

"Yeah, well," Grundish shrugs and scratches at his beard again, not sure how to respond to Jerry's nonsense. "I just mean that I have to go to the bathroom. Where's your bathroom?"

"All right. You're going to have to go back the way we came. Once you get outside, you're going to take a left, walk five feet or more from the doorway, and then turn to face the building. And there you have it."

"So, just piss outside. Got it." Grundish turns and leaves the room the same way he came in.

As Grundish exits, he hears Turleen get excited. "Why Jerry Mathers, you old dog. Is that what I think it is over in the corner?"

"I don't know, Miss Turleen," says Jerry. "Why don't you go take a look?"

"Oh Jerry Mathers, you old fool! You still have my moss-covered, three-handled family gredunza that I gave you years ago, you do. Why, you still must have a warm place in your heart for me or my name's not Turleen Zurn Rundle. And to think I've stayed away from you all these years. Why I oughta…"

Elsewhere in the metal warehouse, Dora drags Askew by the hand to a tiny alcove behind a stack of storage boxes and bailed newspapers. "Let me suck your cock," she says to Askew. "You are so brave and you protected me from that cat. I'm gonna suck your cock good." She tries to unbutton Askew's shorts. His flabby midsection exerts a substantial amount of force on the waistband of his shorts, making it hard for Dora to undo them.

"Wait a minute," says Askew. "Slow down, Dora. You're moving too fast. I like you, too. But this don't feel right." Askew's throbbing boner curses his uncharacteristically active frontal lobe. "You're my hostage. It just seems to me like rape or something if we do something right now. I might be a little goofy in the head right now. But, I ain't no rapist."

"Awww. You're sweet but not all that bright, huh?" says Dora. She drops to her knees and slaps Askew's hands away from his waistband. "I ain't no hostage. Turleen told me I could go whenever I wanted to and that you boys weren't going to hurt me. Anyone coulda told that. I just came along because I ain't got nowheres else to go. And you boys and Turleen all seemed kind of nice. You all seemed like a family. And, however messed up you all may be, you got each other. And I like that. So shut up and show me what you're packing in here." She slaps Askew's hands away again and works at the strained button holding the pants up.

"Wait just a minute," Askew stalls. "Can we just talk a little bit? You seem nice. Maybe we should get to know each other better."

"All right, Mr. Askew," says Dora as she returns to her feet. "Tell me about you. What do you wanna do with your life?"

"Okay," says Askew. "That's better. Let's talk a little first."

"Let's. Tell me what you wanna do with your life."

"Well," Askew hitches his thumbs in his pockets and rocks onto the balls of his feet, "Grundish and I got plans. He's always been my best buddy. Always watched out for me. Grundish and I got plans if we ever get out of this mess. I don't wanna be *bragabocious* but, oh boy, once we get going, we ain't gonna stop." Askew gets excited as he starts to talk about the plans, and he paces back and forth while talking.

"You're kind of a nut. But, you're nice, too," says Dora. "Tell me about the plans."

"Me and Grundish are gonna save up enough money to get a big boat, like a yacht. Or maybe we'll buy a shut-down oil platform. Whatever it is, we're gonna be out in international waters. Out where the government ain't got no *exterdishun* powers. And we're gonna run a brothel, maybe run some gambling, maybe grow weed. We're gonna be a den of *inequity*, but a fun one, mind you. We're gonna get rich. Grundish is gonna let me be in charge of the girls. And there won't be nothing illegal about it because we'll be in international waters, and the government won't be able to do a damn thing about it. We'll just be out there, a big *tentation* to U.S. residents and only a short boat or helicopter ride away."

"That sounds expensive to start up." Dora reaches into Askew's front pocket of his shorts and pulls out the crushed pack of Blue Llamas. On the way out of the pocket, her hand brushes against the side of Askew's turgid schlong and makes him twitch momentarily. She extracts two cigarettes and gives one to Askew. He lights her smoke and then his. She continues, "You're gonna need a lot of money. Do you have enough?"

"No, not yet," sighs Askew. "We're gonna have to work on that when we get down to Mexico."

"You're really not all that bright, huh?"

"What?" asks Askew defensively.

"You ain't gonna earn enough money down in Mexico. Your idea sounds good. But, you're gonna need somebody to finance things for you."

"We'll figure it out," says Askew, not enjoying having holes poked in the plan. "Grundish is real smart. He'll make it work."

"I'm sure he will. No doubt. But you need to think about financing. And I can help. I've got money stashed away. All I do is work and save. Right now I have over a hundred-grand saved. And I know lots of whores. I can find plenty of girls who'd be happy to work for guys like you and Grundish."

"I don't know," says Askew. "This is our deal, me and Grundish. What would you want out of it?"

Dora sits on a stack of storage boxes and sucks at her cigarette. She looks at Askew shyly and tells him, "I just want to be involved. Be a partner. Not have to sell myself anymore. So whatta ya say? Can I get in on the action?"

"I don't know. I suppose it would be okay. But, I get to be in charge of the girls. That's the deal. I'm in charge of the girls."

"That's cool," says Dora, "you're in charge of the girls. So, am I in then?"

"Yeah. I'll talk to Grundish. He'll be okay with it."

They sit and finish the cigarettes in silence, neither knowing what to say. "So, uh, you ain't my hostage then?" Askew asks slyly and moves closer to Dora again.

"Hell, no! That's what I'm telling you mister." She moves toward him and drops to her knees.

"And you want to be here with us?"

"Hell yes, I do! Now shut up and whip it out." Dora reaches out and manages to pop the button and undo the zipper on Askew's pants.

"Can we still pretend that you're my hostage?" Askew asks with a grin.

"Mmmrgghhhhhhh," Dora says, indicating a yes as well as she can with her mouth full.

Outside of the warehouse, Grundish walks around looking for Askew and Dora. There's nobody to be found except for Alf the Sacred Burro, now staying close to his apple tree. Grundish plucks a ripe apple from the tree and holds it out on the flat surface of his upturned hand. Alf's lips tickle Grundish's hand as the burro accepts the fruit from him. "Fruit from the tree of life, my friend," says Grundish. "Enjoy."

Alf stomps one front foot several times and sprays a joyful donkey bray. His lips curl up into a donkey smile. Grundish smiles back. A string of thick donkey saliva hangs from the side of Alf's mouth. Gravity slowly tugs at it until the string breaks halfway toward the ground, leaving part of the strand to fall to the earth in a rounded spit globule while the remainder of the drool snaps back toward the donkey's mouth and continues to hang from his lip. Alf stomps his foot again and smiles at Grundish.

"I understand, old man," says Grundish. He plucks another apple from the tree and feeds it to Alf.

Grundish sits in the front seat of an old, bright orange, VW minibus with the driver's window permanently open. On the passenger seat beside him is a load of apples picked from Alf's tree. Just outside the van, with his head resting on the door and breaking the plane of the open window, is Alf, staring at Grundish with seeping eyes and whinnying occasionally to catch his attention.

"Neigh," says Alf to Grundish. It's what he says. He's never considered excuse me or hey you. Just neigh suffices for a donkey.

"Here you go, Old Boy," answers Grundish, grabbing another apple and feeding it to the donkey. Absentmindedly scratching the burro's dirty brown head, Grundish thinks about his friend and the girl he disappeared with. He ponders how Dora fits into the equation of Grundish plus Askew. He and Askew have been friends for so long that Grundish can't imagine doing most things without Askew. Neither Grundish nor Askew has ever been capable of a sustained relationship with a woman. Not that there weren't ever women. There were the occasional short-lived relationships, usually terminated over issues related to arrested development in Askew's case and actual arrests for Grundish. Their friendship is the longest enduring human bond either has known. *Hopefully*, thinks Grundish, *hopefully Askew is just getting up in her guts.*

And, then he'll get her out of his system, and we can get on with our plans to scoot out of here and down to Mexico.

Alf nudges Grundish's arm with his nose and lets out a low squeak. Grundish grabs another apple for the ass and scritches[36] his head again. Alf has found a new friend. The old dreams of starring in a donkey show in Mexico are long forgotten for him. Alf is satisfied to merely laze about with somebody willing to scritch his head and feed him apples. *A donkey lives a long time*, thinks Alf, *and eventually realizes that this is what it is all about*. He nudges Grundish's arm again to get another apple. Alf chomps on the juicy fruit and swallows. He steps away from the van and horks up a hairy, brown, vomit-ball.

"Grundish!" Askew and Dora walk around the junkyard yelling.

"Grundish!" He hears but doesn't answer. Instead he hands another apple to Alf and rubs a soft spot on the burro's head right between the ears.

"There you are. Where you been, buddy?" asks Askew, appearing in front of the van, holding Dora's hand. They flash dopey grins brought on by orgasm-induced endorphins, and look like a couple of eighth-graders who have just, for the first time, partaken in the sport of bumping uglies.

Grundish looks sideways at Alf. *Shit*, he thinks, *Askew was in there getting poontang. Maybe even stuck it in her fart-box, for all I know. And the way things were looking when I left, Turleen and Jerry probably dusted the cobwebs off each*

---

[36]Yes another made up word. Scritch seems like a better word for the act of scratching an animal's head affectionately. Credit is given to Marcus Eder, author of *Rorschach's Ribs* for the word.

others goods and went at it. And look at me, stuck out here feeding apples to a broken old donkey. His mind momentarily drifts back to his encounter in the Git 'n Go bathroom with Velda. He peels himself away from the memory and looks from Askew's face to Dora's and back to Askew's again. "This is not good," he mutters to Alf. "Not good at all."

"Come on out, Pal," says Askew. "Jerry wants to have a little meeting with us if we're planning on hiding out here. And we all just disappeared on him. He and Turleen are waiting inside for us."

Grundish, Askew and Dora leave Alf at the front door of the building. The donkey tries to follow them inside. Grundish tosses an apple away from the door in order to get Alf to move far enough away for them to get inside without being chaperoned by the burro. Inside of the building, the sound of hooves and horseshoes clanging on the side of the metal building rings out as Alf vents his frustration at the indignity of being ditched by his new friend. Inside, the group convenes again.

"We all need to talk about your situation," says Jerry to no one in particular. His old bones carry what little meat there is on his body around the enormous living area, stopping to rub a cat here and there. "I won't criticize what I don't understand. But I need to know what's going on." He picks up a scrawny tiger kitten by the scruff of its neck and cradles it in his arm. "You boys appear to be in some trouble from what Turleen's told me. Is that about right?"

"Uh, yeah, you could say that," answers Grundish. He sits atop a wooden crate with his legs crossed Indian-style. "Some stuff went bad. Askew there shot a man while robbing his castle, not to mention the rest of the shit that went down. I guess we're what you would call *on the lamb*."

"Okay," nods Jerry. "From what Turleen tells me, you both went a little crazy and some people got hurt. She says you went more than a little crazy," he jabs one long, crooked, finger at the air in Askew's direction. "Is that fair to say?"

Askew and Dora sit back in a stained love-seat with their arms around each other, beaming broken, crooked, smiles fit for a public awareness scare-tactic poster about proper oral hygiene. Beaumont sits tensed on an arm of the couch near Askew, shooting daggers at Dora's head with his eyes. "Yes sir," says Askew. His smile fades. "I went a little batshit crazy. But the people that we hurt were bad apples. Dudes who do some *heenous* shit. Ask Grundish, he'll tell you."

"It's true Mr. Mathers," agrees Grundish. "Askew did kind of lose it. But the people he hurt were some real Fuckers. You don't believe us, you can ask Turleen."

"Well, I'm not going to ask her about that now. That little lady's plumb tuckered out after our, uh, reunion." A Turleen-shaped lump under the purple covers of the waterbed snores contentedly in a gentle, wheezing rhythm. "And, I don't care about all that now," Jerry's teeth chatter as he shivers in the ninety-degree temperature of the room. He drops his kitten to the floor and pulls a knit beanie cap on again, crossing his arms to contain body heat. "If Beaumont and Alf both think you fellas are all right, then you must be. I just can't afford to have some wingnut going loopy here and bringing the authorities down on my compound. I've been living a clean life for a long time now, and I don't need anybody snooping into my situation. I've sacrificed to get where I am. And I know you give something up for everything you gain. Everybody does. But I've really given up a lot. And I'm nice and comfortable now." His teeth chatter, belying the proclamation of comfort. "And I don't want no change. I don't like change, and I don't want none. So let's talk about what you boys need to do. Turleen tells me you've got plans. Let's hear them."

"You tell him, Grundish," says Askew. "It's always so beautiful when you talk about it." Dora wraps both of her arms around Askew's arm and gazes at him.

"Well, Mr. Mathers," starts Grundish. Jerry paces around the room, his lanky form hunched over. He grabs a walking stick carved from the branch of a tree and continues to move about nervously while Grundish talks. "First we need to get down to Mexico. Then Askew and I are gonna scratch up some bread so that we can buy a big ship. And we're gonna anchor it in international waters and run a whorehouse and marijuana dispensary without the government fucking with us. It'll be a real first class act. But like I said, first we need to get out of the country without getting arrested."

Jerry stops and spins in the direction of Grundish, pointing his stick at the large bearded man; his speed and agility surprise Grundish. "You boys are dumb as dog turds, ain't you?" He stares at Grundish, waiting for an answer to what, at first, sounded like a rhetorical question.

"Uh...no," answers Grundish.

"No, sir," says Askew, feeling defensive. "We ain't no *astral* physicists or nothing but we ain't no retards either."

"Well, how you boys gonna get from here to Mexico?"

"I don't know. Maybe a boat or something," says Grundish. "We kind of didn't really have a whole lot of time to plan this. It all sort of just happened."

"You boys have fake passports or IDs?"

"No," says Grundish, his tone changing to one of slight irritation. "We didn't have time to, and I wouldn't have known where to get something like that anyway. I been trying to stay out of trouble since I been out of the joint."

"And what about money? Do you have any money to get you by in the meantime?"

"Mr. Mathers," says Grundish. The volume of his voice rises a notch. His face flushes with a slight pink tinge. He rises from his sitting position and takes several steps toward Jerry. "I understand that we fucked up and we're unprepared. It ain't a good situation, and if I could go back and do things differently, I would. If I could, I'd jump in a time machine and go back and slap some sense into me and Askew. But I can't. And I appreciate your letting us stay here until we figure out what to do. But, I don't like the way you're talking down to us. I know we ain't the smartest guys you've ever run across. But we're trying, man. We're really trying to get ourselves out of this hot water. And, if it's going to be a problem, we'll just get Turleen, and we'll all leave you in peace."

Jerry straightens and steps up to Grundish, looking down at him. He puts his hand on Grundish's shoulder and says, "Now, don't get your granny-panties in a bunch, Son. I'm just asking some questions to help you figure some of this out. If Turleen hasn't told you, I know a thing or two about being on the run. I'm gonna help you, and I'll try to be more gentle so as not to make you boys cry. But we have so much time and so little to do." Jerry stops, scratches his chin, looks sideways, and shivers. "Strike that; reverse it. You know what I'm saying."

"So, what do you suggest?" asks Dora, her left eye blinking at Jerry, making him blush. "Because we are gonna need any help we can get with getting out of here and setting up the ship."

"We?" asks Grundish with more than just a hint of incredulity. "What's she talking about, Askew? Sounds like she's planning on coming along. This ain't no pleasure cruise. You, me and Turleen gotta get the hell out of here, and we can't have this girl coming along and mucking things up."

"She ain't mucking things up," answers Askew. "And she ain't just some girl. She's my girl. We're gonna be in a *mahoganous* relationship, and she wants to come along. And I want her with us."

"Well, what's she gonna do to help out? She's barely an adult and has no real skills that are gonna help us run our operation. What's she got that's gonna help us?"

"Would you listen to yourself?" Jerry interrupts, scowling at Grundish. "You ain't no smarter than my donkey that just lays around in his own sick. What's that girl do for a living?"

"She's a whore[37]," answers Grundish.

"And who do whores hang out with?"

"I don't know. I guess probably other whores."

---

[37]What's the difference between a dead prostitute and a Corvette? I don't have a Corvette in my garage.

"You guess probably other whores[38]," Jerry sneers at Grundish. "Of course, other whores. And you need whores for your boat. What are you planning on doing, putting a help-wanted ad in the newspaper? That little girl can help get you set up."

"Yeah," says Askew. "And, she's got start up money for us. Cash-money, Bro. So, she's gonna be our partner."

Grundish returns to his cross-legged pose on top of his crate. Silent. He rubs the top of his head, trying to stimulate a thought. His face goes slack, and then the furry beard begins to move and his teeth form into a half-smile. "How much money does she got?"

"Over a hundred-grand," answers Dora. She smiles at Askew and kisses him on the cheek. "And, I'm willing to put it up for a one-third interest. I can get the girls for you. I can even help keep them under control."

"Yeah," says Askew, suddenly flustered, "but that's my job. I get to take care of the ladies. Ain't that right Grundish? You always said that I get to take care of the ladies."

"Yeah," agrees Grundish. "Askew gets to be in charge of the ladies."

"Okay, Baby," agrees Dora, "you're in charge of the ladies. I'll be available for consultation if you need me. So

---

[38]Humans are not the only animals that participate in prostitution. Adelie penguins have been observed conducting transactions for sex. Some of the female penguins have been observed "turning tricks" for stones used to build their nests. Typically the females already have a lifelong mate (as penguins do) but will copulate with single males in the flock in exchange for stones.

what do you say, Mr. Grundish? Are the three of us going to be business partners?"

"Well," concedes Grundish, "if Askew wants you that bad, I guess I can go along with it. But, you really have that money?"

"There you go," says Jerry. "You're all getting along. That's flipping wonderful. But we have to get you guys out of here, and out of the country. The first step is gonna be getting you fake passports."

"How are we going to do that, Mr. Mathers? We don't know anybody that does anything like that."

Jerry taps his walking stick on the ground several times and grins. "I'm calling my friend, Chancho. He can help. But before I do, I have a little business proposal for you boys, too."

Alf the Sacred Burro disappears behind a lime-green VW van and awaits the return of his new friend with the hairy face. A kindle of oil-stained kittens appears from under the van and rubs affectionately against the donkey's legs. Now that he is untethered, Alf is finding his way around the junkyard and discovering what he has been missing. Mostly it's more of the same, junked autos rusting out where they stand. The old heaps are dead, dying or disinclined to drive. Spaced throughout the yard are blighted live oak trees being strangled to death by great, clinging clumps of Spanish moss. Jerry never sold any of the vans or even any of the parts to people. He once told Alf that he didn't sell his babies to assholes. To Jerry, pretty much anybody who wanted to buy one of his cars was an asshole. Alf cowers behind the green van because he hears the roar and rattle of the station wagon that always brings the Mexican. That's what Alf calls the cruel little man who kicks at him and pelts him with apples when Jerry isn't around, the Mexican. To Jerry, the short, brown man is known as Chancho. Alf remains behind the van, hoping not to be discovered.

Simulated-wood panels span the sides of Chancho's Plymouth Fury wagon. The faux-wood grain is intended as a complement to the creamy beige sputum-toned paint. Peeking around the corner of his hiding place, Alf sees the driver's side door open. Below the door, two snake-skin boots plant themselves firmly on the ground. The silver-plated tips of the boots can inflict sharp pains on a donkey's ribs. The sun glints off of the tip of one of the boots and scares Alf into a full hiding position behind the van. Extending up and out of the boots is five-feet and one-hundred-ninety-eight pounds of gold-toothed, ill-tempered, donkey-hating, illegal alien. A cowboy hat holds down the thick, black, bowl-cut crop of hair on Chancho's *cabeza*. The gold-toothed smile fades, the wispy moustache droops in sadness, and Chancho's pitted features go slack with disappointment when he sees that Alf is no longer tethered to the side of the building. Chancho slams his door in frustration, causing the one remaining hub cap on the other side of the car to fall off. He lets himself into Jerry's building.

Chancho waddles through the labyrinth of stacked storage boxes, litter boxes, and assorted debris, kicking mange-afflicted felines away from his feet and stepping over cat turds. His strut is that of a pigeon, with the silver tips of his boots clacking on the floor like a lazy tap-dancer trying to work up momentum. His pock-marked face wrinkles in disgust at the overwhelming stench of cat piss. Chancho does not like animals. Chancho does not like people either, with the exception of his mama, Jerry, and the pretty girls.

When he reaches the door to Jerry's living quarters, Chancho takes off his dirty cowboy hat and gently sets it on the ground beside the door. He rolls the pudgy fist of his right hand in the palm of his left, cracking his knuckles. The smile on the stout man's blemished face is momentarily warm and genuine as he readies himself for battle. Turning the door knob as quietly as he can, Chancho throws the door open, turns his volume up to eleven and lets out a warbling war cry as he dives through the air, landing on his shoulder and rolling to reduce the impact. He pops up to his feet, hands balled in front of him, and readies himself for hand-to-hand combat. "Come on and get me, *Cabron*!" he yells, his hands held up and ready for fisticuffs.

Off to one side of the inner sanctum, just prior to Chancho's bursting into the room, Jerry and his company were enjoying a dinner of meats Grundish boosted from the Buttwynn house. Turleen, well-rested and feeling sassy, cooked a pork tenderloin in Jerry's microwave. Grundish, utilizing years of cellblock cooking experience, made what he called Dorito Burritos with ingredients from Jerry's vending machine. The recipe for the burritos went a little something like this:

> Take one packet of ramen noodles and crush them up. Do the same with a bag of spicy Doritos, and mix the noodles and Doritos together. Throw in a package of nacho cheese and mix some more. Mix all of the ingredients in a bag and add a half-cup of water heated in the microwave. Squish them all together and flatten it out. Let it get mushy and dig in.

The Dorito Burritos sit in the middle of the card table the group is gathered around. Only Grundish and Askew pick at the burritos.

"You know," says Askew with a glob of cheesy noodle sauce running down his chin, "this is some awesome shit. I have always loved your prison recipes. Although I do hate that you had to be in the hoosegow to learn your *culimnary* skills. You people don't know what you're missing here." He scoops up another mound of Dorito Burrito and crams it in his mouth. Grundish nods at him, scoops up a large helping for himself, smashes it on top of a chunk of pork, and spoons the whole mess into his maw. Soggy bits of Doritos and ramen cling to his beard.

"Well," says Dora with a crooked smile, "I've put some bad stuff in my mouth before. But I just don't think I can stomach that. I'll just stick with Turleen's tenderloin. Thanks anyways, Grundish."

"Me too," agrees Jerry. "Hell, I shouldn't even be eating this meat. But damn, it's tasty. And I've denied myself a lot of things in my life. But tonight I'm gonna let loose. Turleen, Baby, please bring me some more of that meat. I don't care if it does make my stomach cramp up and gives me the Hershey squirts. I don't care if it takes a year off of my life. I'm happy. I've got my girl here again, and I'm happy. Bring me some more food, Darling." His voice trembles as he calls out for another plate of food. "And one more cup of coffee, too, if you don't mind."

"Turleen," says Askew, "once you get Jerry more meat, you should try some of Grundish's masterpiece. I *exspecially* think that you'll like it. Then again, perhaps it's not the healthiest thing for someone your age to be eating. You know..."

Before Askew can finish his conflicting thoughts, a scream gashes the air, trailing off of the crazed flying-Chancho like a ripped banner streaming from an airplane. Just as Chancho pops up from his roll, sets his battle stance, and screams "come on and get me, *Cabron*[39]," Askew's brain tries its best to evaluate the situation. The thought rolls around in his head and finally settles in that the man in the middle of the room is a threat to everybody's safety. He pushes past Dora, knocking her to the floor from her seat. Letting loose with a bloodthirsty yowl of his own, Askew charges the stocky man in the middle of the room, tackling Chancho at waist-level and slamming him to the floor. Still screaming one long incomprehensible shriek, Askew climbs on top of him in a full mount, pummels the man's fat head with hammer fists, and drops vicious elbows into his face. Chancho, stunned by the unknown attacker, covers up his face and strikes at Askew's head with his elbows. He bucks Askew off of him and jumps on his back, throwing fists under Askew's arms and connecting with his jaw.

Grundish watches his friend trade blows with the unknown man and is impressed with the ferocity with which Askew brawls. As a matter of honor, Grundish allows his friend to fight his own fight. He lets the affray go uninterrupted for several minutes, watching as the two men throw each other into storage boxes and bloody each other's faces. Askew continues to shriek his battle howl,

---

[39]Cabron is Spanish for bastard. More fun Spanish vulgarity: cagar is to crap; puta is whore; mierda is shit; cojones are testicles.

sounding something like a sick cat being stuck with a hot poker.

"Grundish," shouts Dora, pushing at his back. "Get in there and help him. You're best friend needs help."

Grundish reluctantly stands up. "Maybe I should step in," he says.

"Hold on there, Boy," says Jerry, grabbing Grundish's arm and stopping him. "That there is Chancho that Askew is wrastlin' with. He does this with me all the time. He shows up and I try to surprise him, maybe jump on his back and try to beat the shit out of him. We wrestle around, punch and kick each other a little bit – just some harmless fun. Let those boys go at it. It's not like they're gonna kill each other. The worst they'll have is some black eyes and bruises. And all of the pretty has already been knocked out of Askew's face well before today. No offense, Darling," he nods at Dora.

Dora's left eye goes berserk with tics. One side of her mouth turns up into a feral sneer. She snaps at the men, "Well, if you men ain't gonna help my man, then I guess it's up to me." Before they can grab her to hold her back, Dora is across the room and fully committed to the battle. Askew, though, has already gotten the best of Chancho, and stands above him, stomping on the man's fat head. Each time Askew's foot comes down, it makes a squishy thud. Dora unites with Askew in the ruthless attack, standing beside Chancho, stomping and kicking at the ribs and chest of his motionless body while Askew crushes the man's skull, his sock-gartered legs pumping with relentless ferocity on the bloodied head, reshaping the skull to the point where the cowboy hat will no longer be a proper fit.

Grundish and Jerry tacitly agree that the fight has gone too far and step in. Grundish grabs Askew from behind and drags him away from the bloody splotch on the floor where Chancho's still-warm corpse is sprawled out. He throws Askew into the loveseat and stands above him. "No more!" Grundish shouts. "No more. It's over." With his shirt half torn off from the fight, Askew's flabulous gut is exposed. Hanging from his neck is a rawhide strap threaded through what appears to be two human ears. Grundish cringes at the trophies around his friend's neck and momentarily ponders where the second ear came from, the blond boy or Buttwynn.

Askew sits back into the loveseat; his insides are shaking like a leaf on a tree. A flap of torn skin hangs from his forehead and droops over one crazy bugged-out eye. His broken and bloodied smile chatters despite the heat in the room. Askew stands but makes no move toward Chancho. Jerry has already coaxed Dora away and escorted her to the loveseat.

"No more," repeats Grundish, blocking Askew's opportunity to return to Chancho. "It's all over."

"I know," says Askew. "I know. But I'm wild as a bug and all shook up, man. I gotta get outside and breathe some fresh air. I can't take it in here. I need water. Dora, grab me a cup. I saw a pump outside. I need fresh air and water."

"Wait just a minute," says Jerry, sensing Askew's manic energy. He runs to the other side of the room and returns with a jug of water. "Take this. You won't get any water from the pump out front. It don't work because the vandals took the handles. But there's plenty more water in here if you're thirsty."

Dora takes the water jug and holds onto Askew's arm, walking him out of the room and out of the building. On the way out of the building, lurking in the cluttered network of halls and false walls made of boxes, Beaumont the cat lies in wait for Dora. Just before exiting the building, Beaumont launches a surprise attack on Dora's head, leaping from atop a file cabinet, his stomach covering her face. He locks his claws into the sides of her head and digs his teeth into her flesh, scraping them on her skull. She drops the jug of water and dances a drunken jig, flailing and smacking at the enraged animal. Dora's muffled scream and whirling form alerts Askew that something is wrong. Wired on adrenaline and half-crazy, Askew acts without thought. He grabs the wildcat, plucks him once again from Dora's head, and flings the cat into the door. Once again, the sock-gartered legs deal out deadly punishment, this time on the dazed cat, mercilessly snuffing out Beaumont's ninth life.

Askew picks up the jug of water dropped by Dora and exits the building. Leaving the smashed tomcat's carcass in the entryway, Askew stumbles outside, the glaring sun forcing his pupils to constrict to pinpoints. Blood trickles from the torn flesh on his forehead and burns his eyes, clouding his already-blurred tunnel vision. He blindly staggers and bumps into Chancho's station wagon. Dora trails him and helps roll Askew onto the hood of the car. "I'm so thirsty. So fucking thirsty," he says. Twisting the top off of the gallon jug, he downs most of the container of dihydrogen monoxide. "Aghhhhh," he groans and dumps the rest on his head. "I need more. Need water. Get me more water," he tells Dora.

Alf the Sacred Burro remains behind the lime-green VW van and watches Askew squirm uncomfortably on the hood of the car while Dora returns to the building. Sensing something off about the moaning mortal – something sick and sour – Alf stays his position, hoping that soon the fur-faced man will return to him with a good supply of apples. It seems to Alf that the ratio of brown lumps regurgitated to the number of apples consumed has recently been thrown seriously out of whack, with the scale tipped heavily in favor of vomit balls. He feels queasy and respiration is a chore. But, for the time being, Alf does not feel like venturing out from his safe place. Alf will wait for his friend or Jerry before he shows his donkey face again.

Dora returns to the inner sanctum and finds Grundish and Jerry hefting Chancho's floppy ragdoll remains onto a rolling metal table. Jerry leans over the body and gently slaps the fat, dead face several times. "I know, Amigo. I know, my friend," he says. "Just remember, death is not the end." Jerry wipes at a tear and steels his heart against the flow of useless emotions. He looks around the room at the blood and the damage to his property and shakes his head. In an effort to divert his attention from the fate of his friend, Jerry lists off the damage in a monotone voice. "Broken bottles. Broken plates. Broken cutters. Broken saws. Broken chairs. God damned broken laws. Broken bodies and broken bones." He takes a deep breath and feels like he's choking. "God damn. Everything's broken."

Putting her hand on Jerry's shoulder, Dora says, "I'm sorry about kicking your friend while he was down, Mr. Mathers. I di'nt know nothin' but that he was trying to hurt my man. I di'nt want Mr. Chancho dead or nothin'." Her left eye involuntarily winks at him but fails to lift his spirits. "Do you want help wheeling him out or anything?"

"No, no, no. It ain't me, Babe," answers Jerry. "I'm not the one wheeling Chancho out of here. I can't do it. Grundish, there, is gonna take care of it for me. I need to just sit down and talk with Turleen. I'm planning on eventually hooking up with you all on the floating brothel business. But, I need to work out the particulars with sweet Miss Turleen before she tries to leave me again." He looks at Chancho and tears roll down his cheeks. Jerry turns away. Turleen puts an arm around his waist, and they walk out together.

"I can help you, then," says Dora to Grundish. "You want my help?"

Grundish shakes his head and says nothing.

"It wasn't his fault you, know. Askew thought that man was a cop, or an attacker or something. He had good intentions."

Grundish just grunts and starts to wheel Chancho's body out of the room.

"Can't you say nothin'?" asks Dora. "Can't you say that it's gonna be all right? Or that you know Askew didn't mean to do no harm? You can't be mad at him about this, you know."

The cart stops and Grundish turns toward Dora. "I can't tell you it's gonna be all right. Askew just killed another person. That makes three people he's killed in the past week."

"I know that. He's a little off right now. I'm worried about him, too. Heck, he killed Beaumont on the way out. But he's trying to get himself under control. He told me. He don't know what's come over him. But he don't like it, and he's trying to control it. Please don't be too hard on him."

"Don't be too hard on him," Grundish gags on the words. "Don't be too hard on him! Do you realize what he just did? He killed the guy who had our tickets out of the country. The guy who was gonna get us fake passports.

Now we can't get passports. And you know why? Because dead people can't do anything but sit there and rot. Dead people do not make fake passports." He holds Chancho's cold hand up in the air and lets it slap back down to his lifeless belly. "Does he look like he can help us right now? And did you say he killed that cat? Christ! He's out of control."

"Well, the cat attacked me again," she says. "And can't you just get somebody else to get passports for you guys?"

"No. No we can't! I don't know anybody that does that type of thing. Do you? Jerry sure doesn't. This greasy dead piece of shit here was Jerry's only friend. So Jerry don't know nobody else that can help. We're fucked now. And if you haven't noticed, your new boyfriend is turning stone-cold psycho. He's cutting off ears as trophies and wearing them around his neck. Oh yeah, and he keeps killing people." Grundish turns and pulls the cart out of the room, leaving Dora alone in the middle of the rubble.

On a shelf against the wall, Jerry keeps all varieties of bottled water. Spring water in sixteen-ounce bottles. Filtered water in gallon jugs. Five-gallon plastic bottles for water dispensers. Green glass bottles with sparkling water flavored with lime. Dora grabs three gallon jugs of water, wrapping her arms around them, hugging the jugs to her chest. Her face and head itch from the gashes left by Beaumont but she can't scratch at the uneasy tingling with her arms full. She hurries out of the room to return to Askew.

With the jug hoisted above his head and water slamming down his throat, Askew soaks up the hydration, drains the second gallon jug, and tosses it to the side. His crapulous slug-form reclines on the hood, slow-baking him under the blazing sun. "More water," he grunts at Dora.

"Baby," she says, "shouldn't you slow down with the water? You're gonna bust your gut or something. Just pee out some of that water you have in you before you have more."

"Narghhhh," he grunts, eyes closed, barely acknowledging Dora's presence. "So thirsty. More water." He grabs another jug from beside him on the car and twists off the top. *Psychogenic polydipsia*[40] puts its foot on Askew's chest, pries open his jaw, and dumps the third gallon of water down his gullet. Askew's eyes flutter; his heart strains out a syncopated Latin rhythm. The muscles slacken and his head falls back, smacking the hood hard enough to leave a dent.

A whoosh of fresh air slaps Grundish in the face as he exits the building. Air that smells like a Florida autumn. Like dry leaves and plants and earth. A smell that usually feels like a new start to Grundish. Clean air, not like the fuming stench of cat urine in the building. On the hood of Chancho's station wagon, Dora sits crying and cradling Askew's lumpy head in her lap. "He's dying or sick or something," she blurts out at Grundish. "Help him."

His face betraying no emotions, Grundish looks at Askew laid out unconscious on the car and at the empty water jugs thrown about on the ground. He turns away

---

[40]Psychogenic polydipsia is an uncommon mental disorder characterized by excessive water-drinking in the absence of a physiologic stimulus to drink.

from the scene without a word and reenters the building. When he returns, Grundish has four bottles of lemon-lime Gatorade. He hands them to Dora. "Here. He's got water poisoning. He does this sometimes. Try to make him pee and keep feeding him these sports drinks. He needs the electrolytes. When he's done with these bottles, go get more out of Jerry's vending machine and keep pouring them down his throat. Otherwise, he'll get more brain damage than he already has." Grundish fishes a pack of Blue Llamas and lighter from Askew's pocket and turns away again. Alf watches with a satisfied donkey grin from behind the green van as Grundish smokes and plucks fruit from the apple tree.

Askew finds himself holding his breath and swimming in an upward direction. The swirling murky muck slows his numbed appendages. Nearby, a naked infant dog-paddles through the ooze, chasing a one-dollar bill stuck on a fishing hook. The line from the hook drags the dollar bill in the same direction that Askew swims. He flails his arms and legs harder, struggling through the sludge, desperately seeking the surface. Seeking oxygen. His chest tightens. His lungs burn. Just as he is ready to gasp the brown sludge into his body, his head emerges from the slime. He devours the available air, huffing it greedily. A water snake glides by and twists its head toward Askew. The snake hisses and continues to swim toward the shore. Askew follows the serpent to the water's edge and lies back, his legs still in the water and his top half reposed on *terra firma*. When he regains his breath, Askew pats at his pockets for his cigarettes.

And then from out of his head comes Buttwynn. Bloated, bloodied, battered, deceased, Buttwynn wearing thick glasses and a huge gingham apron with pockets. He stands in front of Askew, hands on hips, one ear missing, and stares disapprovingly at the shriveled trophies strung around Askew's neck. And he speaks to Askew. And the voice is Grundish's. "Give me my ear back, you little bastard." He grabs at the rawhide tie around Askew's neck and pulls, snapping it. The ears fall on Askew's gut. Buttwynn snatches the ears and holds them in his palm, examining them to determine which is his. First he throws the darkest one into the water. He examines the remaining *pinnae*, furrowing his brow at the cartilaginous pieces, and finally selects one to stick back to the side of his head.

"You done bad things," says Buttwynn in Grundish's voice.

"I didn't mean to do no bad things. I couldn't help it. I really mean it. I couldn't control myself. And when you became confrontational with me, I lost it."

"You never thought about Grundish, though, did you? He's been your best friend all your life. Always taking the rap for you when things got hot. If somebody was gonna go to prison, it sure as shit wasn't you, was it? If someone wanted to beat your ass, he was always the one jumping in and throwing down for you."

"I know," says Askew sadly. "He's my best buddy and I keep fucking up. I told him I knew I fucked up."

Buttwynn interrupts him. "Grundish could be having a good time right now if it wasn't for you. He could be sitting in a pool room playing Eight Ball. Or he could be making sweet love to Miss Velda, laying her down by the fire, possibly developing a mature adult relationship. Maybe even settling down with her. But he has to take care of you, doesn't he?"

"I know, Buttwynn. I know. I'm sorry. I'll just run off into the swamps and build a chickee hut. I'll kill my food and keep to myself where I won't ruin nobody else's life."

"You're just saying that," snaps Buttwynn. "You're always saying shit like that. You know God damn well you ain't never gonna do it. You'll just stick around and stew the b'Jesus outta Grundish all the time."

Askew says, "I might as well go away. Grundish ain't gonna let me be in charge of the ladies now."

Buttwynn dissipates in the air in front of Askew's eyes and in his place appears Beaumont the cat, now grown to human adult size, with huge boot marks stamped all about his body. Beaumont sits on his haunches in front of Askew, licking at the boot marks, twitching his ears and whiskers at him.

"Be in charge of the ladies?" says Beaumont, also in Grundish's voice. "You crazy sum'bitch. You ain't fit to lick the ladies' boots. You'd ignore 'em. Probably never make 'em actually work. Hell, you'd just be bustin' a nut in all the employees and never see to it that they're actually earning their keep. You'd let the ladies go to crap."

"I would not ignore them or bust a nut in 'em," says Askew loudly. "I'd take care of the ladies. Dora'd help me. And she's the only one I'd be screwing."

"The hell she is," says Beaumont. "You'd ruin the whole operation. Just like you do everything else you touch. Lord knows Grundish has done everything he can to jack you out of the sewer, but you don't ever appreciate it.

If you think Grundish is gonna let you tend to the ladies now, you've gone even crazier than you already were. Grundish ain't gonna let you be in charge of nothin'. He's gonna put the boots to you, just like you did to me. That's what he's gonna do."

"No, he ain't. Grundish ain't never laid a hand on me. He's my best friend, and he's nice to me. He ain't gonna hurt me."

"Well, he's finally tired of your shit," says Beaumont. "He's gonna beat the shit out of you and then go off and start up his own floating whorehouse without you. He's gonna leave you, you crazy bastard."

"He won't do it," shouts Askew. "He's my best pal. We stick together through thick and thin. We're in it together for the whole *kitten caboodle*.

"He's gonna kick your ass and then split," says Beaumont. Softly, over and over, Beaumont tells Askew, "He's gonna leave you alone you crazy bastard. He's gonna leave you all alone. He's gonna leave you ya crazy bastard."

"He ain't. I tell you, he ain't." Askew puts his hands over his ears and scrunches his eyes shut. "Oh! Grundish, help me, Pal." When he opens his eyes, Beaumont is gone. Askew is still on his back, half in and half out of the water. His heart is leaping through his chest, and he is gasping for breath again. When he settles and regains his composure, Askew pats his torn shirt pocket, looking for his cigarettes. His pocket is empty.

"They're all gone. Your friend took them," says a voice that draws Askew's eyes in its direction. His vision takes in Stubbs the dog and Idjit Galoot both sitting beside him, wagging their tails. Stubbs offers Askew a Sordes Pilosus cigarette. "Maybe you should try one of these. They're my favorite brand."

Askew sits up and accepts the offering, turning it in his fingers, studying it, running it under his nose and sniffing it. "This ain't menthol, is it?" he asks suspiciously.

"No, Mr. Askew. It most certainly is not menthol," answers Stubbs. "Trust me. That is one fine tobacco cigarette I'm offering you."

"I'm guessing it's French or something like that, from what I can *gleam* from the brand name," says Askew. "Am I right or something?"

"Yes, something like that. Go ahead and rest a moment. Enjoy the smoke. Then you will need to come with us."

Somehow the cigarette is already lit. Askew takes a long drag on it, feeling the smoke expand in his lungs. He cranes his head back to exhale, blows the thick smoke out, inhales, and blows more smoke out once again. "Wow," sighs Askew. "That is a tasty smoke."

"We told you," agrees Idjit Galoot. His sad and seeping eyes scan Askew's badly battered mug. "Now, if you don't mind my saying so, you have some nasty cuts on your face. Can I cleanse those wounds for you?"

"Sure, man," says Askew. "That'd be real cool." He lays on his back smoking, the cigarette lodged in the gap between his front teeth. Idjit licks at the lacerations on Askew's face, loosening the coagulated crusties, sometimes gently gnawing at the stitches. The cigarette burns down to the filter and Askew flicks it out into the water. The fireball fizzes out and a catfish mouth emerges from the muck, whiskers twitching, and snatches the butt, swallowing it before the other fish can get to it, only realizing too late that it isn't food. Askew pulls his face away from Idjit's enthusiastic cleansing tongue. Dog-breath-aroma clings to his face.

"Now that you've enjoyed a smoke, you have business to attend to. Please follow us," says Stubbs.

"Yes, please walk this way," advises Idjit. The dogs turn and walk toward the junkyard, their synchronized tails wagging back and forth, metronome-like, to some unheard rhythm.

Askew manages to work his way to his hands and knees, still unable to stand. He crawls behind Idjit and Stubbs. Gravel punctures the skin on his hands and knees as he drags himself toward Jerry's warehouse. The palms of his hands are dimpled from pressing down on pebbles. The three of them reach an orange VW van with the roof-top popped. In front of the van, stuck in the ground, is a sign. The sign makes little sense to Askew. It reads:

TONIGHT IN THE VAN
FOR MADMEN ONLY
PRICE OF ADMITTANCE, YOUR MIND
NOT FOR EVERYBODY
DORA IS IN HELL

"What the fuck?" grunts Askew. "What's that mean?"

"That is for you to figure out," says Stubbs. "You are a madman. You can get in. Perhaps you would benefit from sitting a spell in the van."

"Uh, okay," Askew shrugs his shoulders and tries to stand, still feeling as if his body is being held close to the surface of the planet by a double dose of gravity. He gives up on trying to stand and starts to climb into the open sliding side door, sitting on the floor at the edge of the open doorway. "Would you guys mind bumming me a couple more smokes for while I'm in here?"

"I'd be glad to. I have a fresh pack here. You can have it," says Stubbs, moving closer to Askew, the pack held in his teeth. "I've been meaning to quit anyway."

Askew grabs the cigarettes from Stubbs' mouth and wipes slobber from the cellophane wrapping. Two small indentations mar the pack where Stubbs' canine teeth slightly pierced it. Askew slaps the top of the pack against his dimpled palm, packing the smokes, and peels the wrapper from the top. "I think I'll have one more before I go in. Can I borrow your lighter?"

"You can have it, too."

Askew takes the lighter from Stubbs' mouth and wipes the slobber on his shorts. He lights his cigarette and begins to smoke. "Hey…" he says to the dogs, starting to thank them for their help. But, when Askew looks up to say thank you, Stubbs and Idjit Galoot are gone. Standing in their place is Alf the Sacred Burro. Askew works his way to his feet and finds himself unsteady, shaky, bordering on convulsive. He draws hard on the smoke and exhales, inhales, and exhales again before he clears the smoke from his lungs. His head feels three sizes too big and sluggish.

Alf sizes up Askew. "Look at you," says the Sacred Burro. "Standing palsied at the gates of death yet afraid to die. I guess I can't really blame you. It's not your time yet, though. So don't be freaked out about going in the van."

"What do you mean standing at the gates of death? I'm not dying, am I?"

"Well, you are currently in the midst of water intoxication delirium. In case you don't remember, you just chugged three gallons of water and passed out. And this isn't the first time you've done that, is it?"

"Doh!" says Askew, slapping himself on the forehead. "I did that again, huh? I'm not real sure why I do that sometimes. I guess I ain't quite right in the head. I just get so thirsty when I'm stressed out." He rubs at his gashed forehead where he just slapped himself. "I ain't gonna die from it, am I?"

"At this point you've caused additional minor brain damage. Your brain is swollen. It's too big for the space allotted in your skull. So it's basically crushing in on itself in your head. Luckily, the portions of your brain that control your respiration and temperature haven't been affected yet. But, you have done irreparable damage to the part that manages your impulse control. Before it gets any worse, you need to drink some sports drink to replenish your electrolytes. And you need to piss. Piss a lot."

"Is there anything that you can do to, like, I dunno, help me?" asks Askew.

"Yeah, all your sickness – I can suck it up. Throw it all at me. I can shrug it off."

"Okay," says Askew, thinking to himself that the beast of burden is talking nonsense. "But there's one thing, donkey, I don't understand. Why are you here? Why are you telling me all of this?"

"I'm here to help you. I'm the helping kind of donkey. And I've made something for you." Alf arches his back and begins hacking, gagging, and contorting himself into unnatural positions until he ralphs up a hairy brown lump at the feet of Askew. "Take that. It will bring you good luck."

Askew picks up the donkey-loaf and sniffs it. "Wheeee-ewww!" His head snaps back involuntarily as if kicked in the jaw by an invisible foot. "That smells like rotten throat cheese, man. What the fuck is it?"

"It's a bezoar[41]. A wad of undigested vegetable fibers and hair that has accumulated in my stomach in a hardened mass. It is said that bezoars have mystical healing powers and can drive away evil spirits. Keep it in your pocket and no harm may come to you. At least that's what they say."

"If you say so." Askew flicks his cigarette and studies the bezoar closely. It looks like a turd with a beard and is hard like a rock. He pockets the good luck charm and eyes Alf suspiciously. "How is it that you seem to know what's best for me? You're a donkey, no offense intended…"

"…And none taken…" Alf's ears twitch in response to a horsefly buzzing around them.

"…But, you seem wise for an animal. And I feel like I can trust you. Why is it that you know so much?"

---

[41]A bezoar formed from hair is called a trichobezoar. Rapunzel Syndrome is a rare intestinal affliction in humans which results from eating hair and causes the formation of a trichobezoar. The human gastrointestinal tract is unable to digest human hair, so, trichobezoars usually need to be surgically removed. A bezoar in the large intestine is known as a fecalith.

"A donkey lives a long time," Alf says cryptically as he turns to walk away. "Now get in the van. And don't forget to drink lots of sports drinks."

Inside the van Askew folds the back seat down into a bed. He grabs a bottle of water from a cooler full of ice and lays back, smoking and drinking more fluids. The barely-audible strains of a sitar creep down Askew's acoustic meatus and gently sing their song to the tympanic membrane. A whiff of patchouli tickles his nose. "Smells like hippies," he says to himself, smiling. "Like unwashed, filthy, happy, happy hippies."

"It's a hippy van, Daddy-O," giggles Dora as she climbs into the rear of the mini bus. She's wearing only a poncho and has a bright yellow Black-Eyed Susan tucked into her hair. A red peace-sign is painted on her cheek. "Put away that water. You've already made yourself sick with that stuff. You need one of these." She holds out a bottle of lemon-lime Gatorade.

Askew recaps the water bottle and tosses it toward the front seat of the van. "Hey, Baby," he smiles at her. "What do you think of this here minibus? It's kind of groovy, ain't it?" The sitar music increases ever so slightly in volume, occasionally accented by foreign language chants. Askew chugs the Gatorade. "Come over here and lay next to me. I've missed you."

Dora strips away her rancid poncho, and lies out naked by the door. "You want me to come up there, Baby?"

"I don't just want you to. I need you."

"Here I come." She rises from the floor and slinks up the bed on all fours, her back bowed downward and hind quarters tilted up, like a pussy in heat presenting to a tomcat. The tempo and volume of the sitar increase in intensity.

Askew blows a thick cloud of smoke that forms a gray, smoggy ring around the top of his head. "Kiss my aura, Dora," says Askew, grabbing her hair and dragging her face up to his. Kissing her so hard that her teeth smash his lips, making him bleed.

"Oh, yeah," she smiles, her teeth glistening with his blood. She leans in again and deep kisses her man.

Askew pulls Dora's head back by the hair and stares into her eyes. "You want some more."

She says, "yeah, Baby," and they roll off the bed onto the floor, groping and probing, slapping, tickling, ripping off Askew's clothes until all he is wearing is a pair of black socks held up by garters. And then he is in her, fucking with great fervor. Mounting her from behind, doggy-style, he closes his eyes and jack-hammer pounds, gripping tightly onto her hips to keep her from being knocked away by his deep lunges. Askew thinks about how he loves the view from behind, the visual of the penetration, the nice round ass tilted up toward him. He likes reaching around and grabbing at the tits as they flop in time to his thrusts. The sitar and Indian chants build in volume and intensity, the rhythm driving Askew's hips forward and pulling them back in great violent bursts. He opens his eyes to enjoy the view and instead of a smooth, rounded ass, he sees a furry tail wagging and his member forcefully pounding a crusty dog asshole.

"Ouch!" snaps Stubbs. "No lubrication and no reach around! Hell, you can't even scratch me behind the ears while you're doing that?" He attempts to skitter away, his sphincter momentarily seizing up and pulling Askew with him, rectal walls prolapsing, forming a fleshy pink sock on Askew's member. "You're a lousy date," says Stubbs as he clumsily pulls away from Askew. "Give me a cigarette."

"AW JEEZUS! AW JEEZ! WHAT HAPPENED? WHAT THE FUCK? AW FUCK! JEEZ!" Askew launches himself from the van, landing on his hands and knees, retching up fluids and chunks and more fluids. His stomach continues to heave even when the warm flow of vomit ceases. "I wanna shoot myself," he says to the open van door. "I can't believe I just boofed a dog. Oh, God!"

"Calm down," says Stubbs from the open door. "It's not like I enjoyed it either. I prefer to be with the ladies myself. And if I do have to do something like that, I definitely would opt for pitching over catching. Especially with your passionless, mechanical thrusts. But, somebody had to get your mind out of the gutter and urge you to purge some of that water. Now, get up and take a piss."

"You mean you did that to make me puke?" Askew wipes his mouth with a shaky forearm.

"You're going to die if you don't eliminate a lot of your water, and quickly. Now take a piss."

"You made yourself look like Dora? You used her feminine *wilds* to seduce me just so you could make me puke?"

"Well, let's put it this way: I didn't do because I wanted to shit blood for the next week. Now piss. And give me a cigarette when you're done. I love smoking after sex."

Askew grips the van and pulls himself to his feet. Placing one hand on the minibus and leaning forward with his body at a forty-five degree angle from the ground, he lets loose with a thick, powerful spray of urine. His free hand pushing down on the still partially-erect cock, directing the flow into the ground. The sound, like a cow pissing on a flat rock, continues for what seems like minutes.

"There. Now don't you feel better?" says Stubbs. And he did feel better. Askew's head felt like it shrank three sizes that day, right back to its original circumference. Askew's shrunken head nods in the affirmative.

"Now," says Stubbs, "pull another Gatorade from this cooler in here and pound it down. And when you finish with that one, drink another."

Askew climbs back in the minibus and lights two cigarettes, handing one to Stubbs. He gets dressed and avoids eye contact with the dog who sits on the floor wagging his tail at Askew, making sure he drinks the Gatorade.

"We don't have to tell anybody about this, do we?" asks Askew, still averting his eyes.

"I'm a dead dog. Who am I gonna tell? Besides, you think I want it going around that you pink-socked me? Mum's the word, Mr. Askew. Now I advise that you chug down one more of those beverages and swim back to the world of the living."

On the hood of Chancho's station wagon are Dora and Askew. Dora sits cross-legged with her back erect. Her ass edges up to the bottom of the windshield. She holds Askew's head in her lap and drains the last of the Gatorade bottles into his open mouth. Unconscious and pantsless, his sloppy bulk splays out on top of the hood like a dead and bloated baby manatee drifted ashore. The fluids constantly drizzle from his nozzle as they are replaced by the green elixir of sugar, carbohydrates and electrolytes. "Askew," Dora says, "can you hear me? Can you feel me near you?"

With a grunt and a sputter like an old Buick trying to start, Askew stirs and stalls, vapor-locked, coughing and seizing. His eyelids roll up to see the clouds leisurely inching their way across the sky. One cloud looks like a duck with a sword jammed into its neck. One looks like a three-legged man playing soccer. And one looks like Dora's face, close and smiling down at Askew. The Dora cloud leans in and kisses the bridge of his nose. "Oh Baby! Oh Baby!" it says. "You're okay. You're going to be okay." The face cloud bursts, she cries and the tears fall like warm summer rain on his face. "I thought I was gonna lose you. I finally find somebody special and then I think I'm gonna lose you."

Askew sits and looks around. It really is Dora. He isn't dreaming anymore. And she cries. But the tears are happy. Askew's right hand grips the bearded bezoar. A warm breeze blows across his exposed genitals, his thick unruly pubes curling upward and swaying like coarse tufts of overgrown grass blowing in the wind. "I ain't got no pants on," he laughs, not really thinking it's funny. "Where'd my pants go?"

"They're right here," says Dora, grabbing Askew's shorts and handing them to him. "I didn't want you to pee your pants so I pulled 'em off for you."

Askew sets the bezoar on the hood of the car and pulls the shorts over his piss-marinated legs. "What about my sock garters? Did you take those off, too?"

"Right here, Baby." She scoots up behind Askew and loops her arms around his shoulders. The socks and their garters dangle from her hands and rest on his chest. Leaning in closer, she kisses his cheek. "We should get you inside. You've been baking out in this sun for half a day. I was afraid to move you."

"God," he wrinkles up his face as he puts on his socks, garters and sandals. "I stink like an outhouse. I hope ol' Jerry in there has a working shower." He stands on unsteady legs. He is slightly stooped and resting his hands on the front of the car. His equilibrium takes leave, and the ground beneath his feet lurches like a giant, spastic see-saw. He sits back against the car and pulls the fresh pack of Sordes Pilosus from his shirt pocket. He pockets the bezoar and fishes around for a lighter. "I'll be ready in a minute. Just let me get a grip on myself here." He lights two cigarettes and hands one to Dora.

"Mmm," she says, blowing out the thick bluish smoke. "Good smokes. Where'd you get these?"

"I don't know, Baby. I think a dog gave 'em to me. Does that sound crazy?"

"Yeah, a little." She smiles and blows streams of smoke from her nostrils. "But you been sick. And a little crazy. You was having some sort of weird dreams. You cried and you shouted. And you was saying something about dogs and donkeys. I don't know. You may still be a little goofy. Whatever. I ain't gonna hold it against you."

"You truly are my angel, Baby. Can you help me get back inside? I don't know if I'm steady enough to walk by myself."

Dora stands and wraps Askew's flabby arm over her shoulder. She helps him return to the building. The sloppy urine-soaked fool wraps his arm around her thin, elfin frame. The two of them stagger back inside. She struggles to help carry his weight. A vapor trail of piss, smoke, sweat and salvation wafts behind them. The more Askew leans on her shoulders, the more he stumbles, and the stronger she becomes. By the time they locate the shower in Jerry's building, Dora is shouldering most of Askew's load. She sets him down in the shower stall harder than she intends, losing her grip on him and letting him hit the ground with a muted thump. She turns on the water – cold water – and sits on the tile floor with him. Holding him. Shivering.

Jerry says, "You can't leave me again. I've suffered without you for all this time." He strokes her *Nice 'N Easy #108* red hair. She moves away from him slightly. "And don't walk out on me now. I'm not sleepy and there is no place I'm going to."

Turleen faces toward Jerry and turns her mouth up into something that looks like a smile, but is still more sad than happy. "Jer Bear. I've missed you all these years, I have. And in my heart, I know you're the one. But I've got something left that I have to do. I've gotta do what I can for those boys. And I can't just settle in here right now, I can't. You know that." She runs her hand over his bony ribcage and kisses him on the neck. "You said you'll be here for me no matter how this turns out."

"And I will, Miss Turleen."

"Well, then let me get these boys to safety. And if I can do that, then you can join me with them."

"And if not?"

"I don't want to think about *if not*, I don't. Let me do what I can for them. You already told me you were in on the plan if things work out for the boys, you did. Don't you back out on me now."

"Well, I don't want to lose you again," he says, pulling her closer, squeezing her tight. "I can't do it again. Your long-time curse hurts, but what's worse is this pain in here." He pulls back and slaps an open palm on his chest. "I can't stay in here. I need some fresh air. You want to come with me?"

They stand and hold each other close. Jerry hunches over her like a vulture, wrapping his wings around her.

Grundish smokes the last of Askew's pack and throws the butt into the small fire burning beside the VW. He sits on a stack of worn tires, staring into the dancing orange and yellow tendrils, the flicking hypnotic flames. The heat tightens the skin on his face and dries his eyes. Alf rests next to the stack of tires. The ancient donkey sits on his haunches, like a dog, and leans over with his head resting against Grundish's side. Grundish pulls his arm free and scratches the sacred burro's head. Alf tilts in toward the scratching hand until a needy spot right behind an ear receives the treatment.

"Urrrrppp!" Alf looses a belch from down low that smells like pickled turds.

"Damn, Donkey. You ain't gotta do that so close to my face," says Grundish. Not harsh, though. Almost affectionate. He scritches at Alf's ears again and lets the vision of the flames take his head elsewhere.

"There you are. We been looking for you." Askew stands in front of the fire, a case of Blatz beer in his arms, a look of calm in his eyes. "You mind if I sit?"

Grundish nods to the stack of tires opposite him. "You better give me one of those brews if you're planning on enjoying my fire."

Askew tosses a can and Grundish snatches it out of the air. He chuckles. "Blatz. Where'd you get this? I didn't even think they made this shit anymore." He grips the ring on the pull tab and pops the can open. Warm foam runs down his arm. The beer is warm and skunky.

"I don't know if they still make it. But I know that Jerry has a store room stocked to the ceiling with the shit."

"Izzat right?"

"Yup. A whole fucking room."

"All Blatz?"

"The whole room."

"You know why they call it Blatz?" asks Grundish.

"Why?"

"Cuz' that's the sound it makes when it comes back up. *BLATZZZ!*" Grundish pretends to puke. Alf chimes in with his own Blatz-like noise, harmonizing his ructus[42] with Grundish.

"God-damn, that is one foul old mule." Askew waves the donkey fumes from his face. "I can smell that shit over here."

They laugh, and when they stop, there's nothing to say. Grundish chugs his beer and grunts for another. Askew tosses one to Grundish, and they silently stare at the fire and drink their beer.

"You're mad at me, aren't you?" says Askew.

Grundish's broad shoulders shrug despite his effort to remain still. He stares at the fire, sips his beer, and scritches Alf's head.

"I mean, you got every right to be. I keep fucking things up. I keep killing people. And then again, maybe it's your fault for egging me on to push things a little further. But I don't want to blame nobody." Askew fumbles in his pockets and pulls out his cigarettes. He shakes one part-way out of the pack and holds it out for Grundish to grab. They light their smokes and Askew continues. "It don't matter whose fault it is. I know that what I done ain't good. It ain't right. There's no excuse for the way I been. And I can't explain it. But something happened to me earlier today. You might call it a near-death experience. You

---

[42]The world record for the loudest burp is 107.1 decibels, set by Paul Hunn in London, England, on September 24, 2008.

might call it *dramatic* brain injury. Whatever it was, I came out of it feeling different."

Grundish shrugs again. "Yeah?"

"Yeah. Like I'm better or something. Normal...normal for me, anyway. I don't feel like hurting people. I don't feel out of control. I don't know where all that came from or what came over me. But I was mad, and crazy and *erotic* in my thoughts. Some of the shit going through my head didn't make no sense to me, but I felt it as strong as I ever felt anything. And then, *whoosh*," he slides his hand smoothly in front of him, "it's like it just washed away with all that water I pissed out." He stops, looks at Alf. In the dark it almost looks like the burro is smiling a rotten-toothed donkey smile at him. "Do you believe me?"

"Yeah," says Grundish. He tosses his butt in the fire and stands to get more wood. "I do. I don't know why. But I do." He lifts a split log and tosses it on the fire, throwing sparks into the air, red hot flecks riding the waves of heat and smoke up toward the sky.

"God, that's beautiful," says Askew.

"Yeah, ain't it? I love sitting around a fire, bullshitting, getting drunk. I fucking love it." And silence blankets them again, leaving them to stare into the flames and contemplate their situation. "Hey, Beer Bitch, give me another beer and another cigarette."

Askew lights a smoke, flicks it at Grundish then fires one up for himself. He tosses a Blatz over the flames.

"I believe you, you know? That you ain't mad at me," says Askew. "You're my only friend, and you always stick with me, even if I am a fuck-up."

"Yeah, so?"

"So, nothing. I'm just saying. But, I'm afraid, Grundish. I'm afraid they're gonna catch us."

"They ain't gonna catch us. How they gonna find us if we just lay low here and wait for the right time to sneak off? You're done with your crazies, and we ain't gonna go nowhere right now anyways. So we'll figure it out."

"But, if they are gonna catch us, I want you to remember…"

"I know…"

"Remember your promise to me. You gotta put me down like a sick dog. I can't be taken alive."

"I know."

"And don't let me pussy out. If I say that I take it back, don't listen to me. That's just me being a pussy. Follow through with it no matter what I say if it looks like we's gonna get caught."

"I know."

"You promise?"

"Yeah, I promise." And then just the crackling of the fire fills the night.

Askew shifts his position as the smoke finds him and blows in his face. It burns his eyes. He moves and the smoke seeks him out, choking him again. He circles the fire and stands on Grundish's side, Alf resting between them. He reaches down and rubs the donkey's head. He says, "We still gonna get a ship?"

"Of course we are. What else have we got to do? Dora's gonna help us. Jerry wants a piece of the action, so he's gonna contribute. I got the brains. We're set once we get out of the country. We just gotta figure that one out and we're good."

"You boys talking about me?" says Dora as she comes around the van and hugs onto Askew's side.

"Nahhh," says Askew. "You wasn't *ease-dropping* on our conversation, was you?"

"No, Baby. I just heard my name as I was walking over here." She grabs the cigarette out of Askew's mouth and takes a long pull. Putting the cigarette back, her fingers linger briefly on his dry lips. "Is everything all right now?"

"Yeah," says Grundish. "I think so." And they sit, and drink, and smoke, and laugh. The three of them and the donkey drunkenly hunch around the fire, with the smoke and ashes climbing toward the stars and the skunked malt beverages flowing freely. Once again, Grundish thinks that everything is good when he has a friend like Askew.

With the sun barely winking over the horizon and Alf the Sacred Burro nestled up to him, Grundish stirs. His temples throb. His body aches from sleeping on the ground. In the VW van Askew and Dora are twisted in a drunken, naked, pretzel of limbs and body parts, stinking of each other's fluids and dead to the dawning day. Grundish stands, stretches, and pisses on the burning remnants of the fire. The embers hiss at the offense and spit off steam. Inside the building, Turleen and Jerry lie awake in bed, holding each other close, sometimes speaking in soft tones, sometimes just taking comfort in the warm feel of time-worn skin on skin.

Askew's pack of Sordes Pilosus sits on a stack of tires next to a half-full can of Blatz. Grundish shakes the last smoke from the pack and lights it. He dumps the flat beer in his mouth, swishes it around, and spits it out onto the burning embers, again receiving a hiss in response. The cool morning air refreshes Grundish and gives him a feeling that it all might just work out. Somewhere, a rooster crows. Alf whinnies and slowly works his way to his wobbly legs, his limbs stiff from sleep and old age. He nuzzles up against Grundish's arm. Grundish smiles at the sounds of Alf wheezing and Askew snoring. The two noises twine around each other in the air, becoming one auditory wreath of labored breathing, accented now and again by the chirp of a red-shouldered hawk. Grundish smokes and leans against his donkey friend, enjoying the morning, relishing the gentle respiratory song of wheezes, chirps, snores and snorts. The red-shouldered hawk flies from the top of the building. It swoops within feet of the top of Grundish's head and utters a sharp trill.

New sounds fill the air. Muffled voices. Car doors. Feet scuffling. Sounds from just outside the front gate of the compound. Clattering and clanking of metal. Offensive sounds that hit Grundish's ear and hurt his spirit. Sounds that mean nothing but trouble.

He throws open the van door and a wave of funk rolls out over him, the odor of jism, sweat, beer and cigarettes. A tangy note of ass drifts under his nose and settles on his moustache. Askew and Dora, naked and unconscious, lie out on their backs, legs and arms tossed over each other. Grundish briefly eyes Dora's glistening pudendum. The puffy padded mound sits dead-center of her sharp, dangerous-looking pelvic bones, covered by a hint of razor stubble[43]. Much of her body is angular and bony and looks as if it would be painful to lie on. Grundish looks away and thinks to himself that the young girl's malnourished body lacks the softness, the fullness, the thick, loving meatiness and neediness of Velda's fuller figure. He looks away, grabs a filthy poncho from the front seat of the van and throws it over Dora.

"Hey, you guys," whispers Grundish, putting his large hands on the top of the van, just above the sliding door,

---

[43]La Maja Desnuda (The Nude Maja), c. 1800, by master Spanish painter, Francisco De Goya, is considered to probably be the first well known European painting to show a female's pubic hair.

and shaking it. "Wake up, guys. I think something's wrong." Askew and Dora stir and roll back over. "I'm serious. Somebody's out there and I think it might be cops."

They scuttle for the building, Askew and Dora trailing Grundish and throwing clothes on as they run. The door slams behind them just before Alf can follow them in. The donkey's hooves slam the side of the building in frustration. The hoof-on-metal clang rails at the indignity of exclusion once again.

"God damn," says Askew. "What's that donkey doing? He's going to draw their attention."

Grundish runs back to the door and opens it, allowing Alf into the building. They scramble through the building, rats in a maze, seeking out Jerry and Turleen. Grundish throws back the door to Jerry's living quarters and the four of them burst in, interrupting a tender moment between the elderly couple.

"The cops are out there," says Grundish, panting. "They're here for us."

On top of the building, they crawl to the edge and look toward the front gate. Just outside of the gate is a congregation of sheriff's deputies, SWAT team members, and a handful of bearded country boys in camouflage jumpsuits cradling twelve-gauge shotguns in their arms. The entire posse is gathered at the front gate. Grundish and Askew stay low and run around the perimeter of the roof, checking all sides of the compound. They see no one anywhere besides just outside the gate.

Jerry meets Grundish and Askew as they descend the pull-down ladder from the roof. "Here you go," says Jerry, handing a megaphone to Grundish. "Get back up there and stall them. I've got a plan, but you're gonna have to buy a little time."

"I don't wanna go up there. This is the Polk County Sheriff's Office we're dealing with here," says Grundish, trying to hand the megaphone back to Jerry.

"Yeah," agrees Askew, wide-eyed. "Those good old boys like to use suspects for target practice." He holds his hands up, palms out as Jerry tries to force the megaphone on him. "No way. Just last month, a whole big crew of 'em opened fire on one guy they was chasing. Said he had something in his hand that looked like a gun. Those boys didn't stop shooting until they ran out of ammo. And it took 'em quite a while, too."

"He's right," says Grundish. "I was listening to the press conference where the Sheriff was giving a statement to reporters at the scene, and the whole time you could hear the guns in the background, nonstop firing."

"Yeah, and it turns out the guy didn't even have a gun. He was holding his cell phone. They blasted him full of holes, and it turned out he wasn't even the guy they was looking for."

"You're right. Those are some bloodthirsty killers. So if you do as I say, I might just be able to keep you alive. Do you want to get out of this alive?" asks Jerry.

Grundish and Askew both nod.

"Then listen to me. You, take this." He hands the megaphone to Grundish. "And this, too." Jerry holds out a Colt Magnum .44 Anaconda hand-cannon, thrusting it toward Grundish, who takes it and jams it down the front of his pants. The towering Skeletor grasps Grundish's shoulders and locks eyes, somehow managing not to look like a complete doofus in his multicolored geometric-patterned sweater and Peruvian beanie cap. "Just do what I say and get up there. Say something, anything, to stall them. Tell them you have hostages. Tell them you'll start throwing dead bodies out unless they back off and give you some space. Can you do that?"

"Yeah. I can do it."

"Good. Then get up there. And you," he says to Askew, "come with me. I'm gonna need a strong young man to help out."

Grundish sits behind a row of oil drums on the roof and peeks out at the front gate. A bottom-heavy deputy lops off the padlock on the front gate with a pair of bolt cutters. Several other officers grab the gates and begin to swing them open.

"Fuck, fuck fuck," says Grundish, fumbling with the megaphone, trying to figure out how to work it. He hits a red button, figuring it to be the power switch, and sets off a siren on the bullhorn that bare-fist punches him in the face with 120-decibel knuckles.

Instead of drawing them in, the siren song sends the officers scrambling from the gate, tripping over each other, and jumping behind their cruisers. They crouch behind their cars, panting, and point their service revolvers and assault rifles at Jerry's building. Several shots go off and slam into the building before the officer in charge can reign the men in. "Hold your fire. Hold your fire," go the shouts through the lead detective's public-address system on his car.

Grundish hits the red switch again and shuts off the siren. With the swell of the siren muted and the various gunshots already fired, silence and stirred-up dust settles over the scene. Instead of just the silence, Grundish's ears throb and pick up a whooshing sound, white noise, static. He studies the bullhorn and realizes that the talk-switch is the black button on the pistol grip.

On the ground, the deputies begin peeking up over their cars. A fat face, adorned with a soup-crusted bushy mustache, rises above the hood of its car and leads its bovine body toward the gate again. His name is Detective Mojado. Mojado is the hostage negotiator and is working the situation in tandem with Detective Carter. Mojado gasps deep, raspy breaths and feels his heart pumping hard, feels his pulse in his temples. The amplified click of Grundish's bullhorn stops him midstride.

"Uhh…don't come any closer," Grundish says into the mouthpiece, more of a question than directive. His unsure voice increases in volume exponentially as it blares from the flared horn of the megaphone.

Detective Mojado takes a tentative step forward again.

"Don't do it, you stinkin' copper," says Grundish, feeling disconnected from himself, not sure how to react or what to say in a stand-off with the law. He always just turned himself in before, when it came down to it. Not this time, though. Lacking the experience and knowledge for such a situation, Grundish falls back on the old mobster movies he used to watch on Saturday afternoons as a kid. "Yeah, see? We got hostages. See? And if you don't back off, we're gonna start a slaughter in here. See? I'll start tossing bodies out. Yeah."

Mojado backs away from the gate and returns to his car. He grabs the handset from inside of his cruiser and speaks over the loudspeaker. "We will not approach the gate again. We don't want to see anybody get hurt. I am here to see what I can do to work things out. My name is Detective Mojado. You can call me Piso. I'm working with Detective Carter. He is in charge, but I'm going to be the one dealing with you. I don't want this to end badly for you or the hostages. So you need to tell me what you want."

"Um…I'm gonna have to get back with you on that," says Grundish into the mouthpiece. "Give me a couple of minutes to think things over." *Smooth*, thinks Grundish, *real smooth. You're really doing a great job. Why don't you call them stinkin' coppers again? Yeah, see? Rocky's gonna rub you out. See? Real fucking smooth.*

"Well, while you're thinking, why don't you tell me who I'm speaking with? Are you Mr. Grundish or Mr. Askew?"

"How do you know our names?" asks Grundish. *Oh nice*, he thinks, *now you've confirmed it for them.*

"I'll tell you after you tell me who I'm speaking with, Mr. Grundish or Mr. Askew?"

What the fuck does it matter now? he thinks. "I'm Grundish. So, how did you know where to find us?" He peeks up over the top of the oil drums and sees men dressed in black, moving away from the other deputies, spreading out along the wall. "Hey, tell those SWAT guys to stop spreading out and come back or we start snuffing out the hostages."

The SWAT members stop moving and look toward Mojado for orders. Mojado speaks into the microphone. "I want everybody to pull in here where Mr. Grundish can see that we're not trying to pull anything sneaky on him." Officers return to the front gate area and squat behind their cars. It looks to Grundish as if they have all returned. "I'm sorry about that, Mr. Grundish. The men were acting on their own there. That won't happen again. Now, should I call you Mr. Grundish, or can you tell me your first name?"

"Just call me Grundish. Now tell me how you found us."

"Do you have a telephone that we can talk on?"

"No, let's do it just the way we are."

"Okay, Mr. Grundish. Have it your way." Sweat beads on Mojado's forehead and drips down, stinging his eyes. He wipes at his eyes and continues. "We got a positive ID on you at the house where you and your friend killed that man in Hillsborough County. The kid that you took hostage gave a description to Hillsborough's sketch artist, and they determined that it was you two fellows in the house. Pretty easy since they already had an APB out on you guys. They checked the phone records from the house and saw that there were numerous calls to the phone number listed for this property. Simple police work really. We just put together a posse and here we are."

Shit, thinks Grundish. *Turleen kept calling here to set things up for us. Her efforts to set up the safe-house made things unsafe.*

"So, Grundish, what I need is for you to let me know what it is you want us to do. You have the hostages.

Obviously you have demands. Let me know what it is that you are wanting, and I'll check with Detective Carter to see if we can accommodate you."

"We just want you to go. To leave us alone."

"Well, Grundish, I'm afraid we can't do that. You have hostages, and we need to make sure they are safe. Can you tell me how many people you have in there?"

Grundish senses somebody behind him and turns to see Askew hunched over and dragging the battered body of Chancho. Askew drops Chancho beside Grundish and says in a low voice, "Tell 'em we have four. That'll keep the heat off of everybody else."

"We have four hostages," says Grundish into the bullhorn. "A whore, a Mexican and two old people. And they're all starting to get on our nerves. So don't push us."

"Okay, now we're getting somewhere," says Mojado. "Is everybody all right? Nobody's been hurt yet, right?"

"Well, we beat up the Mexican pretty good, but he's still alive," says Grundish.

"All right," says Mojado. "Can you tell me the Mexican's name?"

"It's Chancho."

"And how bad are his injuries?"

Grundish looks at the smashed, squashed, and blood-splattered mess of flesh that used to be Chancho's face. "Uh, he's pretty bad. Real bad."

"Can we send somebody in to bring out Chancho? You can keep the other hostages so you will still have plenty of leverage. And we can take care of Mr. Chancho."

"No. No, you can't. We're not releasing anybody yet," says Grundish.

In the distance the soft whir of helicopter blades can be heard.

"Well, is there something we can do for you? A little trade off, maybe, so that you'll allow us to get Mr. Chancho out of there? Maybe we can send in food and drinks for you and the hostages. After you eat, maybe you will be willing to let us tend to Mr. Chancho. Is there any food that you would like in there?"

"How about some pork chops and applesauce?" says Grundish.

"I'll see what we can do. Let me speak with Detective Carter and see about those pork chops and applesauce."

The sound of the chopper's blades battering the air is louder, closer.

"Is that a police helicopter?" Grundish asks.

"That is one of our choppers," says Mojado. "They are just going to be flying over to make sure everything is all right. We won't be landing it on top of the building or anything."

"Tell them to turn away now. And don't bring any more officers here," says Grundish.

"I can't do that, Mr. Grundish," says Mojado. "I'm not in charge. I'm just the negotiator."

The helicopter is now visible to Grundish and Askew in the distance.

"Give me your gun," says Askew.

"No way. We're not getting into a gunfight with these crazy bastards," says Grundish.

"Give me the gun. I'm not going to shoot at them. I'm just going to make them listen to us."

The whirring dot in the sky grows larger. Grundish looks out at the officers, and it seems as if some of them may have moved a few feet closer to the front of the gate. He hands the gun to Askew.

"Work with me here," says Askew. "Tell them we're gonna kill the Mexican if they don't back off and turn the chopper around." Askew stands up, his left arm wrapped around Chancho's chest and his right hand holding a gun to the dangling bloody meatball that used to be his head. Askew drags the corpse around the side of the oil drums so that the officers can see it.

"We said to back off and turn the helicopter around," says Grundish into the megaphone. "See? We're gonna cap the Mexican if you don't. See?"

"You don't want to do that, Mr. Grundish. I don't have any control over the helicopter. That's Detective Carter's call."

"Back the fuck off, now!" screams Askew. The helicopter looms large and loud in the sky, homing in on them. "Back the fuck off!"

"Don't make us do it!" yells Grundish into the megaphone.

"Back the fuck off!" screams Askew again. The helicopter continues its approach and the officers remain in position. Askew puts the gun up to the side of Chancho's head and pulls the trigger twice, blowing off what is left of the front portion of Chancho's face, leaving a gooping crescent-of-a-head and a ragged, ghastly scoop of negative space. Askew throws the body down on the roof. It lands with a flat thud.

"Now, turn the helicopter around and back off or we snuff the old lady next," shouts Grundish into the bullhorn.

The officers all step back from their positions. The helicopter turns and retreats.

"Keep stalling them," says Askew to his friend. He hooks his hands under Chancho's arms and drags him away. "Jerry's working on something for us. You just gotta stonewall 'em a little longer. Make up some crazy demands or something." Askew lifts the roof hatch that leads back down into the building. He tosses Chancho's body down the hole and turns back to Grundish. "Just hold 'em off a little longer. I promise we won't leave you hanging in *lingo* up here."

"Hey."

"What?"

"Gimme a smoke before you go back down."

"I'm out."

"What?" Grundish asks. "Out? How can you be out? You brought a month's worth of butts along."

"I said, I'm out. O-U-T. Out. I guess this looks like a good time for us to quit." And Askew disappears into the building.

"Your friend shouldn't have done that," says Mojado, his voice lacking inflection. He looks around at the blank, shocked faces on the men surrounding him. To lose a hostage like that, right in front of them and not be able to do anything about it is more than most of the men could have imagined. "I'm afraid that we're not going to be able to negotiate with you if that's how it's going to be." Mojado puts the handset back in its holder and barks out orders, unintelligible to Grundish but perfectly understood by the assault team. SWAT members check their belts, communicate with hand signals and move along the fence walls, spreading in both directions away from the gate.

"Wait a minute," says Grundish. "Wait. We're not going to hurt anybody else as long as you stay where you are and don't try to bring the helicopter back. You and your men stay where you are and I give you my word, we won't hurt anybody else."

"I need you to show me that we can cooperate." Mojado grasps the handset and speaks in a tense, clipped tone. The men in black stop and look back toward him. "We wanted you to send out Mr. Chancho as an act of good will. Now I'm going to have to ask you to give us another one of your hostages. How about one of the elderly folks that you have in there?"

"What's in it for us? I don't need your pork chops and apple sauce. How about you provide us with a plane and a pilot and let us go and we'll give you all of the hostages as soon as we're safe."

"I'll check with Detective Carter and see if that's something we can arrange. Can you just send out one of the hostages? You show me your sincerity here, and I'll go up through the chain of command to see what we can do for you."

Grundish pats his pockets, searching for one last cigarette. "Son of a whore," he says to himself, "it looks like I picked the wrong day to quit smoking."

The SWAT team members check the extra clips for their guns. One stoops down and ties a boot as tight as he can manage, almost breaking the sturdy laces. A collective itch courses through the men, an itch to launch an all out assault, firing tear gas canisters and flash bangs into the building, pumping shots into the hostage-takers as they skitter from the building like naked mole rats from a welding torch. They itch to be the hard rain that washes away the scum. Several canine unit guys have their German Shepherds leashed and frothing for bad guys to gnaw on like rawhides. An electricity arcs through the air from deputy to SWAT team member to canine unit.

"Give me fifteen minutes and I'll give you an answer." Grundish counts the men by the gate and along the wall, nineteen[44] of them that he can see, including Mojado. "I'm keeping track of how many of you are out there. I'm going inside for just a minute. When I come back, you all better

[44]Nineteen is the number of angels who are appointed as guardians of hell, according to the Qur'an, (Sura 74:30).

be there or the old lady gets it next. You be straight with me and we'll do the same with you."

"Everybody pull in," orders Mojado. "Everybody in now." The men resume their positions just outside the gate. "You have fifteen minutes to give us a hostage. If we don't have one of them out here, the negotiations are off. We will come at you with extreme prejudice, and we will do anything we can to stop you from harming the others."

Grundish runs from the oil drums and makes such a clatter. He throws open the roof hatch and slides down the ladder. His hands glide on the rails, and his feet do not touch the rungs on the way down. "Askew…Jerry…" he shouts. The names echo back at him from the metal walls and ceiling. "I need you guys here, now."

"They're trying to get things all set up, they are." Turleen hobbles around the corner of a stack of storage boxes. She holds an almost-spent Sordes Pilosus to her lips and takes one last hard drag on it.

"Where'd you get that?"

"You wouldn't believe me if I told you, you wouldn't."

"Well, you ain't supposed to be smoking. You only got one little burnt up lung left, and you can't afford to fry that one."

"Aw, honey, I appreciate the concern, I do," she says. "But you don't need to worry about me. I'm a staunch character, I am. S-T-A-U-N-C-H. And, I don't know that I'm gonna need that lung much longer the way things are looking. If those blue-boys out there come in, I think we're all done for, I do." She touches her hair as she speaks to him and adjusts something on her leg under her red dress.

"Well, uh, do you have any more smokes?"

"That was the last one, it was."

"Fuck!" His left eye throbs, shooting pain through to the back of his head each time it pulses. "Where are Jerry and Askew?"

"I'm right here," Jerry's voice says from around the corner, irritated. "What's going on? I told you to stay up there and stall them."

Grundish rounds the corner. Askew is holding Chancho's corpse steady on top of Alf the Sacred Burro while Jerry lashes the body to the donkey with duct tape. The jackass's legs tremble, and he hocks up bits and pieces of some previous meal. Grundish stares at the bizarre scene, unsure what to think. Alf tucks his ears back and hangs his head low. He dredges up a ripe throat turd and drops it on the floor in protest.

"Well, don't just stand there," says Jerry. "For he that gets hurt will be he who has stalled. What's so important that you had to come down here and leave your post?"

"They want a hostage. If we don't give one of you guys over to them, they're gonna storm the place."

"Then give 'em Dora and make some sort of lame request in exchange for her, like maybe ask for twenty supreme pizzas or something," says Jerry. Objections form on Askew's lips like a nascent cold sore but are not given the opportunity to fester and spread. "I know, Askew, you don't want to lose her. But if you let her go now, she can hook up with you once you're safe. Trust me on this if you want to get out of here alive. Plus, she's better off getting out of here. Do you really want her caught in the cross fire from those thugs out there?"

Askew shuts his slackened jaw and nods his concurrence.

"Okay," says Grundish. But, instead of moving he just stands and stares at the dead Mexican taped to his donkey friend.

"What are you waiting for boy? You don't get up there and talk to them now, they'll be shaking our windows and rattling our walls," barks Jerry. "Get moving. Now! You better start swimming, or you'll sink like a stone."

"All right, I'm moving," says Grundish as he turns. "But, that's a hell of a way to treat a donkey."

Crouched again behind the oil drums, Grundish counts the men near the front gate. Nineteen in all. "Okay," says Grundish into the bullhorn. "Mojado?"

"I'm here. And you can call me Piso."

"Mojado. We're gonna send out the whore. We got her ready to go. But I need you to do something for us."

"Give me your demands, and I'll run them up the chain of command."

"I'm gonna need two cases of Pabst Blue Ribbon (cold), a carton of Blue Llamas, a box of surgical gloves, and twenty supreme pizzas from Hungry Howie's – hold the olives."

Mojado looks over the top of his car to Detective Carter. Carter nods to him and points at his watch. "Okay," says Mojado, "it's going to take us a little while to get all of that together. Now, are you going to want any bread sticks or chicken wings with the pizza? Or maybe a couple of 2-liters of cola? They usually have pretty good package deals, and we might be able to scrounge up a couple of coupons."

"Just the pizza," answers Grundish.

"All right, then. You go ahead and send out the girl," says Mojado. "What's her name?"

"Her name is Dora. And I ain't sending her out until we have everything I just demanded." Grundish knows that he is risking blowing the deal but holds out to stall just a little longer, hopefully long enough to allow Jerry to orchestrate their escape.

Carter nods again at Mojado. Mojado calls a deputy over and puts his hand on the man's shoulder. After briefly conferring, the deputy gets in his cruiser and drives away. "Deputy Ceñal is on his way to the In-n-Out Mart, and we're phoning in the order to Hungry Howie's right now. It looks like we're gonna try to work together on this, right? I mean, we're going to give you what you want, and you're going to stay cool in there. Nobody else gets hurt. Right?"

"We don't want to hurt anybody," says Grundish. "We're cool. Just get us the stuff I asked for, and we'll send out the whore."

Forty-two minutes later: Deputy Ceñal returns, hauling an armful of cheap beer and a carton of Blue Llamas from his back seat. Ceñal sets everything down on the hood of Mojado's car.

"All right, Mr. Grundish," says Mojado into his handset, "we have your beer and cigarettes. The pizza is on the way. Can you come out and get your stuff?"

Grundish eyes the men at the gate. It still looks like the same amount of people. Everybody holding their position.

"I'm going to send the whore out to bring the beer and smokes back to us. I want you to carry everything through the gate, and put it on the ground about twenty feet away from the building. Go back to your position, and I will send the whore out to pick everything up for us."

Detective Carter nods his approval at Mojado. The mustachioed, bottom-heavy man hefts the beer and cigarettes and carries them past the gate, setting them twenty feet out from the building. He backs away again, his eyes fixed on the steel cans that conceal Grundish. A SWAT team sniper sets his sight one inch above the top of the oil drum that hides Grundish, ready to explode his skull with a burst of lead slugs in the event of any shenanigans or skullduggery.

Dora emerges from the front door of the building. Several of the officers with their sights trained on the door pull their guns down when they see that the young, sickly-skinny girl is not accompanied by either of her abductors. She reaches the beer and smokes and bends over, her rump facing the police, the bottom of her ass cheeks hanging just below the high cut fringed edges of her hiked-up jean shorts, showing a sweet crease of flesh where the rounded parts meet the thighs. Emaciated and clearly worn down by her short years, Dora's presentation still manages to draw curious glances from most of the posse.

Just inside the building, Askew opens the door for Dora, careful not to expose himself to the police. Once inside she sets down the goods and embraces her man. "I don't wanna leave you, Baby," she says, her eyes welling up with tears. "If they're gonna shoot you, I want to be here with you. Don't make me go out there." Her arms wrap around his body, fiercely gripping him, holding him tight to the moment.

"Baby Doll, you gotta do this," says Askew, reciprocating with a firm embrace, not wanting to let go. "There's two ways this can turn out for me. Either I get away and you join up with us later, or they put me in the marble orchard. 'Cuz they ain't takin' me alive. I can't spend the rest of my days in some prison, staring out at the real world through some *bob wire* fences." He kisses her forehead. "I think Jerry just may be able to get us out of here safely. But you gotta go along with the program. Otherwise we're both dead meat. And I can't have that. So give me one last kiss before you walk out the door. Give me something to hold as a *momento* until we see each other again."

The amplified voice of Detective Mojado, muffled by the building, interrupts them. "Mr. Grundish. We now have the pizza sitting just outside of the building for you. Please send the girl out to get the pizza. And then I trust that you will release her to us."

"Go get those pizzas, Baby," Askew peels Dora from his body. "I need you to go along with the plan. You understand?"

"Okay, Baby." She retrieves the pizzas and returns into the building. Askew relieves her of the boxes. Before he can say anything, Dora puts a suffocating squeeze on him, planting wet, warm kisses all about his face, crying, oozing briny tears. "Tell me this is gonna work out, Baby. Tell me it's gonna be okay."

"I love you," he says. "I never knew what that felt like before. But in these last couple of days, you've given me something I never understood before. I'm gonna fight like hell to get out of here and be with you." He returns her kisses. Sweaty forehead to forehead, pressed together, he tells her, "now get out there and make it look good."

And with that, Dora tosses the front door back and flees the building, crying, screaming. She flings herself against the barrel-like core of the officer closest to the gate and screams, "It was horrible! Just horrible! Please don't do anything to provoke them. If you cross them, those monsters'll kill those old folks in there." She buries her face into the officer's chest and weeps. The tears are deeply felt and sincere. Tears for her man. She bawls and blubbers and blows her nose on the officer's shirt, leaving a glimmering streak of hot snot. She weeps more and wipes her nose on his arm. "It was horrible. Just horrible."

The farrow of cops at the front gate wallow in muddled frustration – restless, smoking smokes, chawing chaw, shuffling their feet, waiting for the action. Askew scuttles along the edge of the roof, staying low, crouched and ready to drop into a defensive position if necessary. A demented squirrel skitters along behind at a safe distance, zigging with Askew's zigs, zagging with his zags. There are officers nowhere but at the front gate. As far as Askew can tell, the grounds are not surrounded. Much of the area outside of the perimeter of the property is overgrown scrub, vines, palmetto trees and *crotalus horridus*[45]. It would take a bulldozer or a well-fed crew of illegal aliens with sharpened machetes to cut a swath through the growth.

"Mr. Grundish," Mojado's voice blares through his public address system. "Thank you for working with us. We are taking the girl to the hospital to make sure she is okay. I need you to give me an update on the others. The girl told us that Mr. Mathers is your uncle and the elderly lady is Mr. Askew's aunt. Is that correct?"

Askew runs over and says to Grundish in a soft voice, "We told Dora to tell the police that Jerry and Turleen are both *captivated* and being mistreated by us. That way it still

---

[45]Timber rattlesnakes.

supposably gives us two hostages and keeps them in the clear if this goes bad."

"Mr. Grundish? Can you hear me?"

"Uh, yeah. Yeah. I can hear you. We got the old folks here, and we don't got no problem with capping 'em if you cross us."

"Okay. Okay. Listen," says Mojado, "we've been working together, right?"

"Yeah, I guess." Grundish sucks at his teeth, and thinks that one of the Pabst Blue Ribbons would sit just about right in his stomach.

"So, let's all stay calm. Now, you got what you wanted with the beer and pizza and smokes, right? We were honorable, weren't we?"

"Yeah, I suppose," Grundish allows. Askew pulls a fresh pack of Blue Llamas out of his pocket and hands it to him. Grundish takes a smoke and lights it, drawing hard on it. The throbbing in his eye lessens and then subsides, leaving the sclera feeling dried out and raw. Askew pulls a fag from his own pack and catapults it into his mouth.

"What I want to do, then, is hear the rest of your demands. You send out another hostage, and we'll see what else we can do for you."

"Tell 'em we want a dump truck, Uzis, and a garbage bag full of that Jell-O with the fruit salad suspended in it," says Askew.

"What for?" asks Grundish.

"To stall them. Jerry's just about ready to help us get outta here. We just need a little more time. And to make them think we're insane in the membrane, *Esse*."

Grundish addresses Mojado. "We ain't sending the old broad out right now. First you're gonna meet our new demands. Then we'll let her go."

"Tell me what you want, and I'll see what we can do?"

"First," says Grundish, "we want a dump truck with a full load of gravel in the back. And two Uzis with lots of extra ammo. And we want that Jell-O that has fruit salad suspended in it. I'm talking a shit load of the fruit Jell-O[46], like a garbage bag full."

"Let me run that by my superiors," says Mojado. "It may take a while to fill that order. Can you promise me to be calm and not do anything to those people in there while I see if we can meet your demands?"

"We'll give you one hour," says Grundish. "And then I can't promise you anything."

Forty minutes later: "Mr. Grundish, we are still working on your demands. Detective Carter says that we can get you the dump truck, but we're having trouble finding a load of gravel. It might have to be filled with rubber mulch."

"We want gravel," says Grundish.

"And as far as the Uzis, I think you're going to have to understand that they won't let me give you those. How about shotguns?"

Grundish stubs out his fourth smoke, grimaces, and wonders how long they can hold off an all-out assault.

---

[46]Contrary to popular belief, the gelatin in foodstuffs such as Jell-O, does not come from horse hooves. Horse hooves are made of keratin. Gelatin is made from collagen that is derived from cattle bones, cattle hides, and pigskins.

"Well, then you better talk to them about the fact that if you only give us part of what we're asking for, we'll only send out part of a hostage, maybe just a leg and some teeth."

"Just stay calm in there, Grundish. I will do my best to talk to Detective Carter but my hands are tied if he says no. And as far as the Jell-O, that takes at least an hour to make. With the amount you're requesting, it could take us a couple of hours. So you are going to need to stay calm and work with us. I'm doing everything I can to make you happy."

"Well, if I don't have my Jell-O, my dump truck, and the Uzis very soon, we're going to snuff out the oldies and come at you with our guns blazing."

Grundish descends the ladder into the building. The dark building. The warm, un-air-conditioned building. "What the fuck?" he says. "What's up with the lights?"

A flashlight peeks around the corner and shines into Grundish's eyes. It moves closer to him as he blocks the glare with his hand. "They shut the power off on us, they did," says Turleen, flashlight in one hand, half-full jug of wine in the other. "No phone, no lights, no air condition. Not a single luxury."

"Like Robinson Crusoe," agrees Grundish. "As primitive as can be. So they're starting to try to put the pressure on us now. Steam us out."

"It looks that way, it does."

Grundish stumbles his way toward Turleen, unable to see the ground, a moth to the light. Just around the corner, Askew sits on a wooden crate with a Pabst can clenched between his thighs while he stuffs the greater part of a piece of pizza into his mouth. Two battery-powered lanterns and several candles throw an orange glow about the room, mad dancing shadows settling here and there, illuminating Jerry, Chancho and Alf the Sacred Burro.

"What the fuck you doing?" says Grundish to Askew.

"I'm chowing on this pizza. It's killer. You ever had this shit with the garlic flavored crust. It kicks the turds out of Pizza Brothers. I'm gonna have to quit delivering there and get a job with Hungry Howie's." He drains the remaining fluid in the Pabst can and tosses it into a small-but-growing pile of empty cans in the corner.

"We need to stay sober," says Grundish. "Quit drinking that beer, and give me a piece of pizza."

"He's drinking up some courage," says Jerry, looking up from his work on the donkey. Chancho is firmly strapped to the miserable-looking ass. "The boy is shaking in his shoes. He needs a little liquid courage. And you might benefit from a little of that yourself. Go ahead and have one. You're gonna need it."

Grundish grabs a beer from the case beside Askew and pops the top. "All right," he says, and empties the contents of the can down his throat, not stopping to breathe. "There. Now tell me what we're gonna do. Askew says you have a plan. Please share it with me."

Jerry shuffles around the donkey, ignoring Grundish's question. Chancho's corpse is securely attached to Alf. The sacred burro shifts his weight from his left legs to his right, flashes a look of severe irritation, and shifts back again. Chancho's left arm is taped to the donkey's neck. The right arm is propped up in front of Chancho, just above Alf's head. Jerry places a Smith and Wesson .38 in Chancho's hand and duct tapes the fingers around the handle. In the dim lighting Chancho looks like a fierce armed bandito charging forward on a burro. Jerry unwraps a pack of Black Cat firecrackers and tapes them along the top of Chancho's arm. The fuse dangles just off of the dead man's rigor-mortis-locked elbow. Jerry tapes another strand of the fireworks to the shiny black hair on the back of Chancho's head, and two more down the cold stiff back of the rotting meat-form resting on the back of the burro. He twists the fuses together and turns toward Grundish.

"This here donkey and Mexican are two of the few people in this world I give a shit about. Chancho's dead and Alf is so old that he may as well be." Jerry scritches the donkey's head, Alf leans in toward the nails scraping at his scalp. "These two sorry specimens are gonna get you out of here."

"Mr. Jerry. With all due respect, how in the fuck can a sick donkey and a dead wetback get us out of this situation?"

"Son. Just get back up on the roof and stall a little bit more. Leroy over there knows the plan. He'll tell you what to do when the time comes."

Grundish turns his head toward his best friend. Askew chugs another beer, tilts his head back, and releases a deep, bellowing burp that flaps his lips and sprays a fine mist from his mouth.

"So, you're telling me we're fucked?" says Grundish. He grabs another beer and drains it with the ease of a seasoned binge-drinker.

"No," says Jerry, impatient with having to answer questions. "I'm telling you to shut up and go back onto the roof. Buy us another hour and you will be good to go." Grundish grabs three more beers and pauses, trying to think.

Jerry snaps his fingers at Grundish. "Just do as I say. Don't you realize that there must be some kind of way out of here? Well, there is. And I'm setting it up. So, just get up there on the roof and do as I say. Don't think twice, it'll be all right."

"Okay," says Grundish into the bullhorn. "I'm back. And your time is almost up. What's the deal with our demands?" Grundish cracks a warm beer and tilts it down his throat. The warm beer foams and expands halfway down, making for an aching trachea, stinging his epiglottis.

"I need you to be patient with us, Mr. Grundish," says Mojado. "I am working on everything for you. We have the dump truck with the gravel on the way. Detective Carter is running the request for the Uzis up the chain of command, and that looks like it's probably a go. But the Jell-O is slowing us up. We found a hospital cafeteria over in Brandon that can get us a full garbage bag of the fruity Jell-O. I'm sending one of my men to pick it up but it's going to take him at least an hour, maybe a little bit more, before he can be back here. At that point we should be good to go and you can send the elderly woman out."

Grundish finishes off the rest of his beer and lights a Blue Llama. "You have one hour," he says into the megaphone. His voice is gravelly from chain-smoking and slightly slurred from the rapid alcohol intake, making him sound rough and deranged. "One hour. No more extensions after that. If we don't have everything, including the fucking Jell-O, we kill another hostage. I'll do my best to work with you but after an hour, I can't promise you that I will be able to control Askew."

"We will have everything for you," says Mojado. "Just work with us. We don't want anybody else, including you and Mr. Askew, including my men, getting hurt."

"One more thing," barks Grundish into the megaphone. "I'm coming out in front of the building for just a minute. While I'm out there, Askew will be holding a gun loaded with hollow points to the old man's head. If there's any funny business, Askew will paint the wall with the old geezer's brains and then do the same to the old lady. Do you understand me?"

Mojado looks to Carter for confirmation and gets the nod. "You will have free passage in front of the building for the next five minutes."

Exiting the front door, Grundish can feel the sniper rifles trained on him without even looking. The burly tattooed hulk barely looks at the police as he plucks apples from the tree and dumps them into the bucket he carries. A scurvy black cat with a kinked tail rubs against Grundish's ankles and purrs as he collects the fruit. The cat chews on one of the sock garters and Grundish tries unsuccessfully to push it away with his leg. When the bucket is full he pushes the cat away with his foot and returns to the building. Grundish sits down on a crate in front of Alf the Sacred Burro and feeds the juicy, sweet fruit to the donkey.

"It's time for you fellas to go," says Jerry, interrupting a tender moment between Alf the Sacred Burro and Grundish. Alf sits back on his haunches like a dog, munching on the apples and presenting his head for scritching, trying to ignore the rotting dead man strapped to his back. Grundish feeds him apples and drains another beer.

"Where are we going?" Grundish rises to his feet and rests his hand on Alf's head.

"Leroy there knows what to do," says Jerry, nodding toward a passed-out Askew lying face-down amidst a scattering of empty Pabst cans, a burned-out cigarette wedged between his front teeth.

"He's wasted. Shit, not even conscious. How the hell is he supposed to tell me what to do?"

"Just wake him up, and drag him out of here," says Jerry. "Get him going, and he'll know what to do. It's time for you to go now before those coppers claim to have all of your demands. Because just when they make you think they've got everything, they're going to huff and puff and blow the place down. There'll be a battle outside a-raging."

Grundish tosses his floppy, drunk friend over his shoulder and follows Jerry and Turleen through the maze of rooms and storage boxes, past mother cats nursing their kittens, past overflowing litter boxes and bundled stacks of pornographic magazines, through a room populated with decapitated mannequins, the heads all lined up on a shelf and facing the wall. At the back of the building is a door. On the other side of the door is a corridor made from two rows of junked VW vans. The space between the vans is covered with rotting plywood, blocking out any view from above and letting only prying fingers of sunlight force their way past some of the holes and cracks where the wood has rotted through. At the end of the corridor is an opening.

Askew stirs on his friend's shoulder, struggling to get free of Grundish's grip. Grundish sets him down. Askew wobbles on his legs like a newborn colt. He leans against a decrepit van, tossing his head about like a dog shaking off water. "Where's Dora?" Askew says, looking suspiciously around.

"She's gone, Bro," says Grundish. "We got her out of here so she'd be safe. Traded her for pizza and beer. Remember?"

"Oh, yeah." Askew rubs at his inflamed eyes and shakes his head again. He pulls out a Blue Llama and lights it. "Yeah, that's right. For fuck's sake I hope she's all right."

"And we have to skedaddle, we do," interrupts Turleen. She tips her jug of wine and absorbs of the last drops of the vino.

"The lady is right," agrees Jerry. "The time is now. Do you remember the escape plan, Leroy?"

"Yeah, I remember now." Askew smiles his big gap-toothed grin. "I was just a little out of it. But now I'm back in it."

"Well, then get moving," says Jerry, nodding toward the opening at the end of the Volkswagen corridor. "If you boys stick around here any longer, you're going to get us all killed." He grabs Turleen by the wrist and pulls her close. Jerry has to contort his lank frame in an uncomfortable stoop in order to embrace her. He wraps his spindly arms around the red-headed octogenarian and kisses her on the neck, looking like a praying mantis wrapping its spiked forelegs around a beetle and readying to dine. His buck teeth lightly scrape the skin, shooting shivers down her back. "I'll come for you when it's safe," he says. "I promise you that."

Jerry releases Turleen from the embrace and turns back to Grundish and Askew. "You better take care of my lady," he says. "Just do as I've told Leroy and you should get out of this fine. And once you're clear of this area, just lay low. You'll do best for a while to not to show up on the street, unless you wanna draw the heat. Just jump down a manhole and light yourself a candle, if you know what I mean."

And they did know what he meant.

"Look, Mr. Mathers," says Grundish, "I just wanna say thanks and that we never meant to cause…"

"No time for teary goodbyes, Grundish," says Jerry, slapping him on the back. "Turleen is right. You need to scoot now. By my estimate, you've got about fifteen minutes before the fecal matter hits the air redistribution device, and you all need to be as far away as possible."

The VW corridor leads them through a break in the cinder-block wall that surrounds the compound. The gaping orifice at the end of the tunnel spills them out like effluence from a sewer drain pipe, dumping Grundish,

Askew, and Turleen into a tangle of vines, palmettos, and live oak trees blanketed in a stifling cover of Spanish moss. A low, narrow clearing is cut through the overgrown undergrowth. Askew, now awake and sober enough to carry himself, leads the way, running and stumbling through the jungle-like foliage, tripping over roots and rocks now and again and springing right back up to continue the churning and burning of his legs.

Turleen, with her still-swollen ankle, allows herself to be cradled in Grundish's arms as he carries her through the forest. Grundish charges forward, bent over in order to avoid getting his head caught in the mess of vines and branches just above him, occasionally taking a stinging whack in the face from branches snapping back into place in Askew's wake.

Askew leads them, thumping and bumping along the swath cut through the dense vegetation. Out of breath and sweating profusely, they stop as the undergrowth tunnel opens to a clearing. The afternoon sun bakes their already red and sweaty faces. Askew steps slowly toward a car covered with a camouflage tarp. He throws back the cover and squeals like a happy little girl.

"Fu-huck yeah!" says Askew, pulling a set of keys from his pocket. "Jerry told me there'd be wheels here. He said it'd be juiced up and ready to rock. He didn't say it'd be this." In the center of the clearing sits a gleaming, jet-black '72 El Camino SS, flames painted on the hood, mag wheels, and jacked up in the rear like a thick-bodied booty dancer. Chrome silhouettes of well-stacked naked ladies pose provocatively on the mud flaps. In the bed is an untouched case of Olde Frothingslosh[47], the steel rims on the cans slightly rusted. "Good God. It's a '72 El Camino SS. V-8 engine. Fucking turbo-charged automatic beast."

"I think that beer there may be from '72, too, I do," says Turleen.

"I don't know about all the automotive shit. But it looks good to me. Maybe things are starting to go our way," says Grundish. He sets Turleen down just in time to turn and catch the beer can projectile tossed at him by Askew.

"I think I'm gonna need one of them there brewskies, too, I do." Grundish pulls the tab on his and hands it to Turleen. He grabs another can for himself.

"Well, let's chug these down and then get the fuck out of Dodge," says Askew, pulling the tab on his can.

Turleen holds her can up for a toast. "Through the teeth, over the gums, look out stomach, here it comes, it does." They clink their cans together and upend them, spilling half of the skunk-piss-tasting contents down their throats and the rest on their faces and necks. The beer is chunky, hot, metallic and nearly flat, but it tastes like freedom.

"I'm gonna give you the keys," says Askew to Grundish. "I'm still too fucked up to drive. And we don't need to be getting picked up because I'm swerving us all over the road."

"Well, you two cram in the passenger seat, and let's get the fuck out of here."

---

[47]Olde Frothingslosh, the pale stale ale with the foam on the bottom. Brewed by the Pittsburgh Brewing Company. Guaranteed to fit any shape glass.

Grundish turns the ignition. The engine sputters a sickly wheeze and craps out. He questions the engine again and gets the same answer. "Shit! Fuck! Damn!" he shouts at the car and smacks it on the dashboard. He tries the ignition again and the engine roars to life, a low-pitched heavy metal growl that the men feel in their testicles. "Ayyy," says Grundish, cracking a smile and holding both thumbs up in approval. "Let's make like a banana and split, mother fuckers."

They drive out on a dirt road and don't hear the cacophony of explosions and gunfire back at Jerry's building. They turn onto the paved road, following the directions given to Askew by Jerry. Off to the side of the road a group of turkey vultures gathers in a circle, their hooked ivory beaks tearing into a roadkill armadillo, pecking at each other and making easy work of dismantling the creature.

"Mr. Grundish," says Mojado over the loudspeaker of his cruiser, "please return to the roof. We need to discuss your demands." The speaker cracks and feeds back, screeching painfully in the ears of the cops near the car.

Grundish does not return to the roof. Grundish does not speak over the bullhorn. He makes no further demands, nor any additional threats to the wellbeing of the hostages. Grundish is gone from the building, dumping botulism-tainted hot beer down his throat and getting ready to load into a souped-up El Camino.

"Mr. Grundish, we have all of your demands and need to speak with you." A dump truck loaded with gravel backs up to the gate of the property. Three heavily-armed officers lie still, just inches under the surface of the gravel. Mojado grabs a yard waste bag full of fruity Jell-O from Officer Finn and holds it up for anyone on the roof to see. The Jell-O is laden with large enough doses of chloral hydrate[48] to temporarily put Grundish and Askew into comas. "We have everything you've asked for and we are going to need you to send out another hostage."

The absent-Grundish still does not answer. A chill of unease runs through the men. Deputies, SWAT members and the jumpsuit-clad posse all take positions behind cars and the fence, pointing rifles and handguns toward the front of the building.

Detective Carter nods at Mojado.

"Mr. Grundish," says Mojado over his loud speaker again, "we are going to give you two minutes to answer us. We have been working with you. But, if you do not answer, we will storm the building and take you dead or alive. You have two minutes, beginning now."

Inside the building, Jerry feeds Alf the Sacred Burro one last apple and scritches his friend on the head. The

---

[48]The familiar term *Slipping a Mickey* refers to the practice of secretly dosing a person's drink with chloral hydrate in order to incapacitate the person. The terms Mickey and Mickey Finn (the drink in which the drug has been placed) are likely derived from Michael "Mickey" Finn, a Chicago bartender for the Lone Star Saloon and Palm Garden Restaurant. In the early 1900s Finn was accused of slipping knock-out drops into the drinks of customers known to have money, having the incapacitated patrons of his establishment dragged to a back room where they would be divested of their belongings, and then dumping the victims into the back alley.

moribund donkey coughs up a lump onto the floor. He rubs the side of his face against Jerry's hand and looks at him with a sparkle in his eyes.

"*Mis amigos*, it looks like our time together is over on this plane. You've been good friends. " Jerry kisses Chancho on top of what's left of his head and slaps him on the shoulder lightly. He kisses Alf the Sacred Burro on his puke-stinking prehensile lips. The coarse hairs around the donkey's mouth tickle Jerry and remind him of an incident which would be better off forgotten, an incident involving large quantities of tequila and a bisexual Kenny Rogers impersonator. Jerry gently and lovingly slaps at the donkey's face. His eyes mist up as he stands straight and chokes back the emotions, saying to his friends, "If you find yourself alone, riding in a green field with the sun on your face, don't be troubled. For you are in Elysium and you are already dead."

Alf snorts in a way that almost seems to be a chortle. Chancho sits still on the donkey's back unable to form a smile on his non-existent face.

"Brothers," says Jerry, "just remember, death is not the end. For what we do in life echoes in eternity."

Outside, the voice of Detective Piso Mojado barks out a final warning. "Mr. Grundish. Mr. Askew. You have one minute to acknowledge me. If you do not respond, we come in and get you. One minute!" The men around Mojado are crouched behind their cars, muscles tensed, safety mechanisms undone on their guns, fingers on triggers, eyes focused on the front door and the roof, minds and weapons set for the kill. Off to Mojado's left, behind the fence, an assault-team member cracks the barrel of a grenade launcher and loads a tear gas canister into it, snaps the barrel back into position and undoes the safety latch. He aims it at the roof. On the other side of the gate another officer loads a flash-bang canister in a similar launcher in order to stun the hostage-takers.

One long fuse dangles from the fireworks strapped to Chancho's back. Jerry sprays a can of charcoal fluid on the rear of Chancho's head, strikes a blue-tip match against the door, and lights the fuse, waiting as it nears the first string of Black Cats. Seconds before the firecrackers explode, Jerry throws back the front door and whacks the donkey on the ass with his bony hand. Alf the Sacred Burro bounds through the door. The fireworks explode and the charcoal fluid ignites, prompting the donkey and his deceased, gun-wielding, flaming-headed passenger, to leap straight up into the air. They land and charge in a zigzag bucking trend toward the front gate, right at the cops in their way.

After applying his hand forcefully to Alf's backside, and just before the fireworks begin, Jerry sprints back into the building, his gawky legs high-stepping it toward the bowels of the warehouse, knees pumping chest-high, hoping to have enough steel walls between him and the sure-to-be oncoming barrage of bullets to keep his body from being perforated by hot lead slugs. Turning one corner, and then another, and safely out of danger of being shot, Jerry hears a fusillade of gunfire erupt and shots slamming into the metal walls of his building. He runs faster, shutting and locking doors behind him, until he reaches his living room and intentionally runs head first into a wall, knocking himself unconscious.

Having recently honed their marksman skills on an allegedly armed arrest-resistor, the officers outside of the gate are excellent shots. As Alf charges the police, Detective Carter calls down a curtain of fire on the flaming, burro-riding maniac coming at them head-on with his guns seemingly blazing. Chancho, his black hair throwing off great thick trails of flame, putrid charred flesh coughing out streams of dense black smoke from his head, looks like a demon horseman charging up through the ground from the depths of Hades. Carter's men, practiced, accurate, and unduly violent, entirely and surgically remove the top half of the Mexican's corpse from Alf the Sacred Burro with almost no injury to the ass. By the time the officers, SWAT team members, and camouflage-jumpsuit deputies have exacted their meat grinder onslaught of bullets on Chancho and ceased fire, Alf stands still, ten feet from the gate, with his head slung low. Chancho's pathetic remains played the part of a target until there was nothing left of him from the waist up and a semi-circle of gore and gristle spread out to the rear of Alf. Alf raises his head, dredges up a massive vomit-shit log and, with a cough, propels it out several feet in front of him. Aside from one small-caliber shot to his right rear quarter, Alf is undamaged.

Explosions erupt as flashbang grenades and teargas canisters are fired into the open front door of the building. The men strap on gas masks and bum rush the front door of the building, giving a wide berth to the sick donkey with half of a dead Mexican duct-taped to his body. Alf sits, leaning toward the uninjured side of his rear end, and begins to chew at the tape that holds Chancho's legs to his midsection.

"You sure this is what he said to do?" The El Camino weaves through back roads, circumnavigating the beehive they had likely kicked over in Bartow, and finds its way heading west on country roads toward Hillsborough County again.

"Yeah, positive."

"It don't seem right."

"Well, *evidentually* Jerry knows what he's doing. He got us out of a pretty bad situation back there. I think he's gotta know what he's talking about when he tells us to go back toward Tampa and lay low. He gave me directions." Askew pulls a pack of Blue Llamas from his shorts. He takes out two smokes and lights them, handing one to Grundish. Tucked into one of his sock garters is a folded-up piece of notebook paper. He retrieves the sweat-stained note. Unfolding the page, he studies Jerry's handwritten directions. "He's got another place for us to lam it until he can come get us. And it ain't exactly Tampa. It's in Ruskin. Maybe this place won't be as *luxuriant* as the one we just left, but *supposably* it's pretty safe and secure."

"It just seems kind of risky going right back into the area where they're looking for us."

"You pipe down," says Turleen, her voice slightly garbled from the alcoholic slurry creeping and seeping its way through her digestive tract, leaking the central nervous system depressant into her blood. "Jer Bear knows his onions, he does. He got you'se guys out of that hubbub back there, he did. Jer Bear says that if we go anywhere else, you boys are gonna draw attention to yourselves, do something stupid, just like you been doing all along. Listen to Jerry and we'll make it out of this, we will. And by the way, give me that fag. I'm gonna do some living, I am." She plucks the smoldering Blue Llama from Askew's mouth and places it to her lips. The smoke rushes down into her brown, feeble lung and sends nicotine throughout her system, increasing her heartbeat and breathing, releasing dopamine into the pleasure center of her brain, putting a soft smile on her wrinkled face.

"Come on, Turleen," Askew protests. "You know you shouldn't be doing that." He reaches for the cigarette, but Turleen holds it out of his reach and smacks his arm away with her free hand.

"Leroy, you don't know nothin' from nothin', you don't. You drag me along on this crazy caper. We just narrowly avoided getting into what would have been a losing firefight with a hoard of inbred redneck police. I don't know what's gonna happen to us next. I'm going to live like it's my last days, I am. So don't you give me no guff about one little smoke."

"Fine." Askew screws his mangled face up into a pout. "But you don't get no more smokes. Your habit gets out of control fast and I'm gonna *nip it in the butt* right now, before you get yourself addicted again."

"Fair enough, Fella," she agrees, tapping her ashes out of the cracked window. "But you could let me enjoy this one without giving me the business, you could. And you could open me another one of those chunky beers too, if you don't mind."

Askew pulls the tabs on several Olde Frothingslosh cans and hands them out to Grundish and Turleen. "You know, I been thinking about that promise you made me," he says to Grundish, changing from the touchy subject with Turleen. "You know, the one about if it looks like I'm gonna go to prison?"

"Yeah," says Grundish. "I don't really wanna talk about that right now. I know I made the promise and I'll keep it, okay? Just don't bring me down with that shit right now." Grundish shifts his body and pulls at the Colt Anaconda, removing the uncomfortable hunk of metal from his waistband and setting it on the console between the car's bucket seats.

"No, listen. I'm not gonna bring you down. I think we're gonna get out of this shit. But if we don't…"

"Quit talking your shit, and let me drive." Grundish turns on the radio, flips through the dial and stops on *Flirtin' with Disaster*. He turns up the volume to drown out Askew. "Fucking-A right, Molly Hatchet!" He beats rhythm on the steering wheel with one hand and tries to ignore Askew.

Askew turns the song down and stares at Grundish. "I'm serious, Grundish. I gotta tell you this. I've changed my mind. Things have changed. I want to take it all back. If it looks like we're gonna be caught, I don't mind going to prison. I think I can do it. I've got Dora. I'll draw strength from her. She'll stay with me no matter what. I ain't never felt this way in my life before. It seems like prison would be tolerable, as long as I have Dora."

"You know they don't let you have no conjugal visits in Florida prisons, don't you?"

"Whattaya mean?" Askew fumbles at his pack of Blue Llamas for another smoke. A look of concern washes over his face.

"I mean, no sex. Even if you get married to Dora. Your relationship will have to be more on a spiritual level, if you know what I mean."

"No conjugal visits? You serious?"

"Seriously, Bro. I mean, once a week she could give you quickie handjobs in the visitor's park if you don't mind covertly spooging all over yourself while some kid is visiting with his dad at the next table. And as long as you can be inconspicuous enough that the guards don't notice."

"Seriously?"

"No shit, Brother. And if the guards catch her giving you a dishonorable discharge, they'll throw you in the hole and cut off her visitation."

"Well, I don't give a shit. I take it back. My request is hereby revoked. You don't have permission to put me out of my misery even if it does look like we're gonna go down for this shit."

"Good," says Grundish sharply.

"Good," retorts Askew.

"I wasn't never gonna do it anyway." He turns up the music again. The opening riff of *Gator Country* kicks in. "Fuck yeah, two-fer-Tuesday Hatchet."

Askew turns the volume down again. "Now, that's a shitty thing to say."

"What? I like Hatchet. You gonna start blowing me shit about that."

"No. I mean that you were never gonna do it anyway. You, *supposably* my best friend, made me a fucking promise. And now you tell me you were never going to honor it. That's just plain old shitty, Brother."

"Oh, shut the fuck up," says Grundish. "I can't win with you. You're worse than a bitch. Next thing you know, you're gonna start arguing with me about something I said last month that hurt your feelings." He turns the music up again.

Askew stares out the window, stewing, gritting his teeth. "Pull over," he says. "I need to get out."

"Come on. Don't go getting all huffy on me. We gotta keep moving."

"No, seriously. Pull over. I have to go to the bathroom something fierce."

"You can hold it, you can," says Turleen. "I have to go, too, but you don't see me giving in to my weak old bladder, you don't. You need to just put your fingers in your pocket and pinch it or something."

"I ain't fucking kidding. And I don't have to bleed my lizard. I'm talking about feeling a major shit storm brewing in my tropical zones. If you don't pull over now, I'm gonna drop mud in my drawers, and we're all gonna have to marinate in my stink. Otherwise I need to get out about two minutes ago…"

Before Askew can finish his sentence, the El Camino is at a full stop on the shoulder of the road; a cloud of dust and burnt-rubber-smoke briefly envelopes the car. Askew tosses Turleen from his lap onto Grundish and ejects himself from the car, sprinting for the woods at the side of the road, his pants already dropping and exposing his pale, hairy ass as he disappears into a copse of oak trees.

"Well I might as well go and cop a squat myself," says Turleen, disentangling herself from Grundish and letting herself out through the passenger door. "My old bladder can't hold out much longer anyway, it can't." She opens the glove compartment and finds one oil-stained napkin. "I guess this is gonna have to do for me, it is."

Grundish lays his head back against the back of his seat and closes his eyes. The stress of the day, the beer, the hot sun, and then a silent moment. He shuts his eyes and momentarily allows himself to drift off, expecting Askew or Turleen to rouse him upon their return.

"Hey! Boy! Hey!" The sound of metal tapping on the roof of the El Camino wakes Grundish from his catnap. He reluctantly shakes of the sleep. "Hey, Boy! You need to step out of the car with your hands up." A round face with a well-trimmed mustache and mirrored aviator sunglasses has words coming out of its mouth and they seem to be directed toward Grundish. One of the arms that is attached to the body of the cop-face holds a service revolver, pointing it directly at Grundish's head. The portly deputy's name is Henry Pingle. "If you make any sudden moves, I will splatter you all over the inside of that beautiful classic automobile."

Raising his hands and turning his head directly toward the source of the threat, Grundish realizes that he is facing a Hillsborough County deputy. With one hand still pointing the barrel of the gun at Grundish's head, Pingle opens the driver-side door and steps back, allowing Grundish room to exit the car.

"I don't want no trouble, Officer," says Grundish, holding his hands in front of him, palms out, and stepping out of the car. He towers over the cop but tries to make no threatening moves. "I was just taking a nap here on the side of the road. I worked a late shift last night and I'm tuckered out. Thought it's better to be safe and take a little snooze instead of falling asleep while I'm driving."

"You go to work looking like that, Boy? Where you work?"

Grundish looks down at his clothes: blood-stained shirt and shorts, sandals and sock garters. He has not brushed his matted hair or groomed his beard in days, leaving him looking like some sort of demented homeless person or a musician. "Yeah. I work at a slaughter house. I still haven't even cleaned up yet. Listen, I ain't looking for no trouble officer. I just want to go home and go to bed."

"You think I'm a God-damned fool, do ya? You think I don't know who you are?" He steps back several feet from the Grundish towering over him, out of the big man's shadow. "You one of those boys we been looking for. We been looking all over for you and your buddy."

"I'm afraid I don't know what you're talking about, sir. I ain't done nothing wrong. I just wanna go home." He takes one step toward the officer. "I'm tired, and I wanna go to bed."

"Hold it right there!" screams the cop. "No closer!" He jams the gun in the air at Grundish. "Get down on the ground! Face down! And put your arms behind your back! You make any quick moves, and I'll shoot you. Try anything funny, and I'll shoot you. Give me the stink eye, and I'll shoot you. In case you can't tell, I'm looking for an excuse to shoot you, Boy."

"Fuck," is all that Grundish says, nothing more. The word leaks out like the hiss from a deflating tire and drops to the ground in front of him. He goes through a familiar dance with the officer, raises his arms above his head, drops to his knees, lowers himself to his stomach and puts his hands on the back of his head. With Pingle's knee in the small of his back, Grundish feels the clacking of metal as the handcuffs are placed too tightly on his wrists, securing his thick arms behind his back.

"You stay right there, face down," says the cop. He backs away from Grundish and toward his cruiser. "I'm going to my car. And guess what I'm going to do if you so much as start to wiggle around?"

"I'm guessing you're going to shoot me."

"You're not as dumb as you look, Boy. Now just stay there." He reaches in his cruiser and grabs the radio handset, mumbling something under his breath into the microphone.

"Put the radio thingy down and move away from your car!" Askew materializes from the patch of oak trees with one arm wrapped around Turleen's neck and the other arm out of sight, just behind her back. "Do it now, or I blow this old bag's innards right out through her belly button and mess up her pretty red dress."

Pingle's eyes burn behind his mirrored shades. He drops the handset and swings his gun in Askew's direction, and then back toward Grundish. "I have my sight locked on your buddy's head," he screams at Askew. "Drop your gun and let the lady go."

"Fuck that shit, Fat Boy!" Askew, his eyes throwing off sparks of madness, continues to advance deliberately toward Pingle. "I ain't got nothin' to lose at this point. You go ahead and shoot my friend. I'll just plug this irritating old bitch full of lead and then start blazing at you."

"Please! Mister, please! Do what he says!" Turleen begins to weep, her cries verge on hysteria. Her raspy voice cracks with emotion. "The man is crazy! I've already seen him kill three people, I have! If you don't do what he says, he'll kill me, he will!"

Pingle's head swivels on his neck back and forth between Askew and Grundish while his gun stays trained on the man face-down on the ground. Askew stops just on the other side of the cruiser.

"I'm gonna count to three," says Askew. "And if you haven't dropped your gun nice and slowly, I'm gonna paint your car with this old bitch's guts. One…"

"Please! Mister, please! He'll do it, he will…"

"Two…"

Pingle's head swivels back and forth and his features go slack. "Okay," he shouts. "Okay. I'm gonna set my gun down and step away from my car. Don't do anything crazy." He sets his revolver on top of the cruiser and steps backwards from the car, holding his hands up in front of him.

"Good," says Askew. "Now go over there, real nice and slow, and undo the handcuffs on my friend."

Pingle slowly moves toward Grundish and undoes the cuffs. Grundish stands and brushes away the gravel stuck to his forehead and cheeks.

Askew stays behind Turleen, his flabby forearm unintentionally wrapped too tightly around her throat, her face turning red from the limited air intake. "Now give my friend your handcuff keys, and then get over here and lay face-down on the ground in front of your car."

Pingle lies face down in front of the cruiser and begins to sniffle and convulse, trying to hold back the tears. "Please don't kill me," he begs. "Please. I have a wife and kids. They need me. Please don't kill me."

"Shut up, you Fucker," says Grundish.

"Yeah," says Askew. "Don't have a fucking *Grandma* seizure."

Grundish drops one knee solidly in the center of Pingle's back and slaps a handcuff on one of his wrists. He works the other cuff behind and then over the top of the cruiser's steel bumper, fastening the remaining cuff to Pingle's other wrist, chaining him to the front of the car. Grundish rounds the front of the cruiser and retrieves Pingle's gun from the roof. The steel on the gun is already hot from soaking up the sun. Grundish grabs the keys from the ignition and puts them in his pocket. He rips the radio handset from the car and flings it toward the oak trees on the side of the road. The curled cord of the handset catches and wraps around a high branch, dangling out of reach. With the revolver, he shoots one of the rear tires flat.

"Let's go," says Grundish. They all run to the El Camino.

"Just a second," says Askew. He turns and runs back to Pingle. Askew grabs the mirrored shades from Pingle's face and puts them on. "Now listen up, pardner," he says to Pingle, hooking his thumbs in his pants' pockets. "I don't like the way you was treating my friend back there. I'd file a formal brutality complaint against you if I had the time. But I'm in a hurry so I'm just gonna have to take matters into my own hands." Askew grabs Pingle's pepper spray from his belt and blasts the deputy's face with a thick fog of Oleoresin Capsicum. Before he realizes what he is doing, Askew begins slamming the bottom of his sandals against Pingle's back, his legs pumping violently and snapping ribs like twigs.

"Come on! Now!" shouts Grundish to Askew, pulling him away from the injured Pingle. "You're fucking losing it, again. He was on the radio and probably called in for backup. We need to quit fucking around and get out of here, now."

Askew throws the aerosol can at Pingle, bouncing it off of his head and tells the deputy, "you're lucky we're in a hurry, Fucker." They run for the El Camino once again and dive in. Askew scoots in and works his way under Turleen. Before he can even get himself situated and close the door, the El Camino spews a stinging shower of gravel from its back wheels at Pingle.

Askew shuffles around in the car, situating Turleen on his lap. When he finally gets comfortable, Askew looks up and is startled by the cross look on Turleen's face. She cocks her elbow and drives it backward into his nose. Flashes of light and stars float before his eyes and blood begins to trickle onto his lip. "That's for calling me an irritating old bitch and choking me too hard back there, it is" says Turleen. She grabs a Blue Llama from the pack on the dashboard and eyeballs Askew, daring him to challenge her. "Otherwise, Leroy, you did a fine job of getting us out that mess without even having a gun, you did."

The whirring of helicopters and the warbling of police sirens call out to them from somewhere in the distance.

Grundish jams the accelerator pedal to the floor, and the g-force pulls them back into their seats. The El Camino barrels down the middle of the two-lane country road. The sounds of sirens and choppers grow louder.

"You still know where we're going?" asks Grundish.

"Yeah. We're headed the right way."

"They're gonna have a BOLO[49] out for us. That cop back there called in on his radio after he cuffed me. This area's gonna be crawling with pigs."

"Well, we can just find out where they are, then." Askew flips on the police scanner and smiles. "Jerry set this car up for getting away. Let's just take a listen and see what we're facing."

The scanner crackles with the excited chatter of the Hillsborough County Sheriff's patrol cars. *El Camino west bound on 674…Suspects armed and dangerous…One hostage…Road blocks being set up at Route 37, Route 39, Balm Road and Highway 301.*

"Are there any crossroads out this way that we can turn off?" Grundish asks Askew.

"It's been a while since I been out this way but I don't think so. Just the roads where they got the blockades set up."

---

[49]Be on the lookout.

"We have to do something, we do," says Turleen. "Turn off onto the next dirt road you see. We're going to have to get this hay-burner off the road, we are. We can sit it out in the woods until the coast is clear, we can." She grabs another Blue Llama and lights it butt-to butt-with her old smoke.

"She's right," agrees Grundish. He slows the car down to forty and lets it creep down the road as he works through the situation in his head. "We can't go back or we'll run into those cars that we're hearing back there behind us. And if we keep going straight, we're going to run right into it, too. And if there ain't no crossroads, we got no choice but to find a dirt road or just off-road it."

The *thwap-thwap-thwap* of a helicopter's blades chopping and displacing the air becomes suddenly more noticeable. Askew looks out the rear window and sees a small dot in the sky moving rapidly in their direction. "Aww, fuck!" Askew beats his hand against the door, each smack on the door accentuating his monosyllabic mantra. "Fuck!" (smack) "Fuck!" (smack) "Fuck!" (smack) "Fuck!" (smack). "Fuck!"

"What's happening?"

"They're behind us. There's a chopper closing in. If they haven't *holmed* in on us yet, they're going to any minute now."

Turleen sucks hard at her smoke, burning it down quickly with her one gimp lung. She exhales a dense cloud of smoke and flicks her butt out the window. "We need to get off this road now, we do. There's a trail right up there." She points off to the right with one big-knuckled, crooked finger. Like a bony, misshapen divining rod, her digit indicates the spot where they need to turn.

With the fat and fiery center of the solar system paused and squatting itself directly above the souped-up El Camino, Grundish pulls off of the paved road and onto the gravel path winding into the woods. The overgrown gravel road leads to, and ends at, a thick copse of live oak trees that blocks out the sky above them.

"I guess this is as good as it's gonna get unless we want to get out and try to go somewhere on foot," says Grundish. He grabs the Colt Anaconda, steps out of the car, and looks skyward. "These trees'll block the copter's view of us. And if that chopper pilot didn't see us out there, then we might be able to just sit things out right here."

Askew and Turleen both exit the car, both lighting up new cigarettes.

"Give me one of those, too," says Grundish to Askew. Askew slides a pack of Blue Llamas over the top of the car. "Fuck. I picked the wrong day to quit smoking."

"Looks like I picked the right day to resume smoking, it does." Turleen's shaky hand brings her cigarette up to her mouth. The shaking subsides a little while she draws in more smoke.

"She's right," says Askew, his voice high and tense. He paces in a circle, his hands twitching wildly in front of him, a hurky-jerky accentuation of his panicked rant. "We're fucked here! We're trapped, and we ain't got nowheres to go if they saw us come in here! If we go out to the road, they'll find us! If we go back out into view, they'll find us! And if they saw us come in here, we're sitting *ducts*!"

"Don't go getting all bent outta shape yet," says Grundish, his voice low and maybe too calm. "We don't know if they saw us. That helicopter was way the fuck back there. He probably didn't even notice us. We was probably too far away to be seen."

"Well, we noticed him, we did."

"I know," agrees Grundish. "But that chopper is loud and draws your attention. He wouldn't have heard our car and maybe he didn't notice us. We're just going to have to sweat it out here and hope they don't find us."

The trees' canopy blocks out the sunlight and tints everything beneath it with a soft blue hue. From the distance come the sounds of the helicopter, of sirens, of men shouting and dogs barking. Grundish turns his head toward the road and listens.

Askew says, "Grundish."

"What?"

"This is all my fault. Like I told you before, I fucked up. Ain't you gonna *landblast* me or somethin'?"

"What are you talking about?" asks Grundish.

"You know. Like you done before." He deepens his voice and does an off-the-mark impersonation of Grundish. "'God damn, Askew, I'm always having to watch out for you and clean up your messes' and, 'man it would be so much easier if I didn't have to deal with all this bullshit sometimes.'"

"Jesus Christ, Askew," sighs Grundish. "There you go acting like a bitch again. I say something to you one time out of frustration and you commit every word of it to memory and drag it out later to make me feel bad. I suppose you ain't gonna give me no pussy for a month, too."

"Well, ain't you gonna say none of that mean stuff?"

"Sure," says Grundish, his tone monotonous and empty. "You are always trying to fuck up my shit. If I didn't have to deal with your messes, my life would be so easy." He stops and listens to the noise of the men and dogs getting closer. The sirens and the chopper sound as if they are just outside of the grouping of trees. "Fuck. I can't do this."

"What?" asks Askew. "Ain't you gonna give me no more hell?"

"No," says Grundish. "No, I ain't. You'll just use it to emotionally manipulate me later."

"Well, I can go away. I could find my way south and live in the swamps. Build myself a little hut or something."

Grundish shakes his head slowly. "No," he says. "I want you to stay with me. You're like my brother. I ain't gonna have you going off into the swamps."

Askew narrows his eyes and says to Grundish, "Tell me like you done before."

"Tell you about what?"

"You know. About guys like us. About the ladies."

Grundish says, "all right. Guys like us, you know, the ones that work the shit jobs and scrape by, are the loneliest guys in the world. Can't keep jobs. Don't fit in. They ain't got nobody in the world that gives a sideways fuck about them..."

"Not us, though," says Askew, flashing a busted smile. "Tell me about us."

Grundish is quiet for a moment. He grabs a Blue Llama from inside the El Camino and lights it. He takes hit and exhales a bluish plume of smoke. "Not us, though," says Grundish.

"Because..."

"Because I got you and..."

"And I got you. We got each other, man. And we give a sideways fuck about each other," Askew bursts out triumphantly.

A breeze blows through the live oaks, making the Spanish moss dangling from the limbs dance above them. The sirens, chopper, barking dogs and shouting men grow louder, much closer than before.

"It sounds like they're coming this way, it does," says Turleen. "We gotta get outta here." She limps toward the edge of the woods and looks into the distance behind them to see if the police are heading their way.

Ignoring Turleen, ignoring the sounds of choppers, sirens, dogs and shouting men, Askew says, "Tell me about the ladies, Grundish."

Grundish cocks his head and listens to the sounds getting closer to them. "Okay," he says. "Look out at that pond across the way, Askew, and I'll tell you. I'll tell you so good that if you close your eyes you'll be able to see it."

Looking out past the trees, past a flat open area of ground, Askew stares off at the pond and a flock of roseate spoonbills splashing in the pooled water. Turleen continues looking back the way they came, scanning the road for the police.

Grundish raises his gun and his hand shakes. He drops his hand toward the ground again. His eyes flood with tears that silently roll down his cheek. Grundish weeps for the end of innocence, for the darkness of his own heart, for his true and dear friend, Askew.

"Go on," says Askew, still staring toward the pond. "How's it gonna be. We're gonna get a boat. A real big boat, like a yacht. Right?"

"That's right. Maybe bigger," said Grundish. "And we're gonna get a stable of hookers, and maybe some hydroponic equipment to grow weed."

"And tell me what we're gonna do, Grundish. Tell me about the hookers again. About the international waters. And the hookers, like how they'll all have big fake titties and whatnot."

"Well, we'll grow weed, have hookers, maybe some other shit that ain't legal here."

"And I get to be in charge of the ladies. Me and Dora, right?"

"Yeah, you're in charge of the ladies."

Askew giggles. "And we'll live off the fat of their asses." He starts to turn back toward Grundish.

"No, Askew. Look down at the pond. Look past the pond and past the trees. Look past all of that until you can see our boat floating out in the international waters."

Askew obeys him. Grundish looks down at the gun.

"I see 'em coming down the road, I do," shouts Turleen. "They're a comin', they are." She tilts her head up and sees the helicopter drop out of the sky and hover above the main road. Grundish turns his head and looks in Turleen's direction.

"Just stay over there and keep an eye out for us," says Grundish to Turleen.

Askew still stares out past the pond and past the trees, straining his eyes to see their yacht swaying with the waves of the ocean. "Go on, Grundish. Tell me when we're gonna do it."

"We're doing it soon."

"Me and you. You and me."

"That's right. Me and you. It's all gonna be good. No more Fuckers. No more hassles. We're gonna be living the dream."

"I thought you was mad at me, Grundish."

"No, Askew. God damn. No. I ain't never really been mad at you. And I ain't pissed off now. I want you to understand that."

The men and the dogs are close. The chopper moves in toward the trees.

"Let's do it now," begs Askew. "Let's get the fuck out of this shit and get that place now."

"Sure thing, Buddy. Right now. We gotta do it now."

And Grundish aims the gun and steadies it, bringing the muzzle of the hand-cannon close to the back of Askew's head. His hand shakes, and the tears stream down his face. His hand steadies and his finger puts light pressure on the trigger. The hammer pulls back, and the shot booms out over the land.

Askew falls to his knees. Grundish drops to the ground, too. The shot to Askew's head grazed the top of his skull, carving a groove through bone and brain from the front to the back on the upper right side of his head. Not a fatal shot but one sufficient to render Askew a blathering useless fuckwad for the rest of his days; a drooling, shitting, breathing lump of wasting warmth and nothing more.

Grundish's aim, initially dead-on, was thrown off by the perfectly honed and weighted throwing knife sticking into the side of his neck just below his bearded jaw line, parting his flesh and severing his carotid artery. In front of Grundish, Askew remains on his knees, his lungs continue to breath and his heart pumps, pushing gouts of blood out of his head injury in great spurts. Nothing goes through his head except for a warm breeze blowing through the sizeable trench carved into his skull.

Grundish, wide-eyed and shocked, rocks side to side on his knees, trying to keep from falling over onto the ground. Turleen appears at his side and puts one hand on his head to steady him. She gently ruffles his hair. With the other hand she grips the throwing knife and pulls it from his neck and drops it to the ground. A jet of blood pulses from the wound, wetting Turleen's hands and dress. Grundish looks to Turleen. The word *why* forms on his lips, but the only sound is the pop of a blood-bubble that issues from his mouth and dribbles down his chin before he falls over on his side. In the spot of sandy soil, under the lush canopy of the live oaks, Grundish bleeds out, marking his final stand, his business unfinished but his promises kept.

Turleen turns and walks to the El Camino. Shaking a Blue Llama from Askew's pack, she lights it and leans against the car. And from the road, the men and barking dogs and police cars burst into the forest. She straightens her red dress, draws on the cigarette as if it were her last breath, and faces the throng of officers, waiting for their questions.

I owe my deep gratitude to several people for helping me finish Grundish and Askew. First, an engorged, meaty thank you goes out to Sister Mary Catherine of Superfecundation. You are my muse, my editor, my best friend, and so much more. I'm really glad I never acted on the urge to smack you in the mouth when you would question my grammar, wording, sentence structure, etc. Because of your input, Grundish and Askew is a better book. Now get back in the kitchen and make me a sammich.

Mad fucking props and my immeasurable appreciation go out to my friend and fellow Vicious Books author, Marcus Eder. Marcus designed a kick ass cover for Grundish and Askew. Damn, I do like that cover! Marcus is a talented author, musician, graphic designer, ordained minister (licensed to marry and bury), and, apparently, a world class bacon chef. What can't this guy do? So please, check out Marcus's band, Strawfoot, and buy his books.

Finally, I want to say thank you to the people who read my first novel, *Smashed, Squashed, Splattered, Chewed, Chunked and Spewed*, and encouraged me to write another book. It means a lot to know that the massive effort that went into putting that book out was appreciated. So, I want to give a big, sloppy, open mouthed kiss to all of my readers. Um, perhaps that sounds kind of fruity. Maybe I'll just give the kiss to my female readers. Come on, ladies, you know you want it. Don't worry, my cold sores have cleared up and I just ate a breath mint. And for my male readers, I extend my right hand, give you firm handshakes, and say "thank you, Sirs." Thanks to all for reading my shit.

ALSO BY LANCE CARBUNCLE

SMASHED, SQUASHED, SPLATTERED, CHEWED CHUNKED AND SPEWED – Idjit Galoot has a problem. He escaped from his master's house for a brief romp around town, seeking out easy targets such as bitches in heat, fresh roadkill and unguarded garbage cans. When he returns to his house, the aged basset hound discovers that his master has packed up their belongings and moved to Florida without him. *Smashed, Squashed, Splattered, Chewed, Chunked and Spewed* is the story of Idjit Galoot's ne'er do well owner and his efforts to work his way back to the dog that he loves. Along the way, Idjit's owner encounters Christian terrorists, swamp-dwelling taxidermists, carnies, a b-list poopie-groupie, bluesmen on the run from a trickster deity, and the Florida Skunk Ape.

OTHER TITLES FROM VICIOUS BOOKS AUTHORS

RORSCHACH'S RIBS, by Marcus Eder – Escher Smallwater can't sleep in. That's the least of his problems. Two years shy of thirty and recently laid off from his job in advertising, Escher has a lot to deal with in his life right now. Forced to make some changes since losing his job, his lifestyle is gone and suddenly the American Dream seems more like a nightmare. As Corporate Charlie bares his darker side by way of recessions and hiring freezes, Escher has found himself with more time to reassess his life, and he's mad as hell. He will never be a rock star or date a supermodel. He doesn't get carded at bars anymore, teenagers now think of him as creepy, and he prefers VH1 over MTV. He's never been in love, his career path has essentially disappeared and somehow, he and his neighbors have inadvertently become the drug kingpins of St. Louis. A life once filled with Ikea catalogs and cubicles now consist of consumer guerillaism, lesbian strippers and a gold-toothed thug named "Mo-Mo". All this and an impending high school reunion. Maintaining a sense of humor while exploring the darker side of contemporary culture, Rorschach's Ribs explores what happens when the first generation destined to do worse than their parents grows old and starts questioning the American Dream. Through an eccentric, colorful cast of characters and a sharp cynical wit, Rorschach's Ribs delves into a world of layoffs, recessions, target markets and the underbelly of capitalism.

NOBODY PUTS SWAYZE IN THE CORNER: THE TAO OF SWAYZE, by Phil Callaway, Marcus Eder – You got your Tao in my Swayze. Your Swayze's in my Tao. Within the ancient passages of the Tao Te Ching there is great wisdom on how to live your daily life; how to live the "Way". The same life lessons can be found in the sage-like colloquies born out of Patrick Swayze's storied film career. This book pairs the philosophies of the Tao with various quotes from Patrick Swayze's movies, offering inspiration and humor. Proceeds from this book will be donated to help fund Cancer Research. Please visit the publisher, Vicious Books, for more information.

"Hot dog, I do like these fancy French fags, I do!" Turleen tilts her head back and jets two bluish streams of smoke from her nostrils. She shifts in her recliner and stretches her legs, then flinches at the moist tickle she feels on her bare soles. "I guess I owe you this, I do," she says to the dogs sitting in front of her at the footrest. "Well, get to it, then."

Sloppy, slobbery tongues work the bottoms of Turleen's feet, probing the gaps between the toes and then working their way back toward the heels. Idjit gently gnaws at a yellowed and cracked corn, softening it up and removing tiny bits of dead skin. Stubs licks up to Turleen's ankle and then slowly laps his way back toward the toes

"Meat," says Stubs.

"Meat," agrees Idjit. "Like mortadella."

"Yeah. Mortadella."

LaVergne, TN USA
15 September 2009
157945LV00006B/24/P